CHAPARRAL RANGE WAR

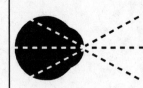

This Large Print Book carries the
Seal of Approval of N.A.V.H.

Chaparral Range War

Dusty Richards

THORNDIKE PRESS
A part of Gale, Cengage Learning

GALE
CENGAGE Learning®

Detroit • New York • San Francisco • New Haven, Conn • Waterville, Maine • London

GALE
CENGAGE Learning·

LIBRARY OF CONGRESS CATALOGING-IN-PUBLICATION DATA

Richards, Dusty.
  Chaparral Range War / by Dusty Richards. — Large Print edition.
    pages cm. — (Thorndike Press Large Print Western)
  ISBN 978-1-4104-6093-6 (hardcover) — ISBN 1-4104-6093-2 (hardcover)
  1. Large type books. I. Title.
PS3568.I31523C43 2013
813'.54—dc23   2013016751

Published in 2013 by arrangement with The Berkley Publishing Group, a member of Penguin (USA) Inc.

Printed in the United States of America
1 2 3 4 5 6 7 17 16 15 14 13

TO MY READERS

I do lots of research for these historical fiction books. I have a great Texas history authority, Charlie Eckhart. He's written me many pages about the Texas Rangers' history and their operations over time. One thing he told me: It was after 1872 that they started to spell *Ranger* with a capital *R.* Because my readers are used to seeing the words *Ranger* and *Rangers* with a capital letter, and because I respect the current name of this proud law-enforcing agency, I am abiding by that spelling convention in this book. Stop when driving through Waco, Texas, and visit their wonderful museum. A very interesting true history of them can be found in all their displays and in their library.

One story is about a local lawman telegraphing to Austin for help in handling a situation that had gotten out of hand. The head of the Rangers sent one man, and the red-faced lawman who met the train asked why he hadn't sent a dozen Rangers.

The Ranger said, "One problem, one Ranger."

When you get time, check out my website, dustyrichards.com. I try to keep up a list of my appearances on the website. I do answer questions from readers' e-mails, which takes time each day. My e-mail address is dustyrichards@cox.net.

In June 2012 I became the president of Western Writers of America. This organization represents so many great Western writers, songwriters, singers, and poets. I want to thank them for electing me. It is a great honor to serve in the boot steps of so many great writers — especially those of my late friend Elmer Kelton.

God bless America and all of you. Western literature is still alive and entertaining you. Thanks for reading mine.

Dusty Richards

ONE

After days of rocking to and fro in his Dietrich Heye saddle while crossing the southern New Mexico/Arizona Territory, Phillip Guthrey thought his eyes felt fried to the core by the glaring sun. With the hipshot horse stopped on the side of the mountain, he could make out the dried-up stage stop and smattering of buildings called a town: Steward's Crossing. A streak of green cottonwoods softened the brownish chaparral-and-cactus-clad countryside where the San Pedro River ran north, bisecting the Tucson stage road. Somewhere off in the spiny brush and tall cactus, some topknot quail kept whit-wooing. A blast of oven-hot air struck his face. He'd surely at last found the true gates to hell, he reflected, then he chuckled to himself. This must be the place where God left his sandals when he finished making the entire world.

Out of habit, he shifted the holster on his

hip to its accustomed place. One thing he still possessed was his scalp, and he hadn't seen an Apache buck except for a few falling down drunk ones since he left Lordsburg, New Mexico. He booted Lobo, his Roman-nosed bay gelding, off his resting spot. Ugliest horse Guthrey'd ever owned, but unless his fortunes rose, he'd be riding him into the next year. Stoutly built with a split mane, the bay stood about fifteen hands, and as Guthrey's old buddy Charlie Stone up in Silver City had said about the gelding, "You couldn't kill that cuss 'less you cut his head off."

Maybe at the settlement down there he could find a drink of sweet water or some good whiskey to cut a trail down his dust-coated throat. Chuckling to himself about his seemingly hopeless situation — trapped in an unforgiving land — he figured his next drink would more than likely only be a double shot of rotgut in some sour-smelling cantina. A nudge with his spur and he headed Lobo off the mountainside back to the Tucson stage road and toward the settlement set under the cottonwoods across the shallow stream.

When he reached the sparse, two-block business district, he spotted three men in the otherwise empty street who were obviously braced for a gunfight, one of them looking like he was just a boy. Wary of being caught in their cross fire, Guthrey checked his horse short of them. In a flash he became doubly wary as the feeling that he was about to ride into something violent and dangerous made the skin crawl on the back of his neck. With Lobo shut down, he tried to decipher the situation from a respectable distance.

"This ain't none of your damn business, stranger," said a well-dressed man standing under the shade on the porch of the corner saloon, smoking a cheroot cigar, and acting like he was in charge. "Just keep moving, saddle tramp, if you like breathing."

The man's words, which were intended to drive him away, stuck in his craw instead. "Looks to me like that boy down there is on the receiving end of a bad deal."

"He got himself into it," the dressed-up man said, not looking aside when he spoke.

"Way I'm looking at this, I don't like the setup. It ain't looking fair enough to me. Them two facing him down are gun hands, and that boy, well, he looks like he ain't old enough to drink in a bar."

"He's old enough to die. What's your name, stranger?" The fancy dresser barely cast a quick glance at him before turning

back as though he had a stake in the out-
come before them.

"They call me Captain Guthrey. Ain't my
given name, but it'll do. What's yours?"

"Harvey T. Whitmore." The man said it
like it should have impressed him.

The gunman on the right never looked
back Whitmore's way. "You dealing your
hand in this, Cap'n Guthrey?"

"That depends. Two of you bracing that
boy ain't really fair. He ain't got a China-
man's chance against either of you."

"Mister, you're butting in where you
damn sure don't belong," Whitmore said
with the snarl of a mad dog.

"I don't see you out in the street bracing
him, Mr. Whitmore." Guthrey squeezed his
eyelashes down a notch and kept his right
hand loose in case he needed to draw.

"Drifter, I can have you shot off that damn
horse with the snap of my fingers."

"Snap them, you son of a bitch, because
that will be the last thing you do on this
earth." After his remark to Whitmore,
Guthrey's chest filled fast with lightning
anger.

"I know him, boss. He's an ex-Ranger
captain, and I ain't having no gunfight with
him." Then the gunman on the right put
his palms out wide and slow-like, and he

backed away.

"Go get your horse, Hanks. You're fired," Whitmore said to him with a wave in the air to discard him.

"Hey," the second ranny standing in the street said. "I'm quitting, too."

Whitmore's eyes flew wide in disbelief. "Some saddle tramp rides into town and you two turn chicken on me? Neither of you will ever get another job in Arizona. I'll see to that."

"I guess this party is all over." Guthrey booted Lobo up the street to where the young man stood. He set the cow pony down right before him. Not even dry behind the ears, the boy couldn't have been out of his late teens.

"Son, how did you get into this mess anyway?" Guthrey asked, rubbing the rim of his calloused hand over the whisker stubble on his upper lip while he considered the youth.

"My name's Dan Bridges." His words came out like a quick dam release. "They — well, someone shot my dad, Harold Bridges, in the back two weeks ago while he was cleaning out a spring up in Congress Canyon."

Guthrey turned in the saddle. He noted that the fancy dresser was gone from the saloon porch. Good enough for the moment. No sign of his two ex–gun hands anymore either. He turned back. "Did you outright accuse them of doing that?"

"I did. Guess I overloaded my ass, mister."

"Kinda," Guthrey agreed and with a frown. Then he asked, "Who is this Whitmore?"

"He thinks he owns this whole country. He's owner of the V Bar 6."

"I could see that part about him. About him thinking he owned everything out there under a cactus." He dropped out of the saddle and pulled down the crotch of his pants and chaps. "What does your family own?"

"We own — me and my sis—"

"We better get out of this street, might be some runaway horse come knock us over." He herded the youth to the side by the hitch rail in front of the saddle shop.

"Yes, sir. They said you use to be a Texas Ranger. Is that so?"

At the side of the street, Guthrey hitched Lobo to a rail. Then they squatted on their heels in the shade of a palm frond porch to palaver.

"I've been with that outfit too. Anyone else around here bucking this guy?"

"He's bought out or run off about half

the folks that used to live around here. My dad wouldn't sell to him."

"So he's got you and your sis left to turn out?" Squatted on the ground with him, Guthrey made a quick check of the area and, satisfied there was no threat, he shifted his weight to his other leg.

"No, really there's others opposed to selling out, but they all go armed and watch everything."

"You have any clue who shot your father?"

"I've been thinking one of Whitmore's range riders. Dad wasn't the first one they caught off by hisself and back shot him. There's been others."

He took a hard look at the boy. "Where's the sheriff? The Arizona law?"

"I heard the biggest donor to his last campaign for office was Whitmore. He's over at Soda Springs at the county seat."

Satisfied there was more to this situation than he knew, he looked around mildly at the near-empty street. "Where did Whitmore go to?"

"I imagine he went out the back way to get more of his hired guns."

"Probably did. How old are you?"

"Seventeen, why?"

"Don't take any offense. I know you're edgy about your father's death, but it's not smart to go up against those kinds of rannies that he's got hired."

"Then what are we going to do?"

"Hold on, I'm thinking." There had to be a way to pin Whitmore's ears back, but at that very moment he didn't know how. He'd heard lots about Arizona's territorial law situation. Each county had a sheriff and, besides collecting taxes, they were the law in that county like it was a state. And you could be wanted in one jurisdiction and ride over the county line and no one arrested you. But that still didn't mean there weren't judges who were no-nonsense providers of the law. He hated seeing injustice, but what was he getting himself into? He was no longer a Texas Ranger, and besides, he was in the Arizona Territory.

"Why don't you ride out to our place to stay for a little while?" the boy asked. "And we can go around and you can see the rest of the small outfits' side of things."

For the moment, Guthrey didn't have an honest excuse not to do just that — 'cept he'd left law enforcement for good, he'd told himself when he rode out of Texas. This wasn't his war. He had no reason to get involved — except for a strong principle about right and wrong that, in this case, ate at him like a starving rat in his stomach.

"Get your horse. I'll go along and see if I can do something for you."

"Whew, thanks, mister. I'll be right back with him."

"Whoa, my name's Guthrey or Cap'n. I ain't no *mister* anybody."

"Thanks, Guthrey." And the boy tore out, about to lose his six-gun out of his worn-out holster. He shoved it back down on the run.

Guthrey closed his eyes in disbelief at the sight of the kid's actions. That boy was damn sure not gun-qualified to get in a shootout. Why, they'd have cut him down till he looked like Swiss cheese. Lord, lord, all he wanted to do was to find some day work on a cow outfit, earn a little change, and get on his way again. He suspected now that was never going to happen here.

In a few hours Guthrey and Dan rode up a well-watered side canyon. To him that meant the potholes in the creek had water in them. Gnarled, twisted trunk cotton-woods told the story that there was water underneath them in good supply. Wind rustled through the dollar-size leaves on a strong current accompanied by the chirps of lots of birds that had taken quarter in them.

The Bridges siblings owned the 87T Ranch. The ranch house was a low-walled affair, log and adobe. Alongside were pole corrals, some outbuildings, and a creaking windmill. A young woman came out and waited for them to arrive. She was attractive enough, with her tied-up red hair looking real bright, and the smile under her freckles was an honest one. She was way too young for Guthrey's tastes, but he planned to be polite to her.

"Where did you go, Dan?" she demanded.

"Aw, to town." He dropped out of the saddle like he didn't want to talk about it.

Guthrey nodded sharply at her and reined in his ugly horse so he could lean his elbow on the saddle horn. All his life he'd rode handsome horses and made it a point especially around women to have a horse he could be proud of. He dismounted quickly and came around the front of his horse's head.

"Howdy." He looked into her green eyes. She was a pretty girl who, by his estimate, was maybe a year older than her brother.

"That's Guthrey. He used to be a Texas Ranger and, well, he saved my life today." Downcast, the boy took off his hat and beat his leg with it.

"What did you do, Dan?" She looked at

him in horrified shock. No answer. She whirled to stare up and down at Guthrey. "What did he do?"

"I'd rather he told you, ma'am."

She shook her brother's arm. "He saved your life? How? Why?"

My, my, she sure was a fiery redhead when she got upset. Guthrey tried not to laugh at her impatient anger, but she sounded more like Dan's ma than his sister.

"I accused them of shooting Dad, and they challenged me to go out in the street."

"Oh no!" she shrieked. Holding her cheeks in her palms, she looked to be beside herself. "What did this man do?"

"His name is Guthrey. You should have seen it. Oh, it was wonderful what he did. First he called Whitmore a son of a bitch. Then when his two gunmen heard Guthrey's name out loud, they got more pale faced than I felt. Whitmore fired one of them and the other guy quit."

"You aren't a gunfighter, Dan. What's wrong with you, doing such a foolish thing? How could I run this ranch without you?"

"We can talk about it later. He's our guest," Dan said.

She straightened her back, recovered her composure, and nodded. "I am sorry for acting so upset, Mr. Guthrey. But he's the

17

only kin I have left alive."

He half smiled. "Now, that's all spilt milk back there; we sure can't sop it up and save none of it. I talked to your brother about it too. I think it was something he had to get out of his system, and lucky there was no harm done. And one more thing, you need to call me simply Guthrey. No *mister* about it. I'm not fancy nor anyone important. I was just passing through and saw some inequities in his situation with those men and him."

"Inequities?"

"Yes, ma'am. Now let's calm down. He's unscathed. That Whitmore knows his pedigree now and I'd like to" — he swiveled around looking for a likely place — "take a bath somewhere, then shave and clean up."

"I'll get you a towel," she said.

He caught her arm. "Now, darling, I have one of those. I just need a place or tub to do it in."

"My name is Cally. Short for California. My mother always wanted us to move on over there."

"Cally, it's my pleasure." He took off his weathered Stetson and shook her hand. He felt they'd made a small peace treaty to get along.

"We have a sheepherder's shower behind

18

the house. No one will bother you and the water will be sun heated — some." She wrinkled her nose at the notion it was warmed any at all.

"Thanks. I can handle that."

"Mister —" she called out. "I mean, Guthrey — do you plan to stay with us?"

"How does that work?" he asked, stopped in his tracks.

Dan looked shocked at her words. "I invited him here, sis."

"I know. I asked him about his plans."

"I'm too dirty to think," Guthrey said and tossed the flour sack towel over his shoulder.

"We can't afford gunfighter wages, sir."

"Who said I'd work for you?" He looked at Dan and then her.

"Well, maybe we need you."

He nodded, then he turned around to make eye contact with her. "The way I look at it, you two are going to need lots of help if you aim to stay here."

Taken aback by his words, she said in a soft voice, "We can talk about it later. Dan can put your horse up."

With a wooden nod to Guthrey, she turned on her heel. "I'll fix some food for us."

The sheepherder shower tub sat on the roof of a shed beside the creaking windmill.

Guthrey took a seat on an old wooden chair and took off his boots, socks, then his vest, gun belt, shirt, chaps, and suspenders, followed by his pants. He was standing like Adam in the Garden of Eden, his snow-white skin under the cool spray of water contrasting with his brown hands as he soaked. Then he used the bar of soap to lather his body, and the strong smell of it ran up his nose. Finished, he dried himself off in the chill of the dry atmosphere that made him feel like it was still wintertime.

On the shade of the porch, he took a straight razor out of his vest pocket and set it on a ledge near a smoky mirror. Then he half dressed, rubbed soap lather through his whisker growth, and mowed it off. Next he pulled on the shower chain to swish off the razor, lathered more soap on his face, and went back with the razor for more whiskers. Finally shaved, he rinsed his face, put the razor back in his vest, and strapped on his gun belt.

He hung his towel on a rack and finished dressing. With his hat in hand, he wiped the grit and dried sweat out of the leather hatband, then placed the hat on his head. Before he went anywhere, he shifted the gun belt on his waist until it fit in the right place. Nice ranch, he reflected, quiet enough after all the towns he'd been in since leaving his sister's place in the Texas hill country. First time an outfit caught his eye in all those hot, blinding, boiling dust-filled days it took him to get here.

Back in Silver City, he had met a widow woman, Claire Johns. Thirty years old, two children, hardworking gal with a nice spread in that higher desert country. But as with so many other of his encounters with eligible women, in the end, he'd kissed her good-bye and rode on. He never had a feeling that he really belonged there. His sis once told him he was too fussy when he'd walked away from another woman back in the Texas hill country. Simple enough reason: He never felt at ease with either of those women. When a man was eaten up inside about little things in a woman's company — and it was about nothing in particular — he better answer his itchy feet and leave.

Cally was ringing a triangle. He was ready to taste her food. The situation with her and her brother looked very bleak to him. How could two teenagers hold a small ranch together with folks like Whitmore blocking their way at every step?

He found the place for his hat on the wall peg inside the big room. The smell of Cally's cooking sure tantalized his nose. His nostrils

21

were still recovering from the prairielike fire that had set up inside them while he was riding over here from New Mexico. The aromas coming to him now smelled good enough to draw saliva into his dry mouth.

"I kilt a chicken for supper," she said. "I hope you like chicken."

"Smells heavenly. Don't fuss about me. I can eat about anything."

"Most men can do that as long as they don't have to cook it."

Amused, he pointed his finger at her. "Darling, you know all about men."

They both were laughing when Dan came inside the house. He blinked at Cally and then at Guthrey with a question written on his face: What was so damn funny?

"We ain't picking on you, Dan. Just poking fun at men in general."

He shrugged. "Fine."

"Hey, in the morning," Guthrey began, "if you don't have anything that needs to be done, let's ride around the country. I want to become more familiar with the land and the people."

Dan agreed. "Sure, we can do that."

"Take your places," Cally said, coming over to the table with heaping platters of food. "Guthrey, you set on that end. Dan sets on this end, and the cook is in the middle."

"We can help —" Guthrey began, still standing.

She dismissed his concern with a head-shake. "I'll handle this end of the deal. Sit down."

"Yes, ma'am." He took his place. The fried chicken truly did smell heavenly. Her biscuits were the right color — brown on top — and the green beans looked freshly picked. Even the flour gravy for the mashed potatoes appeared just right in texture, not watery or too thick to spread. When Cally sat down and nodded, they began to fill their plates. Not much was said during the meal, except Guthrey told her she'd done very well with the cooking and he told Dan he'd better not let his sister run off with some old saddle tramp or he'd be eating lots of burnt, bad-tasting food.

Cally's biscuits were as fine as pastry to him. The sweet cream butter on them was a big treat for a man who for months had been eating food from Mexican street vendor women.

"How long were you in the Rangers?" Cally asked.

"All told, about seven years."

"How was that?"

"I was a Ranger before the war, then the

feds ruled us for five years and there were no Rangers at that time. I came back for the last two years. But Texas legislature has money problems all the time. Their wages are not anything you can count on. If you ask a man to give his life to an organization, you should at least pay him what he has coming to him."

"I can't believe they didn't pay you." Cally looked perplexed.

"Well, they sure haven't. I have vouchers for half my wages over the last two years. I guess they'll pay them someday, but I don't know the date or in what century."

"What have you done without pay?" she asked, looking at him with concern.

"Just that: I did without pay. I finally decided I had to find a real job." He took out his gold pocket watch and saw it was 6:10 P.M., then he snapped the lid shut.

"I bet you've lived by that watch," she said.

"Yes, I did. I always needed to be somewhere or meet someone at a certain time. It's a hard habit to get over."

"We have an unused bunkhouse you can sleep in," Dan said, changing the subject.

Cally waved him off. "That place needs to be cleaned first. No one's used it in a year or more except the pack rats."

Guthrey held up his hands. "Hey, I'll sleep

out under the stars. We can worry about that later."

"I hate for our guest — all right. It's fine, fine," Dan said to his sister, who was looking hard at him.

Later during the night, Guthrey lay in his bedroll and listened to the coyotes yelping. They had owls for their chorus, and he spent a lot of time with their serenade before he fell asleep. Before dawn he was up and rubbing the sleep out of his face. The creosote smell of the desert filled his nose, and a cool breeze swept his face. Peaceful enough place to sleep in. Then a light came on in the house and Cally opened the door. Dressed, she looked decently awake, enough for him to slip down there.

"Morning," he said from the doorway, watching her stir things up to cook.

"Oh, you're an early riser too. Come in. I'm just starting my fixin'."

"Do you need a couple pails of water?"

"Yes, I could use them."

He took two pails and lifted them up with a smile for her. "I can fill 'em."

"Thanks. I'm not used to having help."

"No problem." He went off to where the windmill pipe poured liquid into the watering tank. With the pails filled from the

25

spout, he hauled them back to set on her stand. "I'd milk that cow, but she don't know me."

"If you're willing to milk her, after breakfast I'll make formal introductions. But you're right, a cow that's used to a certain person milking her gets nervous with a new pair of hands on her handles."

"I can milk all right."

"Good. I never turn down help. You were in the war? I'm sorry. I didn't mention it to upset you —"

"No problem. That was a real sorry time for me. I'd never been in many situations where I didn't have a good feeling about how they'd end. Soldiering was never fun. The whole time I was in the army, I had a deep dread in my soul. No way that we could beat them. We had little food, little ammo, and no horses — and we were cavalry. A horseman never feels good walking in the mud. Especially a Texas one."

"Yes, I've been told about the problems you had. Ring the triangle. Dan will wake up." She brought over the coffeepot to fill his cup.

He went to wake the third member of this outfit. "That coffee smells great. I'll be right back."

When he returned, she had put the pot

26

back on the wood range. "You ever have a wife?" she asked.

He shook his head and smiled at her. "Nope, I've never had one."

"That was pretty nosy of me to ask. Sorry. Sit down and eat. Dan'll drag in shortly."

"Cally, I don't really have any deep, dark secrets."

She smiled. "Oh. Shucks, I was going to write a book about a Texas Ranger scandal."

"You'd find out real quick that mine would be pretty boring."

She smiled as she delivered the platter of fried ham and scrambled eggs. Next came the brown-topped biscuits in a pan from the oven, which she set on the board hot plate. Dan arrived, looking still asleep, yawning and stretching his arms to wake up.

"Did you sleep any?" his sister asked him.

"Too hard."

She and Guthrey laughed over his appearance, as it was obvious that he was not totally with them.

"Are you going to be able to show Guthrey anything today?" she asked quietly.

"Sure." He never looked up, busy filling his plate. "I'll be fine."

An hour later, the two men left the ranch

on horseback. Taking the river road north from their ranch's side road, they soon stopped at a wooden gate. Dan dismounted and opened the entrance to the Coalgate Ranch.

"This is Herman Coalgate's place."

Guthrey nodded. He'd been looking at various aspects of the land. Cactus desert on the left and the mixed agriculture land watered by the river on the right. They rode down the sandy lane through the tall mesquite, and some stock dogs came barking to greet them. A short man with his half-curly gray hair edging out of the band of his weathered felt hat met them.

"Morning, Dan. I'm sorry about what happened to your dad. How are things going for you and your sister?"

"Oh, Cally's fine. Herman, this is Guthrey. He sort of saved my hide yesterday in town with Whitmore's bunch."

The man stepped over to shake Guthrey's hand. "Any friend of that boy is a friend of mine."

"Nice place you've got here," Guthrey said, looking at the shallow San Pedro River flowing by beyond the house, corrals, and an alfalfa patch.

"Yeah, Whitmore really wants this place. I have about a mile of river frontage."

"I bet he does want it." Guthrey could imagine how bad the land king wanted this much access to a good water source.

"He ain't getting it though. I wouldn't sell to him anything short of hell freezing over."

Guthrey agreed. "I think several folks feel like that today."

"Herman," Dan said, "Guthrey used to be a Texas Ranger."

"Glad ya came to Arizona. There ain't much law in Arizona, and I know what them Rangers can do. We need some of that around here."

"Herman, a man has some rights in this country. One thing is, no one needs to be harassed by the big outfits. I have no authority here. But as a private citizen I can get mad as hell about that."

"What can we do about it?" Herman asked flat out.

"First I need to meet the folks around here and see what they want to do. There are such things as grand jury investigations if the law's been broken."

Herman nodded. "It's damn sure been broken around here, and many times. This matter did not just happen. They've been running roughshod over lots of us for near three years."

"That's what Dan told me. We've got lots

of ground to cover today. Good to meet you. I'm staying out at Dan and Cally's place, the 87T, if you need any help."

"I'll sure try to get word to you, by golly, if I do."

They rode on and next met Salty Jackson in the middle of the road. Whiskered and a big grinner, he shut down his team and buckboard when they met up.

"Morning, Dan. How're things going?"

"Good enough today." Dan pushed his horse in close to shake the man's hand and introduced Guthrey.

"Nice to meet you, Salty." After shaking the man's hand, Guthrey sat back down in his saddle.

"He's a friend of mine," Dan said. "He's an ex–Texas Ranger."

"Back before the war I was living up by Denton, Texas, and I was a Ranger then. We rode all over looking for horse apples," Salty said.

"Why was that?" Dan asked the man.

"Barefoot mustangs stopped and pooped. If a horse was being ridden, he scattered his out behind him. Looking for signs of Indians, if we saw scattered apples and barefoot tracks, we set off the alarm. The Comanche were among us."

"I'd never thought of that," Dan said.

"It worked to stop surprise attacks on the frontier." Guthrey recalled as a boy wanting to be off fishing instead of being in the saddle and having to Ranger in the hill country around their home.

"He's here to help us," Dan said.

"Good, we can use all the help we can find." Salty nodded at him like a final period on a sentence and picked up his reins. "Sure nice meeting you, mister. Around here we need everyone we can get against them big ranchers. See you at the dance Saturday, Dan." And Salty drove off.

His iron-rimmed wheels churning up dust, Salty soon disappeared toward town. Dan and Guthrey rode on, to meet more of the resisters. Harry Beach with his short wife, Kate, and their four children, and Ira Raines, an older bachelor rancher, were next on the list that Dan had built in his mind. They swung on north and rode through some hills, going home the back way.

They stopped off at one more place. Ted Rawlings and his wife, Lillian, a large, raw-boned woman with teenage children. They operated a freighting and ranch business by themselves. Rawlings was a tough man who spoke of his support for more law and order. Guthrey felt this man would be a strong backer of any efforts to stop Whitmore and to get the sheriff thrown out of office. They shook hands and Guthrey and Dan started back for the ranch.

Guthrey laid out that part of the region in his mind while they rode through the chaparral. His life might someday depend on his knowledge of the lay of this land. They moved through some of the Bridges-branded cows and calves scattered near a small water tank. How many cattle did the two own? The 87T scar on the right side of the cattle made an obvious mark of ownership, as did the two ear notches on the other side that were registered with the brand. An easy way to identify them coming or going.

In late afternoon, they arrived back at the ranch and saw Cally's wash flapping in the wind that was propelling the creaking windmill. In a brown skirt and blouse, Cally looked fresh coming out of the house to greet them. Guthrey and Dan told her about their day as they unsaddled.

"Salty said he'd see us at the dance." Dan spoke to her like that was a question she'd need to answer.

Guthrey paused for a moment before removing the saddle off his horse and wondered how she'd answer him.

"Can you dance, Guthrey?" she asked,

shuffling her work shoes and not looking at him.

He laughed and heaved the rig off his horse's back. "I can sure step on your toes doing it."

"That's all that I need." Then she laughed and nodded her head. "Why don't we? I'm in favor. We haven't done that since before we lost Dad."

"Guess we better go, then," Dan said.

"You two promise not to start any fights?" She looked at them for an answer.

"I don't want to fight," Guthrey said.

Dan agreed. "I don't want to either."

She shook her head. "I suggest each of you buy a new shirt and pants for that event."

His saddle on the hitch rail, Guthrey thanked her.

"Supper around six," she said.

Guthrey heard her and went to the barn. He unloaded the new cartridge revolver model .45 Colt he wore, cleaned the entire works, and lightly oiled the weapon. Since he had not recently fired the weapon, he didn't boil the barrel and cylinders.

"You pay a lot of attention to that gun of yours," Dan said, watching him all the time.

He looked the youth in the eye. "I live by this piece of iron. If it doesn't work when I need it, I'll be dead. It ain't a lot of work considering I am betting my life on it working right."

Dan nodded. "I guess if you think like that — it needs to be clean."

"Tell me about the dance," he said, slipping the weapon back in his holster.

"It's a social. Everyone brings food. Potluck. Then they dance, slow, fast, and faster."

"Do you dance?" Guthrey asked.

"Some. How about you?"

"I can dance. Let's look at the wagon and make sure it don't fall apart going over there."

"Sure, but it's all right."

"Let's look anyway." That boy certainly needed to learn to check on things before they broke down. Maybe his father did all that and never mentioned it to him. Guthrey's grandfather had taught him how to do those things. He made Guthrey respect examining things like wagon gears and saddles, cinches, horse's backs and hooves.

During their inspection of the buckboard, they discovered the wheels needed to be greased and planned to do it in the morning since Cally had called them to come eat supper.

Washing up on the porch, Guthrey and

Dan made small talk about other ranch things. Cally stuck her head out the door. "Are you two coming?"

"Yes, ma'am," Guthrey said. They were coming. This was a peaceful enough corner out of the busy rest of the world. He found that some of his mental guards had become relaxed. That might be all right. He'd been under lots of pressure with his last Ranger job. Time would tell how his stay here would work out.

The rest of the week they spent their days checking range cattle for any signs of screwworms. These flesh-eating maggots attacked any cut in the cattle's flesh and soon killed the victim if not treated. They found several head that needed to be roped and treated with an ether-tar compound. Dan proved to be a good roper and caught anything they found that needed to be doctored or simply checked. Guthrey heeled the cattle's back legs in his rope and held them for him, and Dan bragged about how their two-roper partnership sure beat his one-man operation out hollow.

By Friday, Guthrey's roping had improved a lot too. It had been years since he'd done much cowboying, but he soon fit in place, helping the boy. No problems came up with

Whitmore. If anything, it was maybe too quiet — a man like that never quit doing underhanded things to suit his purposes. He was simply planning for something more.

Two

Their destination Saturday afternoon was the Cane Springs Schoolhouse. Lots of folks were on the dusty road that evening headed for the event. Dan drove the team, sitting on the spring seat with his sister in her new blue dress. Dan had another roan horse hitched behind. Guthrey had borrowed one of Dan's better-looking horses for his ride over, a tall bay gelding Dan called Big Joe. Other people were coming in buggies and wagons. Three boys about twelve years old rode burros and caught up with them.

He could tell they were admirers of Dan's. He'd seen that right off. They set up a big conversation with him about something and beat their burros' butts to make them keep up with his wagon and team.

At the Cane Springs Schoolhouse, lots of folks were scattered about setting up camps around the whitewashed building. Dan drove right to their campsite and told

Guthrey that this was the spot. Plenty of work to do setting up the tent and canvas fly. They'd brought a load of wood for campfires and cooking. Their four horses on a picket line, Guthrey, under Cally's direction, commenced to put up the wall tent. In no time the three of them had it in place, staked in the ground, and she handed down cots and bedding from the wagon to set up later inside the tent.

"It is sure good to have you along," she said to Guthrey when he lifted her by her waist and set her on the ground. "This usually took us forever, just the two of us making camp. Didn't it, Dan?"

Her brother wiped his sweaty face on his sleeve. "Forever. This so far isn't half-bad."

Cally swung a pot of water over the fire that Guthrey had started. "Won't be long till there's coffee, guys."

Women of various ages came by and spoke to Cally. She introduced Guthrey to them when he was handy. He and Dan were busy putting up the canvas fly more for shade than rain protection under the cloudless sky. But it all was part of Cally's "camping" requirements. The setup completed, the menfolk rested in canvas folding chairs, and she prepared supper. Guthrey planned on a siesta if events would let him take one.

"Does Whitmore's bunch drop in here?" he asked.

"Not often," Dan said. "They ain't too welcome."

"I savvy that. But that wouldn't bother them." Guthrey pulled his hat down to shade his eyes and made himself comfortable, stretched out in the chair in the shade.

"Hey, while you get some shut-eye, I'm going to look for some of my buddies and see what's been happening. Rest easy. I'll be back," Dan said.

Guthrey thanked him and was resolved to sleep a little. Children ran around shouting, but he found them no threat to himself and he closed his eyes. Nice to just catch some extra rest.

Not too long into his siesta, Cally whispered something in Guthrey's ear about trouble arriving. His hand went for his gun butt. The sound of her urgency ignited him to be on guard.

"Easy." She held his gun arm. "Whitmore's big man Bud Hampton just rode in with two of his gun slicks, asking for you." Her face looked ashen white.

Guthrey removed his hat and sat up, looking and acting like nothing bothered him. But his purpose was to assess the situation some. Cally was on her knees beside him with her hands in her lap.

"Which one is he?" he asked, leaning toward her.

"See the one that's riding the buckskin horse?" She rose up and looked the other way.

"Yes. Is Hampton wearing that big black hat?" The man weighed about two hundred pounds, maybe more. "That's him, huh? Does he usually come to these events?"

"No, but he's here and he's been asking for you." Her green eyes looked wary and upset.

"Hmm."

"Didn't you order Whitmore around the other day?" she whispered.

"Sure, but there's lots of people here who aren't on his side."

"His bunch don't care. They're ruthless bullies."

He made a face at her. "Did they really ask for me?"

"That's how I know. I heard them when they asked someone coming up this way. 'Where's that blankety Ranger?' "

No rest for the wicked. Guthrey rubbed his smooth-shaven face and tried to wake up some more. "Thanks. You just be sure that Dan doesn't get mixed in this business.

No matter what happens."

She gathered her dress and stood up. "I'll do that. You be careful. Those three men are killers."

He nodded and when he stood up, he shifted his gun belt into place. He set his hat on his head where he wanted it. In no hurry, he started down through the camp after the ones who were seeking him. Some men spoke to each other when he went past them. Not fifty feet from Cally's camp, several men, heads of family, began to get up and follow him. His followers waved for others to join them.

The Whitmore crew reined up and halted their horses close to the front door of the school building. The big man, Hampton, spoke to one of the men in the group standing there, then checked his tall horse again to make him stand still.

Guthrey read the look on Hampton's hard face when he caught sight of him — cold as an iceberg despite the midafternoon heat.

"Folks said you're looking for me," Guthrey said.

Hampton turned with a cold fish-eye look at him. "Your name Gufrey?"

"Close, but not that. My name's Guthrey. What do you need?"

"All these men backing you?" Hampton

gave a head toss at the followers behind him.

Guthrey looked back and then turned to face him. "I think they are. Let's drop those guns of yours, real careful-like, and then you three can ride out of here. I don't want you to wake any sleeping babies."

"I ain't —" Then Hampton must have seen the determination in the faces of Guthrey's backers. "Drop 'em, boys."

From their hard looks around at things, the two men with Hampton didn't appear to like the situation, nor his orders. However, they agreed and dropped their weapons, but not without some grumbling.

"How do we get them guns back?" Hampton asked, his face growing red with anger.

"I have no idea."

"We'll see about this," Hampton ripped out and spurred his anxious, prancing horse around. "You're going to wish you never lived before I'm through with you."

"Hampton!" Guthrey shouted. The anger he felt was under control, but he wanted to answer the man's threats.

"What?" Hampton jerked his horse roughly around.

"Wear your best clothes next time you come asking for me."

"What in the hell for?"

"So they can bury you in them."

42

The crowd quickly parted to let Hampton and his men charge away on horseback. Guthrey knew he'd tossed the gauntlet down for war.

"Can you beat them?" Cally asked when she rushed over to join him, looking upset by the confrontation.

He realized he was madder than he'd intended to let them get him. Those three riding right into a peaceful crowd of men, women, and children, looking for trouble, was not only disrespectful, but a damn belligerent act in the first place. A rude show of force, he'd call it. "I don't know, Cally, but someone needs to stop them from riding in here roughshod to terrorize these people."

She nodded and swallowed hard. "They've never been called to task before — by anyone."

"It's time someone did that, then."

"What about their guns you made them drop?"

"Some men picked them up so a kid didn't get one. I guess those three've got the money to buy more."

She agreed and took his arm possessively, holding her dress tail in her other hand, and she headed him for the open double doors. "Well, Captain, let's go eat and dance. We

43

came here to forget them."

He looked aside at her in amazement, and then with a "What the hell," went on inside the schoolhouse. One thing about California, she was sure a take-charge girl.

The aroma of wonderful food sought his nose when they crossed the threshold. This was going to be a big treat for him; all these ranch women had tried their best to outdo each other. He remembered many such events in the hill country of Texas. His mouth flooded with saliva, and he stood in line behind Cally, looking around for Dan. Not seeing him, Guthrey figured he must be busy visiting with his friends. At least he hadn't gotten into the fracas.

Cally seemed to know everyone, and she stopped to visit with many, introducing Guthrey as her and her brother's guest. No doubt the incident in the schoolyard with Hampton and the other two had everyone gossiping about the ex-Ranger among them. Several times he heard someone say, "He's that Ranger."

If he'd really wanted notice, he'd sure gotten it. Like waving a brightly colored blanket at a mad bull, he'd done that to Whitmore and now to his main man. Twice, counting his running off the two gunmen in town his first day there. He'd better have eyes in the back of his head from here on. Whitmore would have to show he could even the score or he'd lose his hold on the rest of the fear he held over these folks.

"You still thinking about those three?" Cally asked under her breath, sitting beside him on the bench against the wall, their plates in their laps heaped with food.

He nodded and paused in his eating. "To think that those three came here to make trouble, in the middle of all these women and children, still burns me down."

"What would we have done without you?"

"Oh, someone would have stood up and taken charge."

She leaned over to look in his face. "No. In the past they've all run like mice."

"Aw, Cally. People get pushed far enough, they'll rise up. There was a killer in Texas who'd shot several people without cause. His presence scared folks in that small town to death. He made a big mistake — got drunk — and a masked posse hauled him out to a tree, then they drove a horse out from under him with a necktie fastened around a stout branch."

She shook her head. "That won't ever happen here."

He busied himself eating. Who was the sheriff here? No lawman had been on the job in Steward's Crossing when they were fixing to have the gunfight with Dan. No one even went after one as far as he could tell. He needed to meet the man in charge of the law in this country.

"You enjoying the food?" Cally asked.

"I like yours, but some of these dishes are great too."

She chuckled and then looked a little embarrassed. "I am not a great cook."

"Hey, you don't need to deny anything. But what is this?" He fed her a bite from his fork.

"A sweet potato dish," she said.

"I thought so." Then he about laughed. What would people think of him feeding her off his utensil? He needed to be more careful. The two of them, no doubt, were under the scrutiny of many eyes. One day he'd probably ride on, but the redheaded gal seated beside him had to go on living here.

"What's the matter?" she asked.

"What I just did might look bad to some folks. Me feeding you."

She shook her head and ducked her face to hide her amusement. "Oh my, how could you have done that?"

"Well, I did it."

"At times I think you're just a boy inside

46

that shell."

"I ain't. But I forget at times what people might think about my subtle actions."

"I am glad you're so relaxed with me. I'm flattered."

"Your reputation won't be flattered. I'll be more careful from here on."

"You're fine. You want more to eat?"

He shook his head. "I'm too full."

"Give me your plate. I'll go wash them and you can rest. I want to dance. They're about to start playing music."

He laughed at her. "Rest? I'm not that old."

She shook her head. "I want to really dance." She left with their plates and utensils to wash them in a large, soapy washtub, then rinse them in another. She came back in few minutes with her dishes in a cloth poke and set the bundle under the bench.

The fiddler of the small band of musicians was starting a waltz. Guthrey took Cally's hand and swept her toward the dancing area in a fashion that made her throw her head back and nod. "I knew you were lying to me about your dancing skills."

"All left boots," he said to dismiss her words. They swung around, and she shook her head as if in disbelief. The evening proved to be one smooth dance after another. A fastmoving polka left them nearly out of breath, and they went outside to get some air. Her small hand squeezed his hard calloused one as they went out into the cooler night air.

A large bonfire illuminated people standing around in the night, casting large shadows on the outer ring of the yard. Guthrey and Cally slipped to the side to stand by themselves.

His hand felt empty when he released her fingers. She leaned her head against his shoulder.

"I wish this was my way of life every day. Just be like it is here tonight instead of fearing we'll be burned out or run off our ranch. Oh, Guthrey, I would give anything for this range war with that greedy Whitmore to be over."

He twisted her around and hugged her for a quick moment. "It will be. I promise you."

Then he straightened, realizing he'd done the wrong thing in public again. Even in the dark he'd been wrong to do that. Why couldn't he keep his hands off her? He closed his eyes. He needed to escape this situation.

"Shall we go back inside?" she asked.

"Yes."

He led her back into the schoolhouse and

they danced, not saying much till the end of the set. When he released her hand she stood on her toes. "Did you almost kiss me out there?"

Caught, he wet his lips. "You that close, it was very tempting."

With a wink of her green eyes, she whispered, "Good. I thought so."

The rest of the night they danced or sat out. When it came close to quitting time, she asked if he minded taking her home instead of camping there for the night. He agreed and together they took down their things and loaded the wagon with some help from others who quietly thanked him for handling Hampton.

He found himself driving the buckboard home under the stars, with Cally seated beside him. Dan wasn't along. He'd told them he'd ride Guthrey's saddle horse back with his friends a little later that night. Alone with Cally, Guthrey enjoyed the cooler night air. She clung to his arm and for him it felt natural, even comforting. The road was easily visible aside from a few chuckholes he missed seeing that rocked the rig. The bounce only made them laugh, and the trip was uneventful.

In the yard, he lifted her off the buckboard and set her down. Then she turned her face up at him. He lightly kissed her on the mouth. They simply stood there for a long moment in silence.

He swept off his hat for her. "Thanks. You are a generous young lady, Cally. I will mind my manners better in the future."

"I hope not," she said and turned for the house. Beating his leg with his hat, he watched her disappear inside the dark house. Somewhere a coyote howled off in the night. He led the horses off to unharness them in the corral, then went and found his bedroll. He shook his bedding out good to rid it of any scorpions or vinegarroons that might have snuck inside and spread it out.

He didn't go to sleep easily, thinking about Cally and the night's tougher event until he finally faded off.

THREE

In the morning, he milked the cow, put the pail half-full of the strong-smelling hot milk on the dry sink, and went to wash up. Cally rang the triangle for Dan and smiled at Guthrey in the first burst of daylight rising over the mountains to the east. He stood on the porch a moment to view the sunrise.

"Thanks for milking the cow. You're spoiling me." She draped his arm across her shoulders and, laughing, followed him inside like he was dragging her.

"I like spoiling you."

She nodded with a smile. "The dance was great. Would you go to church with me today?"

"I guess I could be bribed."

"Oh, bribed, huh?" She showed him his chair. "You better eat. The pancakes will be cold."

"Dan getting up?" he asked.

"I thought so." Then she looked perplexed.

"I better go look up in his room in the shed."

"I can go."

She pushed him down. "You eat. He sometimes sleeps hard."

"Yes, ma'am."

With a quick kiss to his forehead, she gathered her hem and ran outside the small house for the shed. Guthrey sipped his coffee, holding the hot metal cup in both hands to listen and wait. Soon the sounds of her soft shoes came back and she nodded from the doorway. "He's coming."

Guthrey put down the cup and began forking the pancakes on his plate.

"I guess he didn't get in from the dance until late." She swept her dress under her to sit down.

He agreed. "What time is church?"

"Eleven o'clock. I can pack a picnic lunch for afterward." She looked at him for his answer to the after-church picnic invite.

"Fine. Whatever you want to do."

Pleased about his acceptance, she went for the coffeepot when her brother came into the room.

"Morning to both of you. You two sure had everyone talking last night." Dan slumped in the chair.

"We're going to church this morning."

Maybe that act would help their reputations, Guthrey mused to himself.

"I'm not. I'm going back to sleep. I won't even eat."

"Fine." Cally sounded sharp with her reply.

They found a small crowd at the schoolhouse for the services: several widow women and a few families with children, who were under close parental supervision with orders to be polite, which meant being quiet. The rest were older couples. The preacher was Joshua Harney, a man with a strong voice who belted out hymns and gave a sermon about Jesus speaking to the crowds of those believers who came to see him at Galilee.

When the service was over, there was a small gathering outside, and Guthrey met more of the area residents. A straight-backed thin woman with silver hair introduced herself as Chancey Edwards.

"I hope you live long enough to run Whitmore out of this region. One of his men murdered my husband, George, and a better man never lived. I hope you kill Whitmore and all of his men."

"I'm sorry about the loss of your husband, Mrs. Edwards."

"I'm mad as hell. If you don't kill him and

that man ever rides into my yard, I will kill him."

He shook his head. "Don't. It won't help you."

"It will help me." She turned and walked away.

"She's really bitter," Cally said softly. "Let's go picnic."

"Yes, ma'am."

"Don't call me that. I am not your mother."

"It's my way, Cally. It's hard for me not to be respectful to a woman."

On the drive home, they found a grassy glen under some cottonwoods beside the road. Guthrey tied the horses and then brought Cally's basket down to the site. She spread the blanket and unpacked her food. They ate ham sandwiches and some chocolate cake, washing it down with sun tea.

"Here, you need this," she said, using her fork to feed him the last of her piece of cake.

"Thanks. It tasted good." He looked at her, all prim in her special blue church dress, seated on the blanket. Her beauty had grown since he first met her. Maybe the dress and her red hair fixed up in curls was part of it, but he saw a side to her that he was only now discovering. Her generosity toward him was real, and he had to admit she'd stolen a part of him.

In the next week he needed to meet this no-show sheriff, Guthrey decided. Seated on his butt with his boots and legs spread apart and his arms braced behind him, Guthrey wondered how he'd ever drive the strong forces of evil out of this dry land.

Cally got on her knees, swept his hat off, and kissed him. "You are becoming too serious for a picnic."

Kneeling down beside him, she hugged his neck, pressed her cheek to his, and whispered in his ear, "Are you avoiding me? I'm not some child."

"I know that. I don't want you to think I'm some lurid old man."

"I won't."

"Good. We better get on home, then."

"Whatever you say," she said stiffly. She rose, then bent over, gathering her things to put in the basket.

He didn't want to leave either, but he decided they needed to take some time to think it over before getting into a relationship. Her things loaded, he helped her onto the seat. Nothing he had composed in his mind sounded nearly sincere enough for him to speak out loud to her. Uncomfortable with the turn of events, he clucked to

the horses and they went home in a stilted
silence.

FOUR

The next morning they were civil to each other, but a cold curtain hung between Guthrey and Cally at breakfast. When he finished his meal, Guthrey told Dan he was going to saddle up and go over and meet the sheriff. He knew his words gave Cally a start because she spun around to look at him but never said anything.

"You're coming back here, ain't'cha?" Dan asked.

"I plan on it."

"Good," he said.

"Thanks for breakfast, Cally," he said to her.

"Oh, it was nothing," she said, busy washing her dishes.

He took his bedroll in case he got caught out somewhere. Dan planned to check on some more of his cattle that day, so they parted company. Soda Springs was south and west of Steward's Crossing. Guthrey rode his horse in a jog down the dusty river road. He passed some folks in wagons and waved. It was midmorning before he reached the small village, which looked even less prosperous than Steward's Crossing. Past some adobe jacals and a few more buildings, he saw the faded sign that read Crook County Offices on the front wall of a mud brick building.

He dismounted, shifted his gun belt, then wrapped his reins on the rack. Only a few old Mexican women were in sight along with some yellow cur dogs that barked at him.

Inside the dark corridors of the courthouse, he stopped where a man sat at a telegraph key behind a counter.

"Good morning," he said to the key puncher, who about swallowed his mustache at the sight of him. Guthrey figured his sudden appearance had shocked him or something.

"What do you want?" the young man asked.

"Is the sheriff in?"

The man laughed. "Hell, he don't come in much. Sheriff Killion's got a ranch to run and he and his deputies are all out counting cattle for the tax rolls. You know he's the county tax collector too?"

"I've heard that he does that too."

"Hell, they paid him over twenty thousand for that job last year. County only pays him a couple of thousand to do the law things."

"I really don't care about his pay. I need to talk to him."

"Well, just ride out to his ranch. If he's home, you can talk to him out there."

"Does he have a head deputy I can talk to?"

"That would be Lamar. Lamar Dawes. I'd say he'll be in Rosa's Cantina about this time, sobering up on whiskey."

He frowned at the man. "What happens when they have a crime in this place?"

"Nothing, 'cause, we don't have any crime."

"I find that hard to believe."

"Why, mister, Crook County, Arizona, is a very peaceful place."

He turned to leave since the man had nothing he wanted. "You work the wire for who?"

"The county. The telegraph company couldn't find anyone who wanted to do it. Not enough business for anyone to want to set up a telegraph office here. So I got the job. Wait, that's an army message. I need to hear it. Bet some more Apaches have left the reservation again. They've been doing that real regular lately."

He waited for the man to write out the message.

The operator set down his pencil and began to read the message. " 'Blue Starr and a half dozen bucks left San Carlos Reservation yesterday and were discovered gone at roll call this morning. Headed south for Mexico on fresh horses. Names of others will come later. They are armed and should be considered dangerous.' Hmm, they damn sure will be dangerous."

"What will the sheriff do about that?" he asked.

"The sheriff? Are you talking about the runaway Apaches? Hell. Nothing. He can't spare any men. They're counting cattle for the tax roll. I told you that's where he makes his money. Chasing Apaches don't pay a gawdamn thing."

"Thanks," Guthrey said, disgusted with all he'd learned so far. He headed across the street for the cantina with the faded sign that read Rosa's.

The batwing doors creaked when he pushed them aside. A big man with hunched shoulders standing at the bar downed a shot of liquor. Afterward, he slammed the emptied glass on the countertop. Then he blinked in either disbelief or shock at the sight of Guthrey.

"Who in the hell are you?" The man again blinked his large brown eyes.

"I'm looking for the law."

"By gawd, I'm the law. What the hell do you need?"

"I really wanted to see the sheriff."

"What fur?"

"There are some men running roughshod over the citizens around Steward's Crossing."

"Yeah, who are they?"

"They work for a man named Whitmore."

"Give me one more glass, Rosa, and I'll be fine." He cleared his throat and raised his shoulders to stick out his chest bearing the silver badge. "Mr. Whitmore is a leading citizen of our county. Just who the hell are you to accuse him of anything?"

"You don't understand. His men are riding roughshod over the small ranchers over there."

The deputy cocked a mean eye at him. "Who in the hell do you think you are? I oughta arrest you for trying to stir up trouble."

"Look, Lamar, I'm a former Texas Ranger. I know what I saw over there last Saturday night."

"Why don't you go home, then. We don't

need no gawdamn Texas Ranger in this country. We can handle all the law enforcing here."

Guthrey saw the man's big fist coming at him. He quickly stepped inside the punch and drove his own hard fist into the man's gut. The force of his strike drove all the wind out of Lamar's lungs. The big man went to his knees, trying to gasp for air. Then Guthrey kicked Lamar's hand away from his gun and sent the weapon spinning across the floor. Next he busted him over the head with the butt of his own gun and Lamar went facedown like a poled steer.

"Did'cha kill him?" the short, frowning Mexican woman asked, standing on her toes, trying to look over the bar at the man on the floor in front of it.

"No." Guthrey took the full whiskey shot glass she'd brought over for Lamar and tossed back the contents. The raw liquor cut a trail down his dusty throat and he looked in the mirror behind the bar at himself. Now he would have trouble, but he wasn't about to take a beating from that goon lawman.

He went outside and crossed the street to his horse. Then he changed his mind and stepped back in the hallway of the courthouse. "How much to send this Killion a wire and get a boy to take it out to his ranch?"

"Two bits. But he ain't there."

On the pad, Guthrey wrote, *Check on your deputy. He was drunk and tried to beat me up. He'll have a headache for a while. Phillip Guthrey.*

"Are you serious?" the operator asked, reading the pad.

Guthrey slapped a coin on the counter. "Send it."

"Where can he find you?"

"At the 87T Ranch."

The key operator looked hard at him as if still in disbelief. "You're damn sure enough tough, mister. I hope to see you again."

"You will."

Guthrey rode back to the ranch and arrived there at sundown. Cally came out of the house drying her hands on a towel. "I'm surprised you're back. Dan hasn't come in yet. I'm really getting worried about him, Guthrey. That's not like him at all to stay out like this."

"Where was he going to look at stock today?" He hitched his horse to the rack.

"I'm not sure. He rode west this morning." She ran over and hugged him. "Oh, I've been so worried about the both of you. I think we need to sell out to Whitmore."

Apparently she'd thawed toward him thanks to her concern about him and her brother.

He kissed her and squeezed her tight. "No, don't do that. Dan'll be all right. I'll go look for him."

"I have some food ready. You need to eat first."

He agreed. The daylight was about gone anyway.

She fussed over him as he ate. At last he made her sit down. "You can't get him back here by worrying about him. I'll find him."

"How, in the dark?"

"Trust me?"

"Yes, but — what did the sheriff say?"

"He wasn't there. Some drunken deputy tried to beat me up. But he didn't."

Her fingers covered her mouth, and she looked shocked. "Oh, they'll come and arrest you now too."

"I doubt it. Lock the door. Keep a gun handy. I'll go find Dan."

"When will you come back?"

"After I find him."

"Guthrey, promise me you'll be careful."

"I'll try."

She shook her head like she didn't believe him. "I'll be here."

"Thanks." He kissed her. Then he left the house, found a fresh horse in the corral, and moved his saddle onto its back. With his bull-hide chaps buckled on to protect his legs, he swung aboard. In a few minutes, he started on his way in the twilight, taking a cow track into the backcountry through the chaparral. The horse he rode knew the path, and Guthrey gave him his head, hoping to find Dan if he was injured.

The outline of the mountains to the west stood out against the stars. Grateful he'd drawn a horse that respected the thorny country surrounding them, Guthrey felt that, unless something spooked him, the horse would stay out of the cholla cactus's millions of spines. A canyon's dark depths beckoned to him. If Dan had been in a horse wreck, Guthrey could only hope that the boy was awake and would be able to call out to him. Perhaps Guthrey should have waited until daylight, but a sense of urgency sent him off on this fool's search. Cally had told him it was not like Dan to simply stay away at night because he couldn't get back before dark. He always came back — even if it was full dark.

Guthrey's horse went to the top of a pass between two mountains, then started stiff legged down the other side. He reined up and dismounted to relieve his bladder. The desert spread out beyond him in the silvery light. Some saguaros stood out like fingers pointing at the stars. The strong creosote aroma of greasewood brush filled his nose. The temperature had dropped since he'd left the ranch, he noticed as he climbed back in the saddle.

"Get up, Buck," he said to the horse, giving him a name.

A coyote's howl set off a chorus of them as the pack searched about for a jackrabbit or small deer for their meal. Owls hooted, and the sound of Guthrey's shod horse crushing gravel accompanied him.

Then he reined in his horse to stop. Had he heard another horse nicker? His own mount made a sound deep in his throat that shook him in the saddle. He'd obviously recognized the other animal. Where was he?

The dark form of the other horse came uphill toward him. Guthrey slipped from the saddle and spoke to him. The horse looked sound enough in the starlight. Then he found the tail of the reata still dallied on the saddle horn and broken off about ten feet long. Dan must have had a wreck. But where was he?

With his hands cupped around his mouth, Guthrey called out, "Dan. Dan, where are you?"

He could hear his own voice trying to

penetrate the vast desert night. No answer. He fired his pistol next. The resounding report rolled off across the land and then more silence. Nothing but some distant coyotes howling.

Well, he was closer than before. He might have to wait until daylight to find the boy, or what was left of him. Damn, where could he be? The night's shroud over the land did not answer Guthrey's silent question.

Before he remounted, Guthrey caught Dan's horse by his reins. Later on he might need him. Had this horse strayed from his rider for a long time and traveled a great distance? No way for the cow pony to tell him. He had half the mystery of why Dan hadn't came home. Maybe tracks in the daylight would tell him more. He'd best get himself a place to hang out until sunrise. Dan might be lying somewhere nearby.

Guthrey rode on about a half mile and found some large cottonwoods and cattails — *tules* was what the Mexicans called them. His horse took a drink from the water hole, But Guthrey used the canteen hanging on the saddle horn. The canteen water tasted tinny and warm but it was liquid. Guthrey sure wasn't interested in drinking from some mud hole the roving javelinas might have bathed in.

With both horses' cinches loosened, he hobbled them. With the side of his boot, he scraped a place free of sticks and rocks, then unfurled his bedroll to sleep a few hours until daybreak. Damn, he sure hoped that boy was all right.

The first spears of sunshine peeked over the far-off range of sawtooth mountains, and Guthrey was awake. His bedroll tied back on the saddle, he walked around trying to read signs. Dan's horse had ordinary shoes, so Guthrey could hardly tell it from his own mount. But a horse had come and gone on the cattle trail, so Dan must be farther northwest up the wide basin.

Some cows and calves were coming cautiously toward the water when he mounted up, leaving Dan's horse hobbled by the water hole. Half longhorns crossed with shorthorns, the cows still had a wariness about him he expected. Then he saw a calf following behind with a piece of reata around its neck and the length trailing him. The critter would likely hang that rawhide-plaited rope up on something and starve to death. Guthrey shook loose the rope on the saddle and, standing in the stirrups, fed out a loop.

The cows quickly started to retreat. He

put his spurs to the pony's sides and took off after the calf. His mount cleared a rotting cottonwood log and he was grateful the calf had taken to the grassy open ground near the water hole. When he was close enough, he threw the loop and the pony sat down. Guthrey upended the calf and ran to hold it down.

Its momma stopped and bellowed for the calf to come on as Guthrey sat on top of the critter, looking at the fresh V Bar 6 brand on the calf. Whitmore's mark was on this Three-month-old calf. Then before he jerked loose the extra rope, he looked up and read the cow's brand as she cried for her baby to come to her. She wore the 87T brand on her left side. The Bridges brand. She was their cow, but her calf had a fresh Whitmore brand on it.

What was he into? What in the hell had happened? He straightened up after releasing the calf. He looked all around but saw nothing but chaparral and a handful of cows sounding upset by their bawling. The subject holding his interest ran over to his momma, ducked his head under her flank, and went for some hot milk.

Where was Dan at? He had to be somewhere out here. Guthrey coiled his reata up and tied it on his saddle. His stomach

churned around sour-like and he had a gag-
ging feeling behind his tongue as he sat back
on the polished leather seat and gave the
horse his head. He still needed to find that
boy.

FIVE

Midmorning, having found no sign of Dan, Guthrey crossed a rise into another great grassy swale, and he spotted some buzzards circling. Shocked at sighting those birds of carrion and their interest in a certain piece of ground, he sent Buck off in a hard lope for the place they were focused on. The closer he drew to the object the more certain he was he'd found his boy. Then the figure sat up and shot at a low swooping buzzard with his pistol. The shot dropped the huge black bird out of the sky in a cloud of feathers to flop around in the bunch grass.

"Hold your fire," Guthrey shouted in time to see the haggard-looking Dan fall down on his back. What was wrong? In a sliding stop, Guthrey was off the horse and rushing over to the boy. "You all right?"

"Yesterday." Dan clamped his hands on his injured right leg and winced in pain. "I roped one of our calves that had Whitmore's damn brand on it. My reata broke in the process, my horse tripped, and he fell over on my leg. I must have busted it, and then I kept passing out."

"No problem, I'm just happy I found you. Cally was beside herself last night. I discovered your horse after midnight at some tule water hole. Wasn't much I could do, so I slept till daylight. Saw that calf while I was looking for you, roped him, and got the loop off his neck. Someone had damn sure put Whitmore's brand on him."

"What did you learn from the sheriff?"

"He was too busy counting cattle, they said. His deputy Lamar Dawes tried to start a fight with me. I put the wind out of him and then busted him over the head when he tried to go for his gun."

"Holy shit, they'll swear out a warrant for you."

"So?"

"They may really work you over next time. Boy, they did that to poor Theo Ward. Poor guy was laid up for weeks after the deputy was done with him."

"I'll go plead guilty to stopping a deputy from trying to beat me up. If I can get a judge to accept that, they can't do a damn thing more to me."

Dan frowned hard at him. "How did you figure that deal out?"

"I once had that happen to me down in Caldwell County, Texas. Now, how are we getting you out of here? No way to ever get a buckboard up here. Can you ride, do you think?"

"If I don't pass out again."

Guthrey agreed, then went for his canteen to give Dan a drink. "If you can ride, maybe we can get you home today."

Dan nodded as he swallowed, then he said, "I think you better cut my boot off. It's swollen too tight on that foot. I tried and couldn't do it."

No doubt about it, the sight of Dan's swollen leg shocked him. Guthrey took his skinning knife and began to slice away the boot's vamp first. The flesh ballooned out from the leather incision. Guthrey worried about cutting the boy with his knife, but the boot was finally peeled off his enlarged foot and leg.

"Damn, sorry. You think your leg is broken?"

"I'm pretty certain." Dan's face looked near white.

"Of course we can't see inside you. I don't want to break anything else."

Dan nodded. "I understand. Help me into

the saddle."

"All right, we'll get you on my horse. I'll lead you back to yours. He's hobbled back a few miles. It gets too bad, you tell me. I've got a pint of snakebite whiskey in my saddlebags."

"That might be the best thing I can think of."

It was not easy to lift Dan to his feet, and getting the swollen limb across the cantle and in the seat was even harder. But once he was in the saddle, Dan grasped the saddle horn with white knuckles and his jaw locked hard. They moved at a slow pace.

"You making it?" Guthrey asked time and again when Dan moaned or cried out.

Getting Dan back to the ranch promised to be a living hell for the kid. Step by step Guthrey led the cow pony down the broad grassy swale.

"Guthrey? How are — we — we ever going to stop them from branding our calves?"

"The law."

"But with that damn Killion working for Whitmore, he ain't taking our word for it. Where is the damn whiskey? I need some bad."

Guthrey stopped the horse and looked in his saddlebags for the firewater. In the right side, he found the short brown bottle and

74

removed the cork. "Here. Don't drink it too fast. You aren't halfway safe now on his back. Drink too much and you may fall off."

"I'll be fine." Dan was breathing like he'd run a mile.

With Dan holding the pint bottle on his good leg, they went on. In a while, Guthrey figured Dan was feeling nothing and they were almost to the tule-crowded water hole. He spotted the hobbled horse, who lifted his head and whined at Buck.

"Stay in the saddle," he told Dan and went for the other horse, which was still busy grazing. Thirsty as he was, Guthrey felt grateful for the canteen on Dan's horse. He watered his man down first, who was drunk enough to be singing, ". . . ah, sweet Bessy from Pike."

In a short while Guthrey was on Dan's horse and they were heading into the pass. If the boy could stay in the saddle, they'd be back to the ranch in a few hours. Guthrey could hardly wait.

When the ranch outfit was in sight, he noticed three riders coming off the far slope to their right. Who were they? Friend or foe? He turned his horse back. "I think we've got troubles, Dan. Can you see those riders making that dust coming from the south toward us?"

Dan said, "Uh-huh."

"Grab that saddle horn. We're going to the house, where we have some cover. Hang on, pard."

"I — can — do that."

Gun smoke and the pop of pistol shots came from the three riders. The range was too far, but the strangers intended to kill both of them. Guthrey hoped Dan could stay in the saddle. The ranch headquarters were still a half mile away.

Guthrey charged his mount using spurs and reins. Buck acted like he knew what was coming and broke into a run beside him. They flat raced for the house and some cover. Dan held on to the saddle horn with an iron grip.

The two on their hard-breathing horses covered lots of ground and still the pursuit followed them. Guthrey's back itched, waiting for the first slug of hot lead to strike him. The distance to the headquarters soon became shorter. He could see the windmill.

"Hang tight, son. We're almost there."

Like a wooden Indian, the grim-faced Dan nodded. They swept under the cross-over bar, grateful the yard gate was open. Cally came outside armed with a double-barrel shotgun and tossed it to Guthrey when he dismounted. "It's loaded. I could hear cussing and shooting. I knew something was bad wrong."

"Dan's got a bad broken leg. Get him inside. He's drunk on some whiskey."

She nodded, sober faced, and shouted after Guthrey, "I can handle him."

"Good." He checked the chambers. As she said, it was loaded. With the shotgun in his hands, he started for the corner of the house to stop the incoming riders.

He went on the run around the house to greet them. At the sight of the three riders heading through the gate, he stuck the stock in his shoulder, aimed, and fired. The report of the shotgun hurt his ears. The three horses split, and one went down on his nose and threw his rider. The other two rode in opposite directions. The riders emptied their pistols at him with no results. He was grateful they never stopped moving. At a dead run trying to shoot their empty pistols sideways, they'd be lucky to hit a barn if they had any more ammo in them. The rider on his left went out a small open gate and rode off like the devil was on his coattails. The other shooter jumped off his horse too far away for Guthrey to hit the outlaw with the scattergun. With wire cutters in his hand, the man sliced through barbed wire, remounted, and he too left through the hole

77

he made.

The man facedown on the ground began to moan as Guthrey approached him. His paint horse had gotten up, shaking out a cloud of dust, rattling the stirrups. He looked all right. The cow pony started to drift away but was obviously ground-tie broke and stopped.

"Who in the hell are you?" Guthrey asked the groaning man. Grabbing a handful of the man's shirt collar, he jerked him up on his knees.

"My arm's broken." The injured rider held on to his right forearm, crying out in pain as Guthrey stood him up. Then, seeing that the man's holster was empty, Guthrey shoved him toward the house. His prisoner half stumbled, and Guthrey used the shotgun's muzzle to prod him on.

"What's your name?"

"Bud Jones."

"I mean your real name."

"Jack Nelson."

"Who hired you to do this?"

"No one."

"I'm going to wrench that damn broken arm off at the shoulder if you don't give me answers I want to hear."

He drew back. "Some guy named Hampton. I don't know any more."

"Keep talking."

"I don't know who he was. Big guy."

"Your memory will get a damn sight better when I get done with you."

"Who is he?" Cally asked from the doorway, looking ashen faced and staring at the dust-coated intruder.

"Jack Nelson, he said. You know him?"

She shook her head. "Dan's on my bed. I never saw him that drunk before."

"His leg's broken. There may be more wrong. He roped a calf, his reata broke, and his horse lost his footing, fell, and must have rolled on top of him."

With a grim, set face, she nodded. "When did you find him?"

"Midmorning. I've been coming back ever since."

Nelson sat down on the floor. Guthrey pointed his finger at his prisoner. "You try one thing, I'll tie that broken arm to the other one until I can get you to the sheriff."

He obeyed.

"I'll fix some food. You must be famished," Cally said.

"Thanks. I'm going to hitch up the buckboard. I'll take this one along with me. And after we eat, we can drive him over to the sheriff and take Dan to a doctor."

"Won't Killion try to arrest you?"

"He better not try."

"I can take them. Someone needs to see about the cow and stock here."

"We'll talk later about that." He motioned for Nelson to get up.

"All right," she agreed. "But I know Judge Collier. He lives in Soda Springs. He'll listen to me."

"That might work. Let me hitch up and we can talk more later." He pointed to the open door for his prisoner to move that way.

Outside, the two headed for the corral. Guthrey sat Nelson down on the ground and went about catching the team. With a currycomb and brush, he cleaned them up, routinely checking on the silent outlaw. When the harness was on, he drove the horses over and hitched them to the rig. His job done, he told his man to walk back to the house ahead of him. The man had no choice. It was obvious the impaired arm had him in a great deal of pain.

Inside the ranch house, Guthrey sat him on a chair. Cally had the food out, and before she took a seat, she gave each of them a plate of fried eggs and pancakes. Their coffee cups full, she swept her dress under her and sat down.

"How's Dan?" Guthrey asked her.

"Sleeping so hard that I let him alone."

"That's all right. He needs sleep more than food. Maybe pack some sandwiches for him to eat later. Can we hire a neighbor to watch the stock? And, since you know the judge, you should be with me. I don't trust Nelson here or his buddies who ran off."

"Noble McCoy is an old cowboy. His place is on the way to town. I think we could hire him. He's dependable."

"Good. We'll do that, then."

They loaded a pallet for Dan to ride on. Guthrey tied the moaning outlaw's arms to his body and put him in back too. Then he hitched the saddled Lobo, his bay gelding, to the tailgate in case they needed a mount.

With Cally's basket of food and water in the back, they set out for Soda Springs.

When Cally pointed out a homestead on the way to town, Guthrey stopped at the rickety-looking place beside the road. A rumpled old man came out and took off his hat to wave at her with a smile.

"What brings you and this hombre by here?" he asked, coming over in a rambling walk.

Cally introduced Guthrey to the older cowboy, Noble. "Dan had a horse wreck yesterday. This is Guthrey, who's helping us. He found him. We're taking Dan to

81

Doc's at Soda Springs. That other rascal in back is one of the three people who raided the ranch this morning."

"Raided the ranch? Who were those scoundrels?"

"He ain't saying much," Guthrey said.

"Can you go up and milk my cows, feed the chickens until I can get back?" Cally asked.

"Miss Cally, I'd love to. I'll stay up there. You don't worry about a thing. I can handle it."

"Good, we must run," she said and motioned for Guthrey to drive on. And they left him in the dust.

"He'll do a great job. He took care of things while we made arrangements and had Dad buried."

The tears in her eyes from what that recollection brought on he saw and read. She was weary of all this business and still choked up over her father's recent murder. And Dan's condition added to her concerns. Lots of wrongs didn't make a right moment for her.

Six

They reached Soda Springs, the Crook County seat, in late afternoon. Parked in front, Guthrey handed Cally the reins. After adjusting his gun belt, he reset his hat on his head, and his boot heels soon hit the wooden floor. No one was at the jail. The cell keys had been thrown on the desk, and Guthrey looked around the office and jail cells. Nothing. The sheriff's office and jail cells were dark and empty. He lit a lamp to search the interior, unlocked a cell with the keys from the desktop, and went back to get his man. He jerked the prisoner out of the wagon, hauled him into the office, untied him, and slammed him in the jail. Then he went out, locking the door behind him, leaving the protesting raider in the cell.

"What about me and my arm?"

"You can stay here till hell freezes over. The sheriff will be here in a few days." He went back outside, got in the wagon, and circled the team, listening to Cally's directions to the doctor's office.

Grateful he could see that someone was inside the former house turned office, he jumped down and ran up on the porch. A woman with graying hair came to the door.

"Is Doc here?" Guthrey asked, not knowing the physician's name.

She turned back. "Doc, a man is here. He sounds serious."

A tall man wearing a white shirt came in the room. "Yes?"

Guthrey took him out to the wagon. Doc nodded to Cally on the seat.

"Dan Bridges was in a horse wreck yesterday. I think he broke his leg, maybe more."

Doc looked over Dan where he was lying on a pallet in the wagon. "You have anyone to help bring him inside?"

"Not really. His sister is all."

"Go get Black Jim, Kathryn," the doctor said to his wife, who'd joined them. "He'll help us get the patient inside."

"I'll do that right now." She pulled on the shawl in her hands and nodded to Guthrey as she went by him. "He's a very powerful man who helps us in cases like this."

"Yes, ma'am."

Cally was pacing back and forth beside the wagon. After Guthrey told her that the doctor's wife had gone for help, he saw her perk up.

"What will Killion do when he finds a man in his jail and that you have his keys?"

"Where does that judge you know live?"

"Not far from here."

"When we get Dan inside for Doc to examine, we'll take the wagon over and talk to the judge. If he accepts our story, Killion can't do a thing but hold him for trial."

"Okay."

He hoped he'd settled her down some.

Jim was a big man and Guthrey noticed that his hands were huge when Doc introduced him and Guthrey shook the man's calloused paw.

"Oh, you help me gets him back here, Mr. Guthrey. Then I's can carry him inside. Why, he's just a boy."

Guthrey climbed in and sat Dan up with a struggle. The boy was mumbling, still drunk. Soon they had him in Jim's arms and he was packing Dan like he was a half-grown kid. Cally came along behind the man in the huge pair of overalls who was bearing her brother. Dan was placed on a table in the office and Doc thanked the big man. Guthrey paid him a silver dollar and Jim looked at it like it was too much.

"Stay here," Guthrey said to him. "Doc

will maybe need more help. We'll be back. We need to go see a judge."

Cally looked with concern at her half-awake brother and squeezed his hand when they started to leave.

"We'll be right back," she said and hurried out with Guthrey.

At a house on the side of the mountain, Judge Steve Collier answered their knock on his door. "Yes?"

"Your Honor, my name is California Bridges."

"Yes, yes, I know you, young lady. What can I do for you?"

"My brother had a horse wreck yesterday. Mr. Guthrey here found him and was bringing him back when three men attacked them. They were shooting at the two of them as they raced to the ranch house. Guthrey took our shotgun and shot at one, his horse fell, and Guthrey got him. The other two rode off." She paused. "No one was at the jail when we got here. . . ."

"I locked him in the jail," Guthrey said.

"The sheriff has a man in town. You can go wake him."

Guthrey shook his head. "I came to town to talk to Sheriff Killion yesterday. I found his deputy drunk over in Rosa's. He started a fight with me. I finished it."

"I wondered, when she said your name, if you were that person who beat him up."

"I give myself up and plead guilty. What's my fine?"

"Why, I guess it would be ten dollars for disturbing the peace and insulting an officer of the law. Why?"

"Here's your ten dollars," Guthrey said, handing him the money. "Now, we want that man in jail tried for attempted murder and terroristic threatening, of her and the rest of us."

Collier laughed, flipping the gold coin in his palm. "I know this makes you an unwanted man in the eyes of the law. Who is the man that you arrested?"

"He told me his name, but I think that's a lie too."

Collier looked at her. "You didn't know him, Miss Bridges?"

"No, but what Guthrey is telling you is the truth."

"I believe him."

"The man broke his arm falling off his horse while shooting at us."

"You tell that to Doc?" Collier asked.

"No, but we'll tell him when we go back to check on Dan," she said.

"I'll go find Dawes and handle this arrest business. The man you brought in will be held for trial. And I'll tell Dawes and Killion you pleaded guilty and paid your fine. I'm sure they'll be disappointed, but that's not my worry. What did you used to do, Guthrey?"

"Captained a company of Rangers in Texas."

"I knew you had either military or law enforcement experience. Thanks. I can't believe we have raiders besides those loose damn Apaches. You two don't have any more suspects besides this man you captured?"

"We didn't know those others who escaped," she said.

Behind the judge's back, Guthrey nodded his head at her that she'd done right. "We need to get back to see about Dan," Cally said.

The judge shook Guthrey's hand and bade Cally a good evening.

"Oh," Guthrey said, handing him the key ring. "You may need this."

Collier took it with a laugh. "Good night."

Guthrey drove the buckboard in silence until Cally spoke up. "Why not tell him about Whitmore?"

"Might sound like we were mere gossips. I doubt he'd believe anything about a big rancher. We're going to have to prove that he's behind all this. That will be hard."

"I see what you mean."

He put his arm around her to squeeze her shoulder. "The calf branding, and these raiders, eventually can be dumped on Whitmore's front porch."

Reined up at Doc's office, Guthrey helped Cally down from the wagon and then hitched the horses.

Inside they found Doc washing his hands at a pitcher pump.

"How is he?" Cally asked.

"I'm worried about his hip. Do you think the horse rolled on him?" Doc asked Guthrey.

"Yes, he told me it did."

The physician shook his head. "He may have hip trouble. I can't see inside him, but he may have some pelvis damage in there. I can set his leg, but if his pelvis is damaged it could make him a cripple for life. He'll have to stay here for some time and let things heal. You can stay here tonight, if you like. I have him on laudanum so he'll sleep. Rest is best for his problems."

"Thanks," Cally said, looking at Guthrey.

"I can take a blanket, if you have one, and sleep on the porch."

"I'll find you one. Miss Bridges, come with me. I have a spare bedroom upstairs,"

Doc's wife said quietly.

Cally thanked her and then nodded to Guthrey.

"He'll be all right," he reassured her.

"I hope so," she said and followed Kathryn up the staircase.

With a wool blanket from the doctor, Guthrey went outside and made himself at home in an old stuffed chair on the porch, where he and the crickets shared the night.

As he fell asleep, he wondered what would happen next.

SEVEN

A heavyset man with a gray-flecked walrus mustache sat on a fat horse at the low yard fence. He wore a tailor-made green checkered suit and black silk vest, and a gold chain attached to a watch hung over it. His hat was an expensive white Boss of the Plains Stetson. Clearing his throat, the man woke Guthrey, who had still been sleeping in the chair on Doc's porch.

"You must be the gawdamn Texas Ranger that beat up my deputy Lamar Dawes."

Wide-awake in an instant, Guthrey narrowed his gaze at the man. The sheriff — no doubt. "I settled that last night with Judge Collier. Your deputy was drunk as a hooter. If he tries to arrest me again without a warrant, he may be a dead one."

"Listen to me. I am the law in this county. You mess with me or my men and you will be pushing up daisies."

"A citizen has rights. If your campaign

supporters keep running off and terrorizing small ranchers you'll be in the jail with them."

Killion frowned at him. "What proof do you have of that?"

"Let's start with a calf that belongs to an 87T cow found bearing the Whitmore brand. They still lynch rustlers in the West and his neck can be stretched as well."

"You better not be tied to any lynch party."

"No one knows the identity of lynch mobs. You know that." Guthrey stood up and began to fold his blanket. "Did that liar I had locked up tell you that Hampton hired them to wipe us out at the 87T Ranch?"

Still straight-backed as a top rooster, Killion acted like he'd heard nothing of the sort.

"I'll bet when they send him to Yuma, he'll talk his tongue off. Then everyone will know about your partnership with Whitmore, won't they?"

"You're pretty stupid. You keep alleging I'm part of some gang. You'll never prove that."

"Tell me how stupid I am when a grand jury finds how involved you are with Whitmore in his range-squeeze scheme."

"I catch you doing anything illegal, you'll

do time yourself." Killion turned his horse and began to ride off to control his own temper. "You keep on, Texas, and you'll never see freedom again."

"You better ride on, you may miss counting a cow."

As he stepped inside the open door, Guthrey handed Cally the blanket.

"You shouldn't agitate him like that," she said in a soft voice. "Either he or one of his men'll try to kill you again."

"I want them to try to do something. Then I can get them arrested." He looked down the hall. "How's Dan doing this morning?"

"I don't know; they have him heavily sedated. What if his pelvis is broken?"

"I've worried about that too. But I'm not a doctor. He took a hard fall and was rolled over on by a large horse. That is not a good thing." To him she looked deeply struck by it all. He wanted to hug her and assure her they'd do all they could for him. If they had to, they'd take him to a larger town like Tucson or El Paso. But how would it look if he hugged her right now? Hell with it. He reached out and pulled her against him.

"We'll do whatever we have to do. There's someone somewhere can straighten him out."

In his arms, Cally put her forehead against

his chest. "Oh, Guthrey, I'm lost. I'm sorry."

"Listen, my mother called me Phil. Why don't you start calling me that?"

She looked up at him. "I'll call you Phil. Thanks."

"Good. I just don't want to ruin your reputation. I find myself impulsive around you. I know hugging you might not be proper, but I knew you needed some shoring up."

She squeezed him tight. "I'm glad that you did."

They separated at the sound of someone coming down the stairs. It was the doctor.

"Did I hear Sheriff Killion shouting at you out there?" Doc asked.

"Yes, sir. He was out there threatening me to quit bucking Whitmore, I guess."

The balding physician shook his head in a disgusted manner. "He's not much of a sheriff."

With a nod, Guthrey quickly agreed. "Do you think the boy's hip is broken?"

"I can't be sure, but I'll treat him as though it is just to be certain."

"Then he has to stay here for some time?"

"Yes. Definitely. He doesn't need to be shaken apart, and a ride home in a buckboard would do that."

Guthrey turned to Cally. "Do you have

94

any money?"

"Some."

"Here." He reached into his pocket and gave her three ten-dollar gold pieces. "Don't protest. You need to stay here. I'll go back to the ranch. Me and that old man can see about your cattle. I'll come back and check on you two in a week."

"But —"

Waving his hands at her, he put down her protests. "No buts, I'm heading back to the ranch. You stay here. In a week we can see how he's doing."

"Phil?" She pulled him down by his sleeve and kissed his cheek. The site burned like a brand. She whispered, "Thanks. You two be careful out there."

"I bet we know how. Will I need anything to cook for the two of us?"

"Maybe some flour. Do you make biscuits?"

"Not as good as you do. I'll get some flour on the way back. Listen for what they do about that shooter. And I'll see you in a week and you can tell me what's going on."

"Oh, please be careful." The worry in her eyes knifed him.

Hell with it. He took a deep breath and kissed her hard on the lips, then turned on his heels to go get Lobo saddled and head back to the ranch. As he passed, he said, "Thanks, Doc," over his shoulder.

EIGHT

The sight of the Bridges Ranch in late afternoon brought a little relief to the soreness in Guthrey's aching back muscles. Part of his back problem came from loading and unloading Dan into and out of the wagon, but he could stand all that and would soon forget it if the boy turned out to be all right.

He saw Noble McCoy come out of the house, back his butt to the wall, and roll a cigarette to wait for Guthrey. When he had dismounted Lobo, Guthrey began to strip out the latigos and called out to him, "Everything all right, Mr. McCoy?"

"Where's Dan and Cally?"

"Doc said Dan needed to stay bedfast for a while. I made Cally stay there to look after him. You got anything that you need me to do, Mr. McCoy?"

"Hell, my name's Noble. I ain't no *mister.*"

"That's fine. Just call me Captain or

Guthrey." He shook the man's hard, calloused hand.

"All right, Cap'n. You and me need to keep an eye on the stock, huh?"

"We need to find that calf that's got Whitmore's brand on it and sucking one of the kids' cows."

"Holy jiminy, did they do that?"

"That was what Dan roped the day he had the wreck. His reata broke in the process of his horse falling down and then rolling on him. I caught the calf and got the short length of rope off him so he didn't hang up. Then I brought Dan to the house and three of Whitmore's riders tried to cut us off. I got one, took him to Soda Springs. The other two rode off."

"What did you do with him in Soda Springs?"

"I locked him in the jail. Then I spoke to Judge Collier before Killion got back into town. The judge said they'd hold him until his trial for attempted murder and terroristic threatening."

Noble nodded as if satisfied about the deal. "I heard tell the judge is a tough ole buzzard. He ain't a territory man either. He's a federal judge. They never could agree on judgeships in the legislature, so they got all of them from the federal system."

"He isn't that old. He sounded fair enough to me."

"I was going to wrangle up some supper for myself when I heard you coming. Two minds are powerful smarter than one. What are we going to eat?"

"We can cut off some ham over in the smokehouse. Fire up Cally's range, fry the ham, make some biscuits, and open a Mason jar of something to have with it."

"By jingoes, you are a lot smarter than I am. I was going to boil some pintos till they'd mash and make me some real gas."

Guthrey laughed. "We may have to eat some of that later, but right now I have the plan."

"God bless you for that, Cap'n."

"I'll start a fire in the stove. Can you put that horse up for me and fetch some water? We'll be eating before sundown if we hurry."

"I been batching so long by myself, I don't have any imagination left. I'm going." He gathered up the water pails and went to do his chores.

Guthrey watched him go out the door in his cripple gait. How old was Noble? he wondered. Past seventy? Maybe he'd simply lived a tough life, but Guthrey knew from his experience with his own father: Don't dare tell him he's too old. He might whip your ass for even implying it.

The fire in the stove soon caught ablaze and Noble was back. Water was on the stovetop to boil for coffee. The skillet was hot enough to make the ham sizzle while Guthrey's pan of biscuits was in the oven and starting to really bake. He found a quart jar of canned green beans that he opened and poured into a saucepan on the edge of the main fire spot in the range top.

By sundown they were enjoying their supper. Noble was rambling about being with the Texas Army and Sam Houston at San Jacinto when they captured Santa Anna.

"Damn, I was tired of retreating. We kept asking Sam Houston when we were going to fight that bastard. He'd just shake his head and say, 'When we can win.' Damn, I thought that day would never come. But they got as tired as we did and finally decided we wouldn't ever fight them. And then we struck them hard and we also captured Santa Anna. I wanted to kill him for the Alamo. Sam would not hear of it. Said we wasn't that low. I guess we weren't."

Guthrey nodded. "We better turn in and go find that calf with the wrong brand in the morning. Or would you like to stay here at the ranch and watch things?"

"When my ass starts dragging, I'll tell you."

"Fair enough. You tell me when."

"I might as well get it off my chest. These kids wouldn't have had a chance to survive here on their own with their pa gone. Why did you stop here?"

"I saw that and guess it made me think I weren't doing nothing else right now."

"What I figured. Couple of men I know saw you in town buck them three over that boy that afternoon."

Guthrey nodded. "I might have ridden on that day. But it was too obvious Dan was about to be legally murdered."

"For a fact, he would have been. All right. Good night, then. Ring the triangle. I ain't a real early riser these days."

"I'll do that."

Outside Guthrey undid his bedroll from the saddle and went to find a place to roll it out. The coyotes were yapping and their owl accompaniment carried on the night wind, which was making the windmill creak so loud that Guthrey decided it needed grease. At last under the covers, he mentioned Dan in his silent prayers. Then he rolled over on his left side and went to sleep.

The cow's hoarse bawling woke him early

the next morning. He checked the big dipper. It was close to dawn.

He'd learned how to tell time by that constellation on his cattle drives to Kansas. It was how all cowboys knew when their shift on guard duty was over. He had gone on his first drive as the guy who helped the cook, learned the business and the ropes, then soon drove his own herds up the line. Flooding rivers to cross, tornados, storms, stampedes, the sorry element of bandits, and the logistics, a word he learned in the army. He worked really hard for the three to four months of herding cattle north, had deaths in his crew, pneumonia, snakebites, and horse wrecks. On his last trip two boys were shot in town. Maybe the sight of Dan braced by Whitmore's men reminded him of the Dugan brothers, Tad and Arnold, lying dead in the street that afternoon in Wichita while some drunk braggarts bought rounds of liquor in a saloon and told the world what big men they were. Must not have been too big though. Each one of those three fit in some hastily nailed together coffins made from cottonwood lumber.

He milked the cow first that morning, then went up and lit two lamps in the house and started a fire in the stove. He brought in an armload of small split wood for future

102

fires, then put the coffee water on the stove before he started the bread dough. Noble joined him and laughed.

"By God, I can see you're a man without a woman. Any man this handy has been doing his own cooking for a spell."

"You ever have a wife, Noble?"

He held up three fingers while Guthrey ground up some roasted coffee beans.

"Can you recall their names?"

The old man sat down on a chair at the table. His gnarled hands folded on the tabletop, he nodded. "First one was Claudia. She was my camp follower in the war for Texas, a small Mexican girl who treated me like a king. We were both just kids. When she heard I'd been wounded in battle she tried to get to me. She got ran over by a runaway team and heavy wagon. She's buried in a Catholic churchyard in San Antonio."

His biscuits in the oven, Guthrey straightened and looked at the old man for more of his story. "Number two?"

"I was riding from Austin to someplace up the Colorado River bottoms. I came across a six-foot-tall woman whose wagon was stuck in the mud. She had a big team of horses and they were no help. One would pull, the other one fall back, and after that the other one would do the same thing. No way could she get them both to pull at the same time.

" 'Well, don't sit on that horse and gawk at a woman in trouble,' she said, sounding disgusted with me. 'Either get down and help or ride on.'

" 'Hold on to your britches, lady. I'm coming,' I said. In those days I could take a leather line, whip it out, and cut a small patch of hair off a mule's belly to show him who was boss. My pa told me when I did that I was to whisper, 'Whoa, Jack' and check them with the lines. He also said to do that in a small voice. Second time he'll hear you if he misses it the first time.

"The team consisted of a mare and a gelding that were the worst I ever saw at that trick. So I got on the right side of them, took the lines from her, and shook my head at her offer of the buggy whip she'd been using on them. Next I whipped a line over my back and leaned into the strike, holding them back and said, 'Whoa, Jack.'

"And I took a small patch of hair off the gelding's belly.

"I mean his ears went forward and he stood on his toes. Their owner didn't like it, but I saw that she kept her mouth shut. When I clucked to them, the mare went forward like I thought, and the horse, he fell back in the harness. I did the line trick again at that moment and he joined her and they rolled that wagon out of the mire.

"She looked flabbergasted. I took off my hat and shook her hand. 'How in the blue blazes did you do that?' she asked.

" 'Experience,' I told her.

"Well, her man had been kilt in a war, so we set up housekeeping. Wasn't no sin, we were surviving, and six months later we got married. Eulia and I had us a place west of Austin, and we freighted. Made a good living. Never had no kids, though we sure tried. She took a fever, and after six long days she died. We had five good years. I went back to cowboying. Freighting is boring without company, and I was pretty melancholy about life without her. She was a foot taller than me, and we'd wrestle like two bear cubs. One time she'd win, the next I would."

Guthrey took the biscuits out of the oven and set them on the table, put the skillet of ham-flour gravy on a hot-plate board, and poured them coffee. They ate in quiet, and when they finished, full as pups at a butchering, Noble cradled a tin cup coffee in his hands and continued his story. "Then I met Celia Watson." He chuckled until he had to

105

set down the coffee cup, then shook his white-bearded face. "Now, that was a funny deal. Sweetest but most scatterbrained female in my life. I found her carrying a suitcase on the road to Mogollon, in the middle of Apache country, and back then they were really bad down in that part of New Mexico.

"I rode up and asked her what she was doing there. She said, 'I'm damn tired of working in a whorehouse and so I set out to find me a new job. But I guess I plum forgot how far the rest of the world was away from the Snyder Gold Camp.'

" 'My lands, girl, where are you going?' I said. 'Ain't no town either direction from here less'n twenty miles. And this is Apache country.'

"She set down on her suitcase and dropped her chin in defeat. 'How can I do it, then?'

" 'What are you looking for?' I asked.

" 'A job. It don't have to pay much, just so I get out of wrestling with unbathed old men every night.' She shook her head at me, filled with dread.

" 'I've got me a small place up at Alma,' I told her. I did some day work. It suited her and we had a good life together for a long spell."

"You ain't got a wife now?" Guthrey asked him.

"Lord, no. She died two years ago. She asked me that morning on the road how I was going to get her suitcase and her up there on the horse with me.

" 'Ride double, I guess, and tie the suitcase on.'

" 'That will beat the hell out of walking.' She handed me that carpetbag and it was heavy as hell. I wondered what was in it that heavy. But I tied it on my horn."

Guthrey laughed at Noble's yarn and shook his head. "How come it was so heavy?"

"I asked her. How she ever came that far a-packing it I'll never know.

" 'Never mind. I'll show you later,' she said. She put one foot in the stirrup, and I pulled her up behind me and looked all around for some copper-faced Apache to be peeking at us.

"We finally made it to my place up by Alma. She was a doozy. But sweeter to me than any woman I ever had. I married her a month or so later. She was twenty years younger than me, but that never bothered her."

"What was in the suitcase?" Guthrey asked.

"You won't believe me, but she had gold nuggets that those miners paid her inside it. That's how we moved down here and bought that place I live on now."

"What happened to her?"

"She took sick one day and I got the doc to come there and check her. After he examined her, he came out and shook his head at me. It was her heart. There wasn't anything he could do. It just up and quit on her."

"Did she linger long?"

"Maybe a week of me praying and hoping to God she'd come out of it. But she passed away one night in her sleep. She was so simple and so scatterbrained, I loved her every day we had together. She'd get up and say, 'We going to church this morning or not?' Hell, it would be Tuesday. She baked a pie once and forgot the sugar. Sourest dang apples I ever ate, but I ate it all and never let her know it wasn't good."

Guthrey could see the tears in the corners of his eyes. Noble blew his nose and turned away. "Celia was the neatest thing I ever had, despite her scatterbrained ways. I'd come home tired and she'd crawl on my lap. Tell me how she missed me all day since I left that morning. No one could have been sweeter. And she meant it."

"Well, you've had a great life."

Noble shook his head. "I guess I ain't talked that much about myself in years."

"Thanks, it was a good story to hear. Now let's go find that calf." Guthrey lifted a lid on the stove to check the fire. It would safely burn out. Then, with the door closed behind him, he went into the early-morning light to pick a horse to ride.

Noble was already in the corral, shaking out a loop. "What horse you want?"

"The white one. He looks stout."

Noble tossed the loop over the horse's head and the animal stopped. He was a veteran cow horse, Guthrey decided as Noble dragged his saddle blankets and rig over to saddle him.

They both had their mounts ready in a few minutes and turned the rest out to graze. In the saddle, they rode west to cross over the hills and headed north to where Guthrey had found Dan. They checked several groups of scattered cows and calves plus some resting roan, shorthorn bulls that rose and stretched their backs at the men's approach. There was no sign of the Whitmore brand on any of the calves they looked at.

Noble proved to be a real hand at circling cattle to bring them out of the brush so they could be examined without a lot of unnecessary riding for them. At midday, Guthrey and Noble watered at a tank fed by an iron pipe from a spring. The cool outflow of the spout wet down their mouths and throats as the day's temperature warmed. Their canteens full again, they gnawed on some jerky that Guthrey had brought along.

"This country has some good water," Noble said. "Bridges developed lots of it. Whitmore hasn't done a damn thing but load more cattle on these ranges." Disgusted, he shook his head over the deal.

"Why do the work yourself when you can crowd folks out of where they've done theirs?"

"You've got it." Noble remounted with a little more effort, but he still looked as solid as anyone once his boot soles hit the stirrups.

There was no sign of the wrong-branded calf, though they were searching in the same country where Guthrey had found Dan. "We better go home. There's still tomorrow to go look for him again."

Noble agreed and sat his hipshot horse. "Oh, he'll show up."

Guthrey agreed. They rode back to the ranch talking about the range. A good drenching rain would help the forage, but in the southwest the rain gods were always stingy. Not much difference between west Texas and this part of the desert country in that respect. But this region had a small edge on moisture that came out of the gulf in the monsoon season, according to folks Guthrey had talked to about it. More brush growth and forage than the same latitude in Texas, which he knew would mean there might be better soil out here as well.

In another month, those rains were expected, but the good Lord knew when they'd come. After dark, back at the house, he made coffee and they ate leftover cold biscuits and a jar of canned pork sausage balls heated up.

Noble stood in the doorway as the twilight settled on the land. "When do you reckon Whitmore will try another strike on you?"

"Let him come. I'm ready."

"I don't doubt he will, but next time I figure he'll send six dummies instead of three. By grabs, there's comfort in numbers among a damn lot of cowards."

"There sure is. We can eat now, it's ready. If they come, they better be in their Sunday clothes."

Noble nodded and took his place. "They won't be as easy the next time."

"No, but he ain't hired any Mexicans so

far, has he?" Guthrey asked, pouring them some fresh coffee.

"No, why?"

"He hires some of them tough ones, we may need to barricade up somewhere."

"Guess you ran into them as a Ranger."

"They call them Tigres down there. They aren't the easygoing peons that come from south of the border to find work up here." He took his chair. "I think they can bite barbed wire in two."

"Where do they live in Mexico?"

"Sierra Madres." Guthrey filled his plate, recalling the raid that he and his fellow Rangers had made far below the border to bring back a vicious killer. "Our unofficial invasion of Mexican territory to arrest the bandit chief Gilbert Antago was an international upset deal that Mexico told Washington, D.C., was clearly warlike. But in reality, the *federales* helped us locate him and we caught him hiding in a privy before dawn. We handcuffed and leg ironed him, then put him belly down over a stout mule and headed for Texas. No one was able to hinder us getting him out of that country. In the El Paso jail, we put a ball and chain on him so they couldn't break him out.

"On the way back from Mexico, we finally stuffed some dirty socks in his mouth, we got so tired of his filthy language, threatening us and bitching."

"Did they hang him?" Noble asked.

"Yes, they did, for killing an entire ranch family in one of his many raids above the Rio Grande."

When they rode out the second morning, they both had loaded Winchesters in their scabbards and cartridges in their saddlebags. By then Guthrey really had begun to miss Cally and her cooking. She'd spoiled Dan and him both with her great meals. Their private conversations had somehow been more of a hit with him than he had thought. Things would be better when she returned. Wednesday, he planned to go in and check on her and Dan. He certainly would be grateful to have her cheerful voice back again. And her cooking.

Over the next few days, there was still no sign of the calf they were searching for high and low. They range roped a steer and a yearling heifer to treat them for signs of screwworms. The old man was great on the heel catches. He could effortlessly rope one horse out of a bunch in a pen or wind his reata around a stock cow's hocks and then stretch the animal out.

On Tuesday, they went back in the foothills

where they had looked the first day. Noon-time found them at the same spring-fed water hole. Eating some apple turnovers Guthrey had made in the skillet that morning, Noble was bragging on him.

"You're a pretty good hand at this cooking business." Busy eating the treat, Noble looked to be enjoying them.

"They taste good enough, I guess. You know we ain't seen a soul all week. Whitmore don't have any range hands?" Guthrey asked.

Wiping his mouth with the back of his liver-spotted hand, Noble shook his head. "They travel in groups of three or four when they do come through. That's part of his bluffing folks with his forces. Most of them act like they own all this ground, and the small guys don't belong here."

Guthrey turned his ear to the wind. "I heard someone talking on the wind. We may meet some of his men this afternoon."

"Yeah, I just now saw a black hat over the chaparral coming down that draw out of the west."

When Guthrey stood up, he brushed the dirt off the seat of his pants, reset his holster, and saw a different colored hat bobbing above the spiny vegetation.

"Two of them now," he said to Noble.

The old man rose and stretched. "May be more than that."

Another rider coming off a hillside whistled to his partners when he spotted Guthrey and Noble. It was a loud, shrill whistle and the two in the draw soon appeared on top of the bank still a good distance away.

Guthrey moved to his bay ranch horse and jerked out his rifle. In moments Noble did the same.

"I can handle them," Guthrey said.

Noble nodded. "When I work for a man, I ride for his brand."

"Thanks." He had his eye on the first two.

"Howdy." One of the hands stood up in his stirrups with his hat cocked back and waved at them. "We ain't looking for no trouble."

"You're close enough."

"Hey, me, Jake, and Bob are just out checking on the cattle for our boss, Mr. Whitmore. We ain't borrowing no trouble, mind ya. My name's Howard."

They looked like simple young ranch hands, but Guthrey wasn't taking any chances. "There aren't many of your cattle up here, Howard."

"I know that, but we have orders to check this country. We saw a few head of our

115

stock. We're going to pick up and drive them back south when we go home tonight."

"Good enough. Leave ours up here."

"Oh, we will. You mind if we get a drink? Kind of a hot day."

Guthrey told them to go ahead, sharing a nod with Noble. Then he slid the rifle back in his scabbard. These weren't the hard cases he expected.

When the blond-headed youth who called himself Howard dismounted, he nodded again at Guthrey. "You must be that ex–Texas Ranger?"

"I am."

"Been a lot of talk about you around here. How you beat up that deputy in Soda Springs."

"He was drunk and going to arrest me. He got what he deserved."

Howard held his hands out. "I ain't saying he didn't deserve it, mister. Just repeating what I heard. How do you like working for a woman?"

The working for a woman line about threw him. "Fine, me and Noble here like working for her just fine."

Howard made a face. "Guess I could too, as cute as she is."

"Miss Bridges is a fine young lady." Were they trying to get his goat? If they said one wrong word about her, he'd peel some hide off of them.

The other two looked like the cat had got their tongues, drank, watered their horses, and left the talking to Howard, who Guthrey figured was in his early twenties. The others weren't out of their teens.

In a short while, the three mounted up, tipped their hats, and rode on.

"I thought that Howard boy was going to say too much," Noble said under his breath.

Still watching them ride off, Guthrey nodded. "Let's work north some more today. That calf may be up that way."

"You still ain't talking." Noble chuckled and swung in his saddle. "That youngest one, sitting quiet, I thought would piss in his pants when you confirmed you were the Ranger they'd heard about."

Guthrey agreed. "I guess he was afraid of something. He never said a word the entire time."

"Having a reputation like yours ain't bad, by golly."

"It helps sometimes. The way things are going we'll be getting in late tonight, so let's move."

"No problem. I've enjoyed it all, even trading words with them kids." Then he laughed. "They sure might have done that branding as an order from their boss. That young one sure did amuse me."

"What's that?"

"How close he come to pissing in his pants." Noble stood in the stirrups and trotted his horse, chuckling all the time.

Past sundown, they could hear the Jersey cow complaining as they came over the pass. When they reached the corrals, the light left was just enough for them to see their latigos and peel the saddles and pads off their horses. Turned loose, their mounts went to roll in the dust. Noble headed after a milk pail, and Guthrey started the stove. They were soon in their evening routine.

Guthrey made pancakes and syrup for them along with coffee. He was about ready to serve it when the milker came in with his pail. After Noble covered the pail with cheese-cloth to keep the flies out, he went to wash up. "That is a good cow. I was raised with kicking cows that clubbed me many times when I tried to milk them as a boy."

"Me too," Guthrey agreed. "We had one we called Blasting Powder, and I finally had four bucket-calves suck her instead of milking her. Mom complained, said she had the richest milk of any of our cows. I told her that she could milk her, then. Never heard another word about that cow's milk again. I halfway expected Dad to jump on me about talking to her like that, but he knew the cow well."

"I guess, by golly, in the morning you're a going to town and check on them kids."

"Yeah, we'll eat early and I'll go in and ride back tomorrow night."

"Good. I sure hope Dan is better."

"Me too. I'm tired of cooking."

Noble slapped his legs. "Ha! That's what not having a wife puts on a feller."

Guthrey agreed. Except he simply missed Cally's company more than he'd ever dreamed he would. Her absence made him impatient with himself as the week had worn on. The pancakes even tasted blah. Noble bragged on them, but Guthrey figured the ole man would brag on anything he didn't have to cook.

Way before daylight, Noble nudged him with his boot toe as he slept in his bedroll.

"Get up. I've got breakfast ready."

Guthrey set up. Was something wrong? It wasn't even light yet.

"Come on, it'll get cold. I knew you wanted to start out early today. I'm going to water Cally's garden today and hoe in it."

"You didn't have to do this."

"By grab, I know what I have to do."

Pulling on his emptied boots after he shook them out — in case there was a critter got in them overnight — Guthrey laughed. "Noble, you make a dandy guy to batch with."

"You tell Dan and Cally I said for him to get well."

"I'll do that."

"And leave those dishes for me to wash. You get on up there and find out how that boy's a-doing."

"Noble," Guthrey said, "you keep your guns handy. Since you've sided with us, they'd shoot you as quick as any of us."

He nodded. "You're probably right. I'll do that."

On his own horse, Lobo, Guthrey left the ranch before the sun even came up. The horse was fresh and acted tough when Guthrey boarded him. He intended to push his mount. On the road to town before dawn, he spooked some mule deer grazing beside it. They bounded away in the starlight. Unlike their cousin, the whitetail, who simply ran, the black-tailed ones had a four-legged bouncing-like gait that got them their name.

Guthrey arrived in Steward's Crossing still

half-asleep and never stopped. Then he went west up the steep hill on the Tucson road toward Soda Springs. He hadn't heard much news about the Apaches who had broken out from the San Carlos Reservation, but his isolation on the ranch cut him off from the rest of the world.

Had Whitmore sent those three men he met the day before up there to eliminate that calf? If they had done that, his momma would have been bawling to find him — a sure sign they'd taken him. But since they never heard or saw her, chances were good that he was still up there somewhere.

Guthrey short loped his horse the next few miles. A tough pony despite his ugly head, Lobo had a gait that was smooth enough. In the first peachy light of day, the tall saguaros started to become statues that must have seen the Spanish conquistadors when they came to this land hundreds of years earlier. What if they could talk? He shook his head and nudged Lobo with his spur to go a little faster.

The tules soon filled the wash bed beside the road. Guthrey arrived in the Crook County seat, walking his sweaty horse the last mile to dry him out. He dismounted at a café that was open and had a cup of thick coffee. Commerce had not started for the day, and he marveled at the short time the hard ride had required.

Seated with him at the counter were some obvious workers. They talked about the lack of rain and some man named Nelson who'd broken out of jail.

"Didn't he have a broken arm?" Guthrey asked them.

"Yeah. How did he ever overpower a guard and get away?"

The man turned back to his coffee and commented, "He must have been a tough sumbitch."

"No, he was part of the 'gang' that runs things around here," the burly man beside Guthrey said. "That damn big shot Whitmore's got a passel of them hired to do his bidding. I'd bet that Bridges boy lying up there at Doc's, his wreck was probably caused by them too."

The others down the counter agreed.

"When're we going to get tired of him running roughshod over everyone?" the mouthy one asked. "They run off that family on the Double L place."

"Saul Mitchel?" someone asked.

"He sell out?" another said. "I didn't know that."

"Yeah and left the same day."

The conversation was fast and Guthrey

was trying to piece it all together. The workmen soon left for their jobs. He paid the thickset waitress ten cents for his coffee and went over to Doc's.

At Doc's office, he hitched Lobo to the rail, and a fresh-faced Cally met him halfway to the front door. He hugged her and kissed her on the side of the face. "How's your brother?"

"Better. But Doc is still not sure that he doesn't have more problems inside. The leg is set, and he's still in lots of pain. How are things going with you and Noble?"

"Besides the fact we haven't found the branded calf, all right. I guess you heard that Nelson broke out of jail, and with his arm broken too."

She made a face. "How damn convenient," she said under her breath. "It is so good to see you." Then she blushed. "I've missed our conversations."

"So have I. What're your plans?"

"Let's talk it over with Dan. I'd like to go back home to sleep in my own bed. Be in my own house and tend my garden." He followed her back inside.

"Noble is hoeing in your garden today and plans to irrigate this afternoon."

She shook her head as if embarrassed. "You two may spoil us."

Her brother was propped up on his pillows in the bed. "I thought you two were taking all day to come back inside."

"We had lots to talk about. How have you been?" Guthrey asked, sitting down on a chair beside Dan's bed.

"Better. You all find that calf?"

"No. We've rode every day last week and ain't found hide nor hair of him up in that northwest country where I found you. Treated two head for screwworms. I think we got to them in time."

Dan frowned. "He has to be up there unless someone got him."

"I think his momma moved ranges. There was no bawling cow looking for her baby. No buzzards looking for a meal anywhere we've been either."

"I ain't lying."

"Easy, I roped him too, so I know he was branded like you said. We'll find him. That old man Noble is tougher than I thought. He's a helluva good guy to ride with."

Dan laughed. "I guess he told you about all his wives?"

"Most of it. They were the highlight of his life."

"Yes, I never thought of it like that. Yes, they were."

Cally took a seat on the end of the bed.

"Dan, I'm thinking of going home and looking after the crew. I can't do much for you here. Can you make it without me?"

"Oh, I'll be fine. Doc wants me to stay here for a while and heal. I can use those crutches now and get around. Did you know that guy you arrested broke out of jail?"

"Yes, I heard it all over town when I first got here. Folks are upset. Think he was simply turned loose."

"See how sorry the law is in this county?" Dan shook his head in disgust.

"Don't overload your backside when we ain't here," his sister said. "Whitmore has plenty of allies listening."

"I won't. I simply get mad that Dad's killer is still walking around free as a bird."

Guthrey said, "He won't do that forever. If we can find that dogie we'll have a start on taking him down."

Dan lay back on his pillows. "I know you will. Sis, you be careful. I don't think they care anything about not hurting women."

Guthrey shot a glance at Cally. "Did I miss something?"

"It happened last year —" She looked around to be certain they were alone in the room. "A woman on the Two Star Ranch was assaulted and left for dead. Her husband didn't want any more trouble with them, so he never reported it. Later she told a few of us women that three of the raiders raped her repeatedly."

"Who were they?"

"She said they all wore flour sack masks. But one of them wore a red ruby ring. Poor woman didn't want to talk about who they were, but she slipped talking about that ring. . . ."

"Good morning." The doctor's wife, Kathryn, swept into the room in a fresh starched dress. "Dan, how are you doing this morning?"

"Fine, Miss Kathryn."

"Good. And how are you, sir?"

"Doing all right," Guthrey said. "He thinks he's recovering. I'll be glad when he's back at the ranch taking care of the cattle."

She raised her eyebrows. "We hope it will be soon. Is there anything you need, Cally?"

"No, ma'am." Everyone sort of waited to talk further until Kathryn finally exited the room.

Cally made a face after her exit. "She should have married a preacher."

"What's wrong?" Guthrey asked.

"Oh, tell him, Dan. What she said."

"She told Cally if she went back to the ranch without a chaperone and you cowboys

126

were out there, it would ruin her reputation."

"That's what she told me." Cally shook her head in disgust. "I am still going back to the ranch. You two don't need to do my jobs."

"If Dan can get by here on his own, I can drive you back today."

"I can handle it," Dan said. "Besides, she's going crazy just sitting around here."

"Thanks." She looked pleased at her brother.

"When you want to go back to the ranch, you just say the word." Guthrey was looking out the window at a rider who dismounted at the Texas Saloon across the street. The rider looked vaguely familiar.

"Dan, is that one of those three raiders who shot at us? He's about to step on the Texas Saloon's porch."

Leaning forward, Dan looked hard at the figure, then nodded. "I recognize his hat."

"I wonder where the other one is at," Cally pondered.

"Good question," Dan said.

"What should we do?" Cally asked.

"You two stay here. I'll go check him out."

"You be careful," Cally told him. "That big deputy is still on patrol here."

Guthrey nodded and went out the back

way. He trotted down the alley behind the businesses and crossed the street past the saddle maker's shop. Nothing in sight but some horses at the hitch rail in front of the Texas Saloon. In a few minutes, Guthrey was outside the back door of the bar. Up the six steps, he eased the unlocked door open. One of the working girls sitting on a wood case about screamed at his appearance. He put his finger to his lips. From his vest he took out a half dollar and tossed it to her. She caught it in two hands and smiled.

She hurried over as he beckoned to her with his hand.

"There is a man in there that wears a black hat with a floppy right side." He pointed to that side of his own weathered hat. "He's large. You go out there and check so that he don't know anything, then come back and tell me where he's at and who he's with."

The next half dollar made her really smile when he showed it to her. She raised her hems higher and pranced out of the room, which was full of beer kegs and wooden cases of liquor bottles.

Impatient, Guthrey dried his right hand on the side of his pants. He shook his head over the passing minutes. She sure took her time getting back to him. Then she appeared and came quickly to where he stood with his arms folded.

"He's with a shorter man at a side table," she whispered. "They've been in here before. Calls himself Rip. The other man is Thad, he's sometimes a cowboy."

He paid her the other half dollar.

"I can coax either one of them back here." She twisted, holding the side of her worn dress out from her body.

"Thanks, I can handle them. Were any of their friends in the place?"

She laughed aloud, then covered her mouth with her hands and looked embarrassed at her outburst. "Nobody likes them."

"Good. Stay in here for a while."

She made a seductive pose for him, with her hands on her hips. "You ever get lonely, come find me. I'm Sealley."

"Thanks, Sealley." He straightened, hefted his pistol a few inches from its place of rest in his holster. The revolver was free enough to suit him. Not looking at the men at the table, Guthrey came through the back door and stopped at a place midway down the bar. Using the mirror behind the bar, he made sure there was no one behind the men if he had to shoot either of them.

The two men frowned at each other when

they noticed Guthrey's abrupt entry and how he was staring at both of them. Their look was one of "Who's he?"

"It's him from the —" The one Sealley had called Rip managed to get out. Both men went to their feet but too late, and in that split moment, all hell broke loose. They were too slow. Guthrey had his pistol hammer cocked and ready to shoot them so fast it made the pair blink in disbelief. They let go of their gun grips, released their weapons to settle back in their holsters, and raised their hands in the air.

Guthrey moved in quickly and disarmed them, shoving their pistols one at a time in his waistband, and indicating a direction with his gun barrel, he made them move aside.

"What the hell are you doing with us?" Thad asked.

"I'm marching you up to the jail and filing charges of terroristic threatening."

"You think they can hold us?" Rip asked as if he would be walking out of the hoosegow as soon as he got there.

"I don't have to worry. The sheriff will keep you two." Guthrey stopped his prisoners at the batwing doors. "Stay right there," he warned them.

His original words drew laughter from the

other customers.

"If he don't, the sheriff'll be in court," Guthrey said in a soft voice. "He's sworn to uphold the laws of this territory."

"Yeah, they won't touch him or else our taxes will double," some guy shouted.

The man's words sunk into Guthrey real slow as he herded the two out on the boardwalk. He made his two prisoners move ahead of him, and his plan was to march them down the street to the courthouse.

What if Killion wasn't counting all of Whitmore's cattle? Did the tax count go up on any opposition people who were on the tax rolls? How could he find out those numbers, and how accurate were they? Interesting thoughts.

Both of his prisoners marched a few feet ahead of him. At his direction, they crossed the street without incident. Every business's porch had filled with quiet onlookers. By his estimate, the boardwalks were filled with store employees or folks who were in town to shop. The strained looks on their faces, like they expected something to explode, stabbed his heart. He figured that these quiet people were worried that more blood would be shed in the street this time. In places, the onlookers backed up for him and his prisoners to go by them.

The doors were open at the courthouse. In the hall, he told them to turn in to the jail and ordered them to get into the first cell, which was dark and empty. Then he realized there were no keys lying on the desk or anywhere in sight. He opened the top desk drawer while both men stood inside the cell. He took the pair of small keys he found in the desk and unlocked the chain threaded through the rifles and shotguns on the gun rack. He held on to the four-foot chain too. Then he wrapped it tight around the door and the steel door frame and put the lock on it.

"You think that will keep us in here?" Rip asked.

"I do, 'cause when you escape this jail there will be several consequences ahead for you both. There'll be wanted posters for you two that will say wanted dead or alive. You won't sleep safe anywhere you run. Bounty hunters will be sniffing out every place you ever hid." Guthrey laughed aloud at the vision of them cornered, so scared when the trackers closed in on them that they'd pissed in their pants knowing their certain fate.

"Those wolves will shoot you in the back of your skull. Chop your head off with an axe and stick it in a burlap sack to claim

132

that reward. They never bring live ones back. They don't have to feed a head. That head won't escape them. It don't need a horse to ride either. Simple execution. Before you step out of that cell you better think about the price of your freedom."

"You son of a bitch," Rip said, kicking the metal bed. "I ever —"

"Shut up!" Thad said.

The telegrapher came over to the door of the office and met Guthrey at the hall coming out. He asked in a whisper, "Did you bring in more prisoners?"

"Yes."

"You know that other guy is gone."

"You know where he went?" Guthrey asked him.

The man shook his head and held out his hands to wave off any part of it. "How are you going to keep them in?"

"Swear out a warrant to hold them for trial."

The agent cocked his right eye shut to look at him hard with his other one. "To who?"

"The judge."

"What can he do?"

"Enforce the law."

The agent shook his head. "You don't

know how Crook County law works, do you?"

"It will change." He gave the keys to the telegraph operator to put in the top drawer of the desk for the sheriff and the judge to find, and in moments he came out the front door of the courthouse to meet Cally coming to check on him.

"Someone said you arrested two men and marched them to jail." She looked very concerned.

"I captured two in the saloon in broad daylight. And I threw them in a cell."

"Are they locked up?" she asked in a hushed voice.

He nodded, keeping an eye on everything out in the bright sun. "Is Judge Collier in town?"

"I don't know. But we can go by his house."

Spinning around at the sound of a horse coming on the run, she caught his gun arm, "That's only Freddy Shields. His dad is a rancher."

"Good," he said, hurrying across the road with Cally half running to keep up with him and holding her hem up.

"I remember the judge's house. It's not far." He tossed his head at a house high on the western slopes of the mountain.

"What if he's not at home?" she asked.

He slowed down when he saw that he was winding her. "We simply need to find him and swear out warrants to hold those two for trial."

She gave him a disgusted look. "They let the other guy get away."

"That needs to be stopped. The judge has the authority to do something."

She caught his arm and they halted on the rise. "What if Killion continues to ignore him?"

"Then we may need to go higher up. All the judges in Arizona are federal judges, I understand. They have power. Collier may need to use it or I need to go see the governor."

"Have you ever had this problem in Texas?" she asked when they started hiking again up the open cheatgrass-covered hillside.

"The Texas Rangers have arrested several crooked sheriffs and bad officials over the years. They all went to prison."

"Will that stop Whitmore?" she asked upon reaching the judge's yard.

A collie barked and ran around all excited. The judge's wife came out on the veranda. "Come here, McDougal. Those people don't need to be jumped on."

"He's fine," Guthrey said, and coming through the gate, he dropped down for a minute and shook the dog by his lionlike mane. This was one of those great dogs, a watchdog and partner to his owners, and Guthrey felt a little jealous of her having him. But there was no place in his life for a dog — he didn't even have a place in his life for himself.

"Miss Bridges and Mr. Guthrey, I believe?"

He swept off his hat. "Yes, ma'am. Is your husband home today?"

"Oh, he's coming back from Tucson on the stage. I expect him around noontime."

"I brought in two men who were in on the terrorizing at the Bridges Ranch and put them in jail. I had hoped to swear out warrants for them."

"He should be here in just a little while."

"Thank you. We'll come back then," Guthrey said.

"How is your brother?" the woman asked Cally. "I understand he was hurt quite badly in a wreck."

"He was in a horse accident. He's mending, we hope. He is much better. Thanks, ma'am."

"Sorry my husband wasn't here."

"No problem," Guthrey said to keep down

the missus's concern. He petted the collie again and then closed the gate, keeping the dog in the yard.

They headed back to the doctor's office. To save some time, Guthrey planned to cross the steep open desert going back toward the cluster of buildings. At the real sheer places in the hillside he helped Cally over the rough terrain. The curing spring foxtail and wildflowers, which they walked through to reach the road at the foot of the hill that led to Mexico, were turning brown. On the hard-packed surface at last, they cut across more desert to come in at the back of the doctor's place.

"What if someone gets word to the sheriff about your prisoners and he comes to town to turn them loose?"

"I'll have to make other plans."

She hugged his arm at the foot of the porch stairs. "You be careful. We — I sure need you right now. With Dan down and all, there's no way that I could run that ranch. How's Noble?"

He laughed. "Why, he's tough as a snapping turtle. How old is he?"

"I think someone counted up and he's close to eighty years old."

"He's seen some tough times in his life,"

Guthrey told her, holding the door open for her.

"Did you two get into any trouble?" Dan asked them, sitting up on the bed with pillows behind his back.

"No. But Guthrey arrested two of those raiders over in the saloon," Cally told him. "And the judge won't be back until the noon stage arrives."

"That can be anytime," Dan said, amused. "It depends on how many times they rob it between here and Tucson."

Cally and Guthrey agreed, and Cally went for some coffee for the two of them. Dan didn't want any.

"How did you find the two of them?" Dan asked.

"You saw the big guy go in over there. He joined the other already in the Texas Saloon across the street. The two of them were busy drinking like nothing had ever happened."

"They give you any trouble at all?"

"Just verbal." He dismissed any of the action as just part of his day.

"Do you think I ever knew them?" Dan asked.

"One's named Thad and the other is — oh, Rip. That may be an alias."

Dan shook his head. "What are you going to do now?"

"Wait for the judge to arrive."

Dan nodded, then made a face when he raised himself up by his hands and moved a little, seeking a more comfortable spot. It was obvious to Guthrey that the boy was a long ways from being healed. Did he have more things wrong on the inside? No way to know and now only time would tell.

"Can I fix you two some lunch?" Cally asked.

Guthrey nodded and Dan thanked her.

Unable to simply sit and wait for the judge, Guthrey walked the floor of the bedroom and tried to figure out a way to solve all this business with Whitmore's harassing people and Killion's lack of doing anything. If these warrants failed to hold those men in jail and his plan didn't work, maybe he needed to go to the capitol in Prescott and find the governor. Someone needed to be in charge of law enforcement in the territory and put a stop to Whitmore's terroristic threats and running over the little people — ranchers and small farmers.

The judge appeared when the stage dragged half the dust off West Mountain into town and stopped in the wind-driven catch-up cloud of tan dirt. Judge Collier descended behind a fancy dressed lady, who the driver courteously helped down the iron step to the stool he had placed for her to more easily descend.

His honor recognized Guthrey and walked over to shake his hand. "How are things going?"

"Someone let the first prisoner I brought in out of jail. I have two more of that gang in the jail now, but so far no lawman has shown up at that office this morning that I know about."

"Damn that bunch. I am going to wire the governor to send a U.S. marshal down here to take charge of this county's law enforcement."

"Can he do that?"

"He may have to declare martial law, but he has that authority, if he will take it. You know the legislature has called for an Arizona Ranger force to be initiated in the Territory, but they have never funded it. Too much politics going on up there, and these sheriffs are getting so much money being tax collectors that they can buy the legislative votes to stay that funding."

"I learn something new every day," Guthrey said as they headed for the county offices again.

"I will wire him and perhaps he can have a man here in a few days."

Guthrey agreed. "I guess we can round

up the other one again if he hasn't left the country."

Collier agreed. The jail office was still dark and empty of lawmen. The two prisoners in the cell acted sullen, plus they wanted food and water. Guthrey gave them a canvas water bag and told them the law had to feed them.

"Where the hell is the law at, then?" Rip demanded.

The judge walked in and stood looking at the pair. "I am told by the telegraph agent that there will be someone here shortly. The telegraph agent has sent for them."

Why hadn't he sent for one of them in the first place? Guthrey wondered. Then he smiled to himself. The agent knew that if anyone came the prisoners would be turned loose because Guthrey was the one who brought them in, but the lawmen could not turn down the judge's request to jail these two malcontents. Guthrey owed the bright young man a thank-you.

The same big bruiser he'd had the fracas with at Rosa's came in. He looked hard-eyed at Guthrey, but then, when he saw the judge, he put on a phony smile. He cleared his throat and spoke in a gravelly voice. "Yes, Your Honor, what may I do for you today?"

"We have two felony-charged men in your jail. Be sure they are kept here. Their bail is a thousand dollars apiece, cash money only. If they aren't kept in here you will pay their bond."

"But — but . . ."

"Also, I want that other one that someone released to be brought back here. Put a ball and chain on them if you can't keep them locked up."

"Yes, sir, Your Honor."

"If you can't maintain this jail and office, then I'll place a U.S. marshal here to do it." Collier pointed his finger at the desktop.

The deputy was looking all over and finally collapsed in the chair. "Where are the keys?"

"I don't know where the cell keys are," Guthrey said. "The key for the lock on the chain around the cell door is in the top drawer. I took it and the chain from the gun rack to lock them up."

"Oh, oh, I see now."

"Listen," Collier said, "I expect those two to be here when the grand jury convenes."

"Yes, sir, Your Honor, I understand."

The judge nodded to Guthrey and they left. Outside, Collier shook Guthrey's hand. "We'll get this thing straightened out. I appreciate your help. Where will you be if I need you?"

"At the Bridges Ranch north of Steward's Crossing."

"Watch for word, and thanks again." After they parted, Guthrey went over to get Cally and head for the ranch.

Back at the doc's office, Guthrey hooked up the ranch team and Cally soon joined him.

"I told Dan," she said, loading her things, "that I'd be back next week to check on him."

"We can arrange that."

"You and the judge settled everything?"

"For now anyway. He's going to telegraph the governor to send a U.S. marshal to examine everything about the sheriff's office and its operation. I learned something else."

"What is that?"

"The telegraph agent helped me. When the judge got into town, he sent for that big clown Killion has for a deputy. I figure he knew that bruiser would turn those men loose. But not with the judge there."

"The telegrapher's name is Tommy Glendon."

"I'll thank him next time." Guthrey boosted Cally up to sit on the spring seat, then went around and climbed on himself.

She clutched his arm. "Do you believe we will ever settle all this business?"

"Yes, ma'am. Everything takes time."

"My father has been in his grave hardly more than a month and we still don't . . ."

Guthrey turned to look at her. She was biting her lower lip and tears spilled down her cheeks.

One-handed, Guthrey tore loose his neckerchief and told her to take it. Back in control of the horses, he made them trot, and they left Soda Springs with his horse hitched on behind. It would be after sundown before they reached the ranch. But she'd be home and should feel better if she didn't worry her head off about her brother's recovery.

The trip was long, and it was after dark when he wheeled the buckboard into the yard. Noble came over with a candle lamp to help him unhitch.

"How's the boy?" Noble asked, holding the light up high and smiling at Cally.

"He ain't ready to ride a bronc," Guthrey said.

Noble laughed. "How are you doing, Miss Cally?"

"Fine. Good to be home, Noble. Thanks for helping us."

"Aw, I'm glad to be here. Who else needs

an old busted-up cowboy to help them?"

She hugged him. "We sure do, don't we, Guthrey?"

"You bet. Any problems?"

"Nothing I couldn't handle." He shrugged as they went for the house.

"Anything bad happen?"

"I caught a guy scanning the ranch headquarters with field glasses."

"Who was it?" Guthrey asked as Cally lighted the lamps in the house.

"Said his name was Smith."

"That's an original name, isn't it?" Cally teased and shook her head, busy firing up her range to make supper for the two of them.

"Who did he work for, do you figure?" Guthrey asked.

"Easy enough. He rode a Whitmore Ranch–branded horse."

Guthrey closed his eyes. Was it a good idea to allow Cally to come home? It was just one more thing for him to worry about. He needed an army and had one old man, a girl, and a possibly crippled boy. Where could he find more help? No telling.

In a short while, Cally served up some fried potatoes and scrambled eggs and joined Guthrey at the table with hot coffee. Noble sat with them and sipped coffee.

"Did that Smith tell you why he was surveying the ranch?"

"Told me he was simply hunting."

"What did you do to him afterward?"

"I kept his field glasses and told him I'd shoot him if he ever came back."

Guthrey laughed. "I bet he ran home."

"Well, I loaded him on his horse and emptied my pistol close enough he thought I was shooting at him."

Guthrey put down his coffee and laughed. Cally joined in. "You did what?"

"By golly, I busted some caps close enough he could hear them whiz right by his ear."

They finally turned in. Noble left the house ahead of Guthrey, and Cally walked him to the front door. "Can you believe he did that?"

"He damn sure did it." He kissed her lightly and said good night.

She whispered after him, "Sleep well. I appreciate all you've done for us."

He nodded and went to spread his bedroll near the corral. All his efforts to help had fallen almost on deaf ears. One judge was the only person to really help him. Maybe they could do some good before Whitmore ran everyone out of the country. Guthrey didn't sleep well that night with those thoughts rattling around in his head.

NINE

Before dawn, Guthrey milked the gentle cow and carried the half pail to the house. Cally was up and dressed, working on making bread, but she looked like she'd slept little during the night. He put the milk pail down and then poured himself some coffee from the pot on the range.

"Did you have a bad night?" he asked, seating himself.

The flour flew and she nodded, busy working the dough in her wooden trough. "My family just wanted to ranch here. I'm not sure that was a good idea. We moved here right after the war was over. The Apaches were still running over this part of Arizona. But we never bothered them, and they respected us. Kind of live and let live.

"Mother died of something. The doc never knew what it was. She had the fever, lay in bed listless, and then she slipped away. I thought her death took some of the strength

Dad had away from him. We had some run-ins with Whitmore's men, but that made Dad more determined. I figured they shot him 'cause he was trying to get the others organized to fight their takeover of this county."

"Did they have meetings?"

"Yes. But all that activity ended with his death. They went back into their own shells like turtles. When there was no more talk about doing something, that's when I think Dan went to town and challenged them. Mercy, thank God you came along."

"Things have been quiet since the botched raid, 'cept for that scout they sent to spy on us."

She shook her head. "We simply aren't hearing about it. No one is talking about being threatened, but what we did hear is that they're taking a little cash from Whitmore, less than their places are worth, and leaving without so much as a word to their neighbors."

"I guess I better spend more time in town," he offered.

"Am I interrupting you two?" Noble asked from the doorway.

She smiled at him. "No, we were just talking. Come in. I nearly have breakfast ready."

"Morning. Guess you milked the cow?

She ain't bawling for anyone out there. She's a good gal," Noble said after washing his hands and face, then took a seat. "Kinda like company to have her."

"I already got her," Guthrey said. "But thanks."

"What are we doing today?" Noble asked as Cally brought him steaming coffee in a tin cup and waited for Guthrey's reply.

"I'd still like to find the calf with Whitmore's brand on him. Did you see him anywhere while we were gone?" he asked the old man.

"No, but the way I get around, I figured if I did see him I'd leave him for the two of us to handle together. Broke my leg a few years ago messing with a range calf like that while working him on the ground."

"Good idea," Cally said. "One crip is enough on this ranch. Poor Dan, he must be beside himself not knowing what's going on out here."

"I didn't expect that calf to be that hard to find." Guthrey shook his head. "I found him easy when I roped him and took the broken reata from around his neck."

"That calf has bothered you, hasn't it? Ever since it happened, you've been bothered," Cally said, putting breakfast on the table for them.

"It was rustling. Pure and simple. Better said, it was blatant rustling."

"I can't figure why he had it done." Noble shook his head. "May just have been some of his ornery help's idea too."

"That's a good thought," Cally said.

"For whatever reason, it was a shot at your ranch."

"But it didn't hurt any of us."

"I don't like to be spit in the face," Guthrey said. "Come to think of it, that might have been a red flag insult to get your brother Dan all upset."

She turned from washing the dishes to frown at him. "What do you mean by that?"

"What if they figured he'd come stomping mad to town again and challenge them like he did the day I arrived?"

She dried her hands. "That sounds more like — Phil, you saw that calf last week. Was the brand fairly fresh?"

"Oh, yeah. I think that was what they planned." Guthrey said. "They wanted him mad as hell and ready to expose himself so they could kill him — justified."

"You're a good influence on him," she told him. "He would have done just that if you had not settled him down." With the back of her hand against her forehead, she slumped on a kitchen chair. "All this information shakes my faith that we can ever survive."

"Buck up, girl. That conceited devil isn't going to run us off. We're going to stop him," Guthrey said.

Noble agreed. "He won't ever take over this whole country."

Cally shook her head. "You two are looking on the bright side. All I see are dark canyon walls squeezing us out. On Monday I need to go to town and get some supplies."

"I better go with you."

"I'm sorry. I know you two want to ride the range and check stock."

"No problem. So we better look over things the next couple days," Guthrey said. "You keep that shotgun loaded and close."

"I will. I promise." She rose and went to the door with them.

Noble went on out after asking Guthrey what horse he wanted cut out.

"That white one is good."

"That was Dad's favorite mount. He rode him up there to check on that water hole. Dan was shoeing a horse that day and let him go alone. I worried the white horse made him an easier target."

"I know. I want them to try."

"Oh, don't ride him, Phil. Please, for me?"

"Let them try." He hugged and kissed her.

"Don't worry."

She looked sad when he left. But he had some plans to see if they were surveying his and Noble's activities on the ranch. The spy they sent to keep an eye on them that Noble discovered was no genius. But hiring a paid assassin was not beyond a man like Whitmore. No doubt Cally's father was either shot by one of them or by Whitmore's foreman, Hampton. The rest of his men, Guthrey decided, were probably not open killers. Like the ones he ran off in town that first day he showed up.

An assassin was different. He came to do a job. He was professional. He had an arsenal of weapons. Telescoped rifles that could kill a fly from far away. A small pistol to fit in his hand and kill a victim in close contact. A suitcase of knives with small, thin blades to kill someone in a crowd. Explosives. Guthrey recalled such a setup in Texas where a banker was blown up by an individual paid to do it by a man who hated the banker. The killer looked like a businessman when he checked into the town. In the days before the murder, he inquired about buying a business for himself. If he had brought enough dynamite, he never would have been caught. He must have felt he did not have enough power, so he stole some sticks of blasting powder from a store's shed and dropped a glove in the process.

After the explosion, the merchant told the town marshal that he was missing six sticks of blasting powder from his stock. The local lawman investigated and told Guthrey he felt the glove found on the scene of the crime belonged to the thief. Investigations showed the expensive glove was handmade by a Dallas company. The glove's mate was found in this man's luggage when they decided he was the only one in the town who could have afforded such an expensive item.

The assassin was hung for the death of the banker, and so was the man who hired him. It was another case he'd closed as a Texas Ranger. But in Cally and Dan's case, Guthrey needed evidence or someone to confess to shooting their father. Nothing in these deals was ever easy. Without real law enforcement, it was ten times harder to solve cases like this.

After several unsuccessful days riding the ranch and looking for the calf, Noble and Guthrey returned to the house each night with no more information than they had left with. Sunday night, Guthrey went to get some sleep under the starlight, pondering the events of the past few days. He rolled over again in his bedroll and tried to go to sleep, but it escaped him.

TEN

The next day Guthrey drove Cally into Steward's Crossing for supplies. While she was in the mercantile, he went over to the Lucky Star Saloon and ordered a beer. The place was nearly empty. Some old derelict was scrubbing the floor with a rag mop. Mainly he was mopping without changing water on his mop and making muddy swirls on the floor and singing hymns. Better said, he was trying to sing hymns, but he only knew half the words to them.

The bartender, observing the man's action, finally threw a towel over his shoulder, came around the bar, and went to cussing him out. "You dumb peckerwood, ain't you ever mopped a floor before? Get the hell outa here right now. You're fired. You've made a big damn mess of the floor is all you did." Then, after taking possession of the mop, the bartender shouted, "Sophie, come here!"

A thin woman in a threadbare dress came out of the back room and asked him, "Huh?"

"See what that damn bum did to us? Now mop this floor till it's clean."

"I didn't make the damn mess," she grumbled but went to hand wringing out the mop.

The bartender came back, complaining about the help he could not hire to do the job.

Guthrey nodded in agreement, nursing the beer and hoping for more customers to come in so maybe he could talk to someone who knew something.

"You're the guy bucked Whitmore in the street about three weeks ago," the bartender said, coming down the bar while polishing a glass.

"Yeah. You seen them two gunmen again?"

"You want to do it again with them?"

"No, I want to talk to them if they're still in the country." He sipped on his beer.

The bartender stacked the glass he had finished cleaning and came down close. "What would you pay to know where they're at?"

"Depends how much information you have."

The barkeep looked around before he said

in low voice, "Jewel Hanks is working at a sawmill over in the Chiricahuas. He's some kin to the guy who owns it, or his woman is. I ain't sure. I don't think Larry, who calls himself Sewell, is around. His name in Texas when I first met him was Thomas. Claude Thomas."

No doubt he was wanted in the Lone Star State. Men didn't change their names unless they were wanted or did something sorry in their past. Guthrey put a silver dollar on the bar. "Where did he go?"

"Tucson, I think."

He slid the coin across to the man. "What else do you know?"

"Have they started the damn railroad from El Paso yet? This place is goin' to dry up before it gets here."

Guthrey shook his head. "I don't know. I didn't come that way. My name's Guthrey." He waited for the man to give him his.

"Tim, Tim Wallace."

"I came across northern New Mexico and down through Silver City to get here."

Wallace nodded. "Are the prospectors doing any good up there at Silver City?"

"Some are, some ain't."

"Just like most of those places. There were some good mines up there, the rest are a kiss and a promise. Tombstone's another like that down the road here. They boom and bust. They've got some big payrolls, but there's plenty of bars already there. No need for me to go to that town. Why didn't you go down there?"

"Besides Rangering in Texas, I've spent the rest of my time working cattle. I'm not working at a damn mining job." Guthrey downed the last of his beer.

"I savvy that. You going to ranch here?"

"I'm looking. Thanks." He left the bar mulling over the question of where Whitmore's two hired guns were employed at the time Dan and Cally's father was shot. At the least, they had been on Whitmore's payroll back then. But since their former boss fired them for refusing to face down Guthrey, they might add to Guthrey's information. No telling how tough they were. They knew him or had heard of his rep in Texas. The only way he'd ever learn anything was to go look them up.

A teenage clerk was loading items in the buckboard when he joined Cally in the hot sun. She smiled. "I hurried."

"I told you that was not necessary." He wanted to hug her and kiss her cheek to reassure her he was back, but he restrained himself. When had he gotten so possessive? The last two women he'd courted he hadn't done that with. For certain he did not need a wife at this time. He had no big stake to buy himself a ranch or even a paying job.

When all her things were loaded, he lifted Cally up in the wagon, and she laughed. "I'm not a cripple."

"Just loading you," he said and laughed too.

She looked a little embarrassed and shook her head.

Before he could speak, two middle-aged men rode up. One was long-faced, wore a suit and Western hat and sat atop a good-looking tall bay gelding. He took his hat off for Cally.

"Howdy, Miss Bridges. You doing all right?" She nodded to him, then he spoke to Guthrey. "Are you going to be at the social Saturday night?"

"I can be." They shook hands.

"Carl Brown's my name, and this is Lester McCall." The older man leaned over and shook Guthrey's hand too.

Brown said, "A bunch of us want to talk to you about doing a job for us: taking over as sheriff."

Guthrey looked surprised, but said, "Sure enough there's a need for a better lawman in this county. You think it ought to be me?"

Brown looked around. "Yes. Give it some

thought. We don't need to discuss the details now. It can hold till the social. I wanted to be certain you were going to be there." He reined his horse around. "Miss Bridges, have a nice day. Guthrey, we'll look forward to talking to you then."

The two rode off down the street. Guthrey could see that Cally had a million questions to ask him and he had half that many for those two ranchers about what they wanted from him.

"What did they really want?" She squirmed on the seat beside him as he took up the reins to leave.

"To talk, they said." He made sure no one was coming, then made a U-turn in the wide street. He had plenty of room to turn the team around, and afterward he clucked to the horses to trot. The matched pair of bays stepped out, and he sat back on the seat.

"They sounded very serious. They said something about me taking over as sheriff."

"Sheriff?" she asked in a subdued voice. "My father told them almost two years ago they needed to kick Killion out of office, but few would listen, and the man who ran against him that fall was not too sterling. After the elections, he moved on when he didn't get the job."

"It's spring now. There won't be an election until next November," Guthrey said, shaking his head. "The parties won't choose their candidate till late summer. Maybe. How influential are those two men?"

"They could be strong if they wanted to be. They're leaders in the Mormon Church here. Lots of folks around here are Mormons."

"Well, does that change your plans about going to see Dan this week?"

"I guess I better go on Friday to see him." She looked back and was satisfied that only dust was chasing them.

"We can do that." He still was niggled by the men asking him to talk to them at the dance. They sure had something on their minds that sounded serious. Would he take or seek a law job in Arizona? The sheriff and tax collector job sounded like a good-paying one. Good enough that he'd have a big fight if he sought it. Killion would not hand his badge over on a plate to him, that was certain. And Whitmore was already upset over Guthrey saving Dan. He'd fight Guthrey tooth and nail. Dang, this could get complicated.

"You made up your mind yet if you want to run for sheriff?" she asked, hugging his arm tight.

He shook his head. "I've been thinking what I could live on for that long. It would be after the first of the year before I took office if I did win."

"We could feed you. I mean, you could eat and live at the ranch."

"But everything costs money in this world, Cally. I mean everything, and going from now till next January without any money would be hard."

"But I bet you could win the election. You're the only one who ever stood up to Killion or Whitmore."

"And they'd make sure I was miserable the entire time until I did take office, and possibly after too." He reined up the team and stopped at the side of the road. There were things he needed to get straight with her, and this was as good a place as any. No one was around but some quail calling out in the chaparral.

"Is something wrong?" she asked.

"I guess there is. I want to set some things straight between us. I'm fifteen years older than you are. My living at your ranch is going to ruin your reputation — someone already told you that."

"The doctor's wife, Kathryn, said that, but she's not my mother or my boss."

"No, but I don't want to be the ruination

of your reputation. You are a sweet, caring person and have the right to find yourself a husband and take charge of your own life."

"Why don't you let me decide? I can make my own choices. I don't know what tomorrow will bring. Since my father died, I hardly know who I am. You're a nice guy, older or not. You don't have to be a father to me. I like to dance with you and be around you. I am not going to please bossy people like Kathryn anyway."

"Cally, you have a life to live. I'm a drifter. I've not stayed with much of anything. I thought the Rangers were my place until they proved that you can't count on things, like when my full pay quit coming."

"I figured the war stepped in and first interrupted your life, like it did so many men your age."

"It did. Maybe I should have stayed with cattle and driving them north or wherever. But I lost some men on those drives who left me feeling I hadn't done all I could to save their lives. I made some money and should have built a ranch while the business was so good." He shook his head, feeling he was getting nowhere in discouraging her from any plans he felt she was making with him. "Damn, you aren't listening to me."

"I'm listening fine to you, Phillip Guthrey.

You aren't listening to me."

"Oh, I am."

"No, you're telling me I make you regret not doing some things. For that I am sorry. But you and I were thrown together for a reason. The good Lord has a purpose for all of us. If we belong together, age should not keep us apart. You don't hate my company yet, do you?"

"No. I wanted to warn you . . . I'm not a big sticking-around sort of guy."

"If you need to leave, I will be hurt, but let's wait till that time to make any judgment about our deal. All right?"

He shook his head and picked up the reins. She stopped him and leaned against him. Nothing he could do but kiss her. Damn, nothing was settled. Nothing at all. He sat back and thought for a second, then said, "I have warned you."

ELEVEN

Noble was there when they returned to the ranch. He met them and helped unload Cally's supplies into the house.

"Anything happen?" Guthrey asked.

"Not one damn thing, by golly. It was so quiet I was worried something was wrong," Noble said and laughed.

"Brown and McCall told him," she indicated Guthrey, "that they wanted to talk at the dance Saturday night about Guthrey taking over as sheriff."

"Hmm," Noble snuffed out his nose. "They say any more, like how they'd get rid of Killion?"

She shook her head and went inside.

When she was gone, Noble looked over at Guthrey. "Them Mormon folks are clannish. Guess they've got a right to be. But if they have had enough, maybe you could head up a ticket to beat Killion and make a real sheriff."

"That election is a long time away. Then the job is even farther away. I'm not certain I could wait around that long. But I'll see. They do need a real sheriff here."

"You know, someone once told me that an elected official can be tossed out of office by a petition," Noble said.

Guthrey nodded at the words. "I guess we didn't have that in Texas."

"You get enough signatures and you can call for an election. I heard of them doing it."

"I doubt these folks want to do that."

"You can't tell. Folks are tired of not having any law and order."

Guthrey looked around to be certain Cally wasn't within hearing distance of them. "I've been thinking. Where did they shoot her father?"

"Oh, up in Congress Canyon."

"Did the law ever come out here and check on that murder?"

Noble shook his bland, whiskered face. "No. There was no one around to do that. Three of us went up there and got the body. Dan was too upset to do it himself after he found him."

"I need to look at that place tomorrow. I guess I should have gone up there when I first came here. I simply expected that had been done by the sheriff. Of course, I didn't know how loose the law was up here at that time."

"No one could have expected that." Noble shook his head wearily.

"Was an autopsy done?"

"I don't think so. He was shot twice in the back, kneeling down."

"Were his clothes burned around the wounds?"

Noble shook his head. "Hard to tell. Dan rolled him over when he found him. So his body was dusty anyway when we got up there. We wrapped him in a blanket and put him over a horse. It was a grim day. I took him to the funeral home in town. Mr. Jones and his worker Greg took his body inside."

"I still want to see the setup up there."

Noble agreed with a nod. They carried in the rest of the supplies and found Cally busy making supper. Thanking them, she offered them coffee.

They accepted her offer. With the cups she'd filled in hand, they took seats at the table and she joined them. "Have you two been looking at our older steers? We'll need to sell several to pay some bills and keep afloat. Dan and I planned to sell fifty or so before the hot weather."

"Where do you usually sell them?"

Guthrey asked.

"Oh, sometimes we can sell them here to fill Indian reservation orders. But I haven't heard of any of those lately, have you, Noble?"

"No," Noble said. "I think Whitmore must be filling all that business with Ike Clanton."

She nodded. "There are some butchers in Tucson who bought cattle from us. But we could only take, say, a dozen at a time. They only butcher so many head a day and must feed the rest until they can get them into the plant."

"Who paid the most?" Guthrey asked.

"Butchers in Tucson always paid more than those army or Indian deals. But getting them there was always a problem. It takes three to four days to drive them over there."

"So what do you think?" Guthrey asked the older man.

"Oh, a couple of us could drive thirty to forty head easy to Tucson. These cattle ain't haints like those full-blood longhorns we use to have. Get us a lead bell steer and maybe a heeler dog or two."

"I may need to go look those butchers up and find out what they can use. I've seen several fat two- and three-year-old steers we can pick from the herd," Guthrey said.

"That wouldn't be much of a cattle drive for you, but it's pretty big for us. Supper is about ready."

"We'll go put the horses up and wash up, then." Their chairs scraped on the floor and they excused themselves.

They each took a set of harnesses off the team and put them on the tongue. Noble led the pair off to the pen system. Then they went back to the house. Guthrey regretted that he had not gotten more done that day besides the round-trip. They'd been to town and had no problem with anyone — none of Whitmore's men even showed up.

They were finishing supper when they heard a horse coming hard up the road leading to the house. Guthrey rose and went to greet whoever was riding in. A youngster, no older than sixteen and bawling her eyes out, dismounted and rushed over to hug him.

"They shot Daddy a while ago."

He caught her by the arms. "Is he alive?"

"He was. Mom said to come get you and you'd help us."

"Do you have a team and wagon?"

She nodded.

"What's wrong, Eva?" Cally asked, joining them in the sundown's red glow.

"They shot her dad."

"Who?" Cally asked, running over and hugging the girl.

"Some of Whitmore's men —" Then she broke down crying and her knees buckled. Guthrey swept her up, and Cally led the way back inside.

"Put her on my bed."

"She's the Rawlings girl, ain't she?" Noble asked.

Cally answered, "Yes."

"Noble, go saddle two horses. Little lady, you just lie here." He put her gently on the bed. "Cally, you lock the doors. We'll go see what we can do for her father. You two stay here. We'll be back as soon as we can."

He took a Winchester down from the wall rack and checked the breach. It was loaded. Then he nodded grimfaced at Cally. "We'll do all we can."

"God bless you," she said and patted his shoulder. "Be careful."

In a few minutes Guthrey and Noble tore up the road on their horses in the growing darkness. With the Winchester stuck in his scabbard, Guthrey waved at Cally standing there in the lit doorway. No telling what he would need once they got over there or how bad Rawlings was hurt.

"Ted Rawlings is his name," Noble called

out as they rode hard up the dirt road. "He runs some cows. Hauls freight to Tucson and some to Tombstone. Hard worker. His wife's name is Lillian."

"Yes, I know. Dan introduced me to him. Wonder why they shot him."

Noble shook his head. "No telling, but he has a bad temper."

Guthrey nodded that he had heard the comment. At last, they walked their hard breathing, sweaty horses in the starlight on the final mile to the Rawlingses', a place Guthrey remembered visiting.

A red-faced, rawboned woman in a wash-faded dress came to the door, the light from the inside spilling out from behind her. "Howdy, Noble and Guthrey," she said to them, then turned to Guthrey. "I'm sure glad you came. I have a problem with Ted. Maybe you can talk to him."

"How is your husband? Do we need to take him to the doctor?"

"He's in bed. Come with me."

The big man was shirtless, with his upper body bandaged in torn-up sheets that were stained from his blood seeping into them. He tried to sit up.

"Don't get up."

"They kinda outnumbered me."

"Where were you shot?" Guthrey asked,

171

looking hard at him in the candlelight.

"There're bullets in my chest." Rawlings made a face of pain.

"Deep?"

"They're in me."

"We better take you to a doctor," Guthrey said.

"Hell, what can he do?"

"Get the bullets out."

Rawlings shook his head. "My brother was shot in El Paso. We took him to a doctor down there as fast as we could. The sawbones cut an artery trying to get the bullet out, and he bled to death. I'm letting these damn bullets stay right in me."

Guthrey decided he wouldn't be able to talk him into being treated. "Who shot you?"

"One of Whitmore's men. Name's Ruth. Carl Ruth. He and two more —" Rawlings's coughing stopped his speech. When he recovered some he began again. "They rode up and accused me of killing a steer belonged to Whitmore."

"They have any proof?"

"Hell, no. They came looking for trouble was all I saw."

"You knew Ruth?"

"I'd had words with him before. They took a steer of mine last year and sold him to Ike

Clanton. The brand inspector told them they must pay me for him, and it took three months to get my money. And I only got it after I told Whitmore I'd take the damn money out of his hide."

"Did Ruth ride in and accuse you of stealing a steer?"

Rawlings looked upset. "Yeah. He rode up and then sent his two men looking for signs and accused me of slaughtering one of their steers."

"Did they find anything?"

"Hell, no."

"When did the shooting start?"

"I told Ruth if he ever came back and upset my family again, I'd kill him." Rawlings stopped and nodded, and it was obvious from his face that he was in pain from the bullet or bullets in his body. He swallowed hard. "They all three started shooting at me. I got a bullet in Ruth and one of them boys he brung with him before my knees crumbled."

"You reckon either of them will die?"

"I hope to hell they all die."

"If you won't go to the doctor, what can we do?"

"Go get that sumbitch for me."

"I'm not a killer, for you or anyone else. I want this range war stopped, and I mean

173

stopped. You were a damn fool to spark them into a shoot-out. We can maybe get enough people to throw Killion out of office and break their stranglehold, but gunfights only get innocent people hurt." Guthrey turned to leave.

"Guthrey?"

He stopped in the bedroom door and looked back.

"You going after them?"

"I'm going into town to see if they're not as dumb as you are about seeking a doctor to treat your wounds. I figure you have less than two weeks to live. Better get your business into shape while you're still conscious — you're leaving a widow and your children to deal with them."

"They killed my brother getting his bullet out —"

Guthrey shook his head. "Nothing I can do for you if you won't listen to me. I'm sorry, ma'am. Come on, Noble."

"You don't think he's right about not getting treatment?" she asked.

"He's not right. Doctors make mistakes, but they try. His brother might not have lived, but they tried to save him is what it sounded like to me."

She nodded. "I see what you mean."

Guthrey and Noble went outside to their horses.

"Where are we headed?" the old man asked.

"To find Ruth and the other injured man and see what's what."

"You think Ted lied to us?" Noble mounted his horse and checked him.

In the saddle, Guthrey started the horse toward town under the quarter moon rising in the east. "No, but I promise he'll die if he doesn't get medical help."

The old man looked back. "I guess we did all we could for that ornery old man."

"I wished he'd listened to me." Guthrey shook his head in disappointment. "We've done all we can do here."

"What if we find Ruth?"

"I intend to take him to jail for terrorizing them."

"Will the judge keep him in jail?"

"I hope so. Ruth had no authority to accuse the man of theft. He needed to file a warrant and have the sheriff serve it."

"Our sheriff don't do that."

"He ain't right either."

They reached Steward's Crossing, and Guthrey took to the bars but learned nothing about Ruth or any of the others. Noble came back to Guthrey after he got some

175

information from a man Guthrey had tried talking to earlier without luck. The two met at the horse rack, unhitching their horses.

"Ruth was taken in a buckboard to Soda Springs earlier tonight. He was unable to ride a horse."

"What about the other wounded man?" Guthrey looked at the nearly empty dark street, waiting for Noble's answer.

"He was only scratched. His name's Kyle. He went to heal up with some Mexican woman in the mountains, according to what was told me."

"Why won't anyone tell me anything?"

"They don't want any trouble with Whitmore."

Guthrey nodded. He savvied that.

Near midnight, Guthrey and Noble reached Soda Springs, and the lights were on in the doc's house-office. A hardcase holding a rifle stood guard on the porch. Noble frowned at Guthrey.

"Let me handle him."

Noble nodded.

"What do you want?" the guard asked.

"I understand they brought in a badly wounded man?"

The man started to swing his rifle around, but he had waited too long. Guthrey moved in, gave him a hard knee to the crotch, and

ripped the rifle away from him. He slammed
the rifle butt in the man's chest, and the
man went to his knees with a moan. Going
by, Guthrey shoved him down.

"Watch him with a gun, Noble," Guthrey
said over his shoulder and went through the
lighted door. Doc looked up at his entry.

"He going to live?" Guthrey nodded at
the passed-out man under Doc's knife.

"He should. Why?" Doc frowned at
Guthrey.

"I'm having him held for murdering a
man over above Steward's Crossing tonight."

"Sounds like you have more problems."
Doc shook his head and went back to work
on his patient.

"What do you want to do with that bird
on the porch?" Noble asked from the doorway.

"Tie him up. He's an accessory to murder
too."

"I can do that."

Doc shook his head in disbelief. Then he
chuckled. "You get enough of them in that
jail, you may bankrupt the country feeding
them all."

"I consider that would be a good deal.
Then they wouldn't be riding high horse
over everyone on the river side of the

county."

"Can I gag him?" Noble asked.

"No, we better not."

"He better shut up or I will," Noble said, sounding displeased.

"Hell, he gets too mouthy, stick a sock in his mouth."

"I may just do that, dad gum him anyway."

"Doc, I don't think your patient's going to run away. I'll be sure that dumb deputy collects him before he's well enough to flee."

"That will be fine. Who did they kill?"

"They shot a rancher, Ted Rawlings. His brother was shot in El Paso a few years ago and they rushed him to a doctor. Getting the bullet out of him, they hit an artery and he died. Now Rawlings is going to die because of it. He's got, I think, at least one bullet in his lung and wouldn't come in with us. So by the law he will die at the hands of your patient."

"No way to convince him to come in, huh?" Doc asked, dropping a lead bullet in a pan from the jaws of his forceps.

"No, and I told him to get ready to climb in a box. His days are numbered."

"Must have been a clumsy surgeon did that."

"We tried to get him to come and be treated. I'll go see Dan for a minute, and then I guess we'll go back after we have the papers on them two filled out."

"Be careful. This range war must be getting tougher," Doc said after them.

Guthrey went into the back bedroom and Dan was awake, braced up on his pillows. "Everything all right?" Dan asked.

"Yeah, now. One of Whitmore's gun hands rode out to Ted Rawlings's place with two men. Carl Ruth told his men to search the ranch for evidence that Rawlings killed a Whitmore steer. That's illegal; he had no search warrant or even the authority. Words came to action, and they gunned Rawlings down. He has some bullets in his body and refuses medical attention, since his brother died on an operating table in El Paso over bullet removal. I told Rawlings he'd die."

"My God, he will."

Guthrey shook his head. "Nothing me or Noble could do."

"How bad off is Ruth?"

"Doc says he'll probably live to stand trial." Guthrey lowered his voice. "Cally can't come to see you until Friday. That all right?"

"Sure. Something else wrong?"

"The Mormons want to talk to me at the dinner-dance Saturday night about taking over as sheriff."

Dan nodded. "I'm not surprised they want you to take the sheriff job. Are you going to do it?"

Guthrey nodded. "We'll see."

"That would put you right in front of Whitmore's guns." Dan frowned at him. "Let me know what they say when you talk to them."

He agreed and clapped Dan on the shoulder. "Keep healing. We'll keep cowboying."

"Thanks and be careful. You too, Noble."

Noble had made his way into the back bedroom. "I will, Dan, don't worry about us. We're going to get to the bottom of all this smelly business."

"You get well," Guthrey said, fatherly-like. "We're going back tonight. I don't like Cally being alone up there."

"I'm fine here. You take care of your business, and I'll look for you two when you get time."

Guthrey and Noble took the tied-up guard to the jail. When they got there, a grizzly faced old man woke up in the chair behind the desk and frowned at them.

"Who in the hell are you two?"

"We have another prisoner for your jail," Guthrey announced. "His partner is over at Doc's being treated for lead poisoning. You will need to jail him too when he wakes up

180

tomorrow."

"By God, I'm about to run out of room and places to put them."

"Well, pappy, you may need to build a larger jail to house them all." Guthrey took the rope off their prisoner, and when the old man opened the cell, he shoved him inside.

"Hey, there ain't no bed left in here," the man grumbled.

"Sleep on the damn floor," Noble said. "You wouldn't be in there if you'd minded your own damn business."

The man shook a fist at him. "I get out of here, you old galoot, I'll stomp your ass."

"You can try, but then they won't need room for you except in a box at the cemetery."

Guthrey laughed at Noble's promise and went out to the telegraph part of the building. He used a piece of paper and addressed it to Judge Collier.

Judge, the man we jailed last night (John Doe — he wouldn't give us his name) was involved with wounded man (Carl Ruth) who's now at Doc's after terrorizing a rancher, Ted Rawlings, who will die from the gunshot wounds they gave him while he was protecting his wife and

181

family. Two others were with Ruth on this raid. I will try to apprehend them. Phillip Guthrey.

He left two bits on top of it for Tommy to deliver the message to Collier in the morning. Then he and Noble headed back for the ranch under the stars. The sun was peeking over the eastern horizon when they reached the lighted house. Cally rushed out to hug Guthrey, and the Rawlings girl stood back in the doorway.

"How is Ted?" Cally asked, burying her face in his vest.

"They shot him, but he won't let a doctor look at his wounds. So he's going to die."

Cally glanced up and blinked at him. "He what?"

Guthrey told her the story and Eva, his daughter, added, "I believe you're right, Guthrey. He just hates doctors."

"So you saw Dan in town?" Cally asked. "How is he?"

"Fine. He said we were excused from coming back until after we talk to those men at the dance. But he wants to know how that works out and what their plans are."

"I will have the food ready shortly. When did you two eat last?"

He hugged her. "How long, Noble?"

"Maybe a week." They all laughed.

"You two put those horses up, then clean up. Eva and I will fill your hollow bellies."

They took their mounts to the corral. Unsaddling them as the day burst open, Guthrey's eyes burned in the bright light. A good sleep would be a big deal he'd enjoy. The muscles in his legs and back felt stiff and sore as he tossed his saddle on the corral rail.

"I don't know about you," Noble said. "But I'm about caved in."

"Me too. After we eat I'm going to sleep for two days."

He and Noble headed for the house. How much more would Whitmore try? He was no doubt a long ways from being through with his business of running folks off the land. How could he be stopped? What would come from him next?

At this point Guthrey was too tired to even think about it.

TWELVE

Guthrey's awakening was slow. He had been sleeping on Dan's cot and emerging from hard sleep; he sat up and rubbed his eyes.

"You said to wake you up," Cally said, seated on the edge of the narrow bed.

He nodded. His nakedness was covered by the blanket, but he wondered where his clothes were at. His gun and holster hung on the nearby ladder-back chair. He could still recall her soft kiss that had awoken him. Sweet of her, but she was a good person.

"I have some breakfast ready."

"What time is it?"

"About six in the afternoon."

He nodded. "I'll be down there in a few minutes."

"You all right?" She rose and looked at him with concern.

"I'll be fine. Just slept too hard."

"Eva went home to try to convince her father to go see a doctor."

"Good, she might convince him. He was set too hard for me to move him."

"I'm making you uncomfortable. I can tell. Sorry, I just wanted to be with you by myself for a few minutes."

He nodded. "I know, and I really appreciate you."

"I'm going, I'm going." She hurried to the doorway. "Thanks. You make me happy."

"I'll be out there quick as I can dress."

"Good." And she was gone.

He threw back the blanket and quickly pulled on his pants, then stood and caught his shirt. In a few moments, he pulled on his boots and strapped on his gun. His hat on, he left the shed and headed toward the house.

When his hands and face were washed, he dried them on a flour-sack towel. Cally brought him some coffee and he accepted it with a kiss for her efforts. "Whew, I am still sobering up."

"We have a few days before the dance. What do we need to do?" She set the plates out for him and herself. "I let Noble sleep."

"Good idea. He's a tough old man." Guthrey sipped on the hot coffee, the rich fumes going up his nose. Nice to be back in her company to watch her swish around, setting the table for their breakfast.

He took his place and she joined him. "Well, will you stay and be sheriff if they support your election?"

"I wish I had that answer. If they're serious, I imagine I'd probably run for office. But that doesn't mean I'd be elected. I'd still have to convince the voters. Some voters would consider me a Texan and not vote for me. So it would be no shoo-in deal."

"I think everyone is ready for change."

"Oh, I'm not that sure."

She reached over and grasped his wrist. "Why not?"

"We'll simply have to see." He lifted her hand and kissed it.

She blushed more than usual. "Yes, we will."

Noble slept on. So after the meal, she sat on Guthrey's lap and fussed with him. For Guthrey it was a neat time. They were alone and acting kissy-faced. He hadn't ever shared such a peaceful time with any other woman he could recall.

"Maybe Kathryn was right. We do need a chaperone," he teased.

She threw her arms around him. "Oh, I'd hate that."

He agreed.

They parted company near midnight. He went back to Dan's cot and soon fell asleep.

Sometime before dawn, Noble woke him.

"We've got some company," Noble whispered.

"Who?" Guthrey asked, rising onto his elbows. A moment of shock had gripped him.

"I think they're Apaches."

"Oh, hell, what are they doing?"

"Roping some of our horses right now. They woke me up doing that."

"Go to the house. Wake Cally and be certain that she's all right. I'll go see about the horse thieves."

"I can do that. You be damn careful."

"No problem."

Quickly getting dressed, he checked his Colt and was satisfied it was loaded. All he could do was hope that Noble could protect Cally. He slipped out in the starlight and could hear the horses being chased. Obviously the Apaches either needed fresh mounts or simply needed horses to ride.

In the starlight he could see that one of them was on foot and had a horse on the end of a lariat. The horse was fighting to escape. The Indian must have smelled like an animal of prey to him.

Guthrey fired his pistol in the air. "Leave my damn horses alone!"

The Apache released the rope, horse and

all. Another showed up on foot and shot at Guthrey with a rifle. Guthrey returned fire, and that silenced the shooter. Three braves on horseback swept in, picked up the two on foot, and raced away with them. Were they going away or planning to regroup?

Guthrey hurried toward the ranch house, keeping a lookout behind him until he reached the front door and Cally let him inside.

"Everyone all right?" he asked, taking the rifle she handed him.

"Yes, we're fine. What are they after?" she asked.

"Horses. I expect they needed some to get to Mexico."

"They have never done this before." She shook her head in the soft flickering candle-light.

He hugged her shoulder to comfort her. "Times change. People like that get more desperate as time goes on."

After a short while he went back outside under the stars to listen for any sign of the raiders. The rifle in his hands, he worked his way from shed to shelter building until he was satisfied they had left. What in the hell would happen next?

At sunup, three Apache army scouts and an officer arrived at the ranch. By then,

Guthrey and Noble had counted the horses and knew the braves had only managed to rustle one. Guthrey considered their losses minimal.

"They were here trying to steal horses a couple of hours before dawn," Guthrey told Lieutenant Grayson as they all squatted on the ground by the corral. "I think they were mere boys."

"Yes, they are teenagers, but deadly."

"Oh, yes, they shot at me."

The officer nodded. "They killed a ranch couple north of here yesterday."

"Noble woke me, like I said. I found one of them had roped a horse that was spooked enough he was fighting his captor. Then another boy on foot shot at me. I shot at him and he ran like hell. Then three riders came and swept up the two on foot and left. We later determined they'd stolen a single horse."

"If we capture them, we will return the horse. If we can't recover him, you can apply for compensation from the government office for his value."

"Thanks. We'd like to have him back, but we understand."

The triangle rang, and the three went to the house to eat the breakfast Cally had prepared. Guthrey saw that the officer was clearly attracted to Cally. He acted very proper but left after breakfast, thanking her graciously.

Noble had gone to check on the irrigation water in the garden. Alone with Cally, Guthrey teased her about the lieutenant's interest in her.

"I have been to Fort Grant several times, and I cannot see myself as an officer's wife, thank you."

He laughed, and she brandished her fist at him. "Don't try so hard to get rid of me."

"Oh, I merely saw an opportunity I was afraid you might have missed." He waved at her and went to check on Noble's progress at changing the water set. Noble was just finishing up.

"This irrigation system Cally's father laid out for the garden really worked," Guthrey said to Noble. "The little spring fills the small pond, then the system uses the head pressure so the water flows down the small cemented ditch with enough force to fill three rows at a time. The move is simple enough and utilizes the water available to keep this big garden so well watered."

"Danged if it don't work well," Noble agreed.

"He must have been smart," Guthrey said. "All of his spring setups on the range for watering stock work well too."

"Real smart. He never wore a gun. They killed an unarmed man when they shot him. Do you know why he didn't wear a gun?"

"No, why?"

Noble dropped his head. "Told me he'd kilt enough men in the war. He wasn't fighting that battle again."

"So they couldn't provoke him into a fight and instead they simply murdered him."

"That's about the measure of it."

"What else?"

"It wasn't like he didn't have any guts. With his fists, he beat the hell out of one of Whitmore's men for insulting a lady in town one day. Mrs. Green was practically assaulted by some hand named Bob James. Course James was drunk, like lots of them boys get. He had her bent over, kissing her and mauling her awful open-like. She was a real lady, and I guess Bridges knew that too. He came running over, tore James loose of her, and beat that damn drunk to a pulp."

"James still work for Whitmore?" Guthrey asked.

"I reckon he does. I seen him a time or two since then."

"Did you ever think he could have shot Bridges to get even?" Guthrey asked.

"Damn, Cap'n, I never put that together.

He might have been the one. Now, why didn't I put him down in my mind as a suspect?"

"You see him, will you point him out to me?"

"Boy, I mean Bridges beat him up. I believe his eyes are still black-and-blue from that beating."

"How was Mrs. Green after that event?"

"She was all right. It was a big shame that she happened to be on the boardwalk when James staggered out of the cantina."

"The law should have arrested him." Guthrey shook his head in disgust at the notion of a respectable woman being openly assaulted on the street of a town.

Noble shook his head. "Now, as long as you've been here, have you ever seed any law in the Crossing?"

"No, but they need some law so those drunk rannies walk the line when they're in town. Can we ride up where Bridges was shot this morning?"

"Sure, it's up in Congress Canyon. Not much up there but a spring he developed."

"I want to look the site over."

"I'll just tell Cally to watch the water set. No need to tell her where we're going. It would only upset her."

Guthrey agreed, and they went to the

house to tell Cally they were going to ride for a bit and might be back late for lunch.

It took almost an hour to reach the opening in the side of the mountain that led to Congress Canyon. There were lots of tracks of animals and stock that used the pathway.

The canyon walls began to tower over them, and the way narrowed as they rode into the darker shadows. From the times of flash flooding, the narrow walls showed the high water mark, head high on the two riders. Damn sure not the place to be after a torrential rain fell in the mountains. The country soon widened out and some cottonwoods grew on the banks of the wash with potholes of water in the bed.

They rode up to a stone-mortar dam, and Guthrey could see the water spilling over its lip. Both men dropped off their horses and let them drink. Noble gave a head toss for Guthrey to follow and he dropped his reins and led the way.

There was a pipe coming out of the hillside and it came near half-full of water where it spilled into Harold Bridges's pond. The man had spent some time building all this, and, like the rest of his water setups, it was neat and very strongly built.

"Tell me something," Guthrey asked, still looking over the situation. "You have to come in here by that trail and go out that trail to get away from here, right?"

Noble nodded.

"So the shooter must have been up here in waiting or else he came after Bridges."

"No one saw him or any others come or go." Noble shook his head. "But I reckon that Dan came up here after dark and discovered him. His body was facedown when Dan found him. Right here."

"Was Bridges doing anything? Like repairs or anything?"

"Best I recall, all he came up here for was to inspect the setup."

"Who would have been here, then?"

"Damned if I know."

"Is there any gold or precious metals up here?" Guthrey looked at the high country surrounding them.

"Why would you ask that?" Noble shook his head.

"Let's check around. We're looking for signs of some digging around up here."

"Hell, they've dug up a big part of China looking for another Tombstone in all these mountains and canyons."

"Dan once told me that they owned lots of land. His dad bought several homestead parcels that were patented. What if there was gold or silver, even copper up here, and

Bridges caught someone working it?"

"Hmm." Noble snuffled. "You don't think a Whitmore gunny shot him?"

"I'm trying to figure out why a Whitmore-hired killer would let himself get in this box canyon when he could have shot the man in an easy place to escape from on any given day."

"Damn, that's why you were a Ranger and I was a day-working cowboy all these years. You've got me worked up now. Should we start searching?"

Guthrey nodded. He went one way and Noble went the other. They began a systematic look at the ground for any signs of digging or mining efforts. Working their way through the greasewood and dry bunch-grass, they turned up little with their efforts until Noble called to him from a good distance up the north hillside.

"What did you find?" Guthrey called out.

"There's a rose quartz outcropping up here."

Guthrey soon joined him. He knew about folks finding gold sometimes in such out-croppings. Out of breath, he stopped and Noble handed him a handful of rotten quartz. In the veins of quartz rocks, thin spider gold shone bright in the sun.

"This has been worked some," Noble

pointed out. "There ain't much gold showing here right now, but there could be the
mother lode in this outcropping. Damn,
now I believe what you started on saying
about what might be up here. This may be
what got him kilt instead of Whitmore's men
doing it."

"It sure might be a lead on why someone
killed him."

"I'll be a hornswoggled lizard if you don't
beat all. Simply thinking about all the damn
reasons why Bridges was shot, and we come
up with some gold. Whoever blasted this
outcropping, maybe 'cause Bridges caught
them, they shot him."

"There could or could not be more gold
in this box canyon." Guthrey surveyed the
rest of the area, even the stunted juniper
brush higher up on the mountain.

He put a few small pieces of the quartz in
his vest pockets.

"Well, boss, what now?"

"We're still speculating. I hope that undertaker took the bullets out of Bridges's back.
Knowing the caliber might make our job
even easier."

"And now every whiskered prospector
stumbling around these hills is a suspect for
his murder, right?"

"Yes."

"Are you going to tell Cally?"

"I will somehow. I want us to do some more exploring in that rose quartz outcropping. We'll pick up some blasting sticks, cord, detonators, and a rock drill in town."

"I know an old hand, Pete Karnes, who can keep his mouth shut and who will work this outcrop for a little something."

"No reason to waste time. Let's get hold of him after lunch."

"I can damn sure do that."

"Let's go back. This has not been a bad day, partner."

"No. It ain't."

After lunch that afternoon, Noble excused himself and went out to check on the horses. Guthrey sat at the table sipping a last cup of coffee as Cally dried her dishes.

"You have anything happen so far today?" she asked. "You and Noble both were pretty tight-lipped at lunch. You usually talk about a cow getting old or a calf with funny hide coloring. Just something."

"We went to Congress Canyon this morning. I'd never been up there before. And I was waiting till we were alone to talk about it."

"That was where Dad was shot." She bit her lower lip.

197

"Yes, and I'm not telling you this to upset you further. But when we got up there, I wondered why a hired gun would kill a man in such a place when he could have killed him anywhere in the open range and escaped easier than he would coming out of there."

"That's a good question." She folded her arms and waited for Guthrey to continue.

"Well, Noble and I traipsed all over in the area hemmed in up there." He reached in his vest pocket for the quartz and took her hand to drop the grains of rock in it.

"What is this?"

"Rose quartz, and see those spider veins?"

"Yes."

"That's gold."

Her other hand covered her mouth and her eyes flew open. "Really?"

"There's not much more evidence up there than that. But that outcropping may contain some gold."

She slid into the chair next to him. "Is there lots up there?"

"I don't know. But according to the map you showed me one night, that is deeded land that you own. I also have a new theory of why your father was murdered. It was this — the gold."

"Are you are saying Whitmore didn't kill him?"

"He's been moved down on the suspect list. How many men have been by here in the last two years looking for gold and silver?"

"Several."

"Start making a list of all of them you can recall who came by."

"Oh, that's horrible if he was killed over some gold mine and I've been blaming someone else."

She came into his arms and clung to him. He swept off his kerchief for her to cry into, then he squeezed her tight. "Whitmore's done enough bad things. But right now I don't believe he was responsible for your father's death."

"How will you ever find who did it?"

"Greed. Whoever it was, he killed for this gold once, and he will be back to find it again."

Gentle-like, he patted her back to reassure her. Damn, he was getting more and more pleased when she sought his arms for comfort. But she didn't have the needs of some widow who had experienced deep intimacy with a man before and had needs for it again.

War had taken the boy's life away from

him. The handholding and stealing kisses from some sweet girl had all evaporated in those years. All over the battlefields there had been women without men, some without a living husband. They had had to trade their bodies for food, for security, and some for simple love to heal their losses and replace their departed mates.

Damn war anyway. A decade later, Guthrey was still haunted by memories of the beds he had shared with females desperate to swim out of the hell of those battles they found themselves in. Their lovemaking had happened under the chorus of artillery shelling the farmland around them. One sweet young woman, still exhausted from birthing only three days before, had her newborn beside them in the bed.

She had mumbled, "It's been a long time for me. Him gone. I had to have someone to hold and love me tonight or I'd die. I ain't a whore, mister. I just need a man to love me."

His belly churning on the upset from the reminder, he whispered, "I'll see you later," to Cally and left the house.

THIRTEEN

Late that afternoon he and Noble found
Pete Karnes in his sun-yellowed sidewall
tent. Loaded on three pack-horses they had
with them were the supplies and things
they'd need to search the quartz deposit,
picked up earlier that afternoon.

Pete was short, wore lace-up boots, and
had white whiskers that had been trimmed
so they surrounded his mouth when he
grinned.

"What'cha doing these days?" Karnes
asked Noble.

"Doing day work for the Bridgeses. This
here is Cap'n Guthrey. He's their foreman."

"Glad to meet'cha, Guthrey. Folks been
telling me you're an ex-Ranger and round-
ing up outlaws like jackrabbits." He chuckled.

"Well, we've put a few in jail. Noble tells
me you know mining. We've found a quartz
outcropping on the Bridgeses' deeded land

and need an expert to see if there's any gold in it."

"That could take some work," Pete said with a frown.

"We'd like to hire you to explore the outcropping, and then we can decide about expanding the operation should we find enough."

"What would you pay two Mexican boys to help me? I ain't that tough anymore."

"How much do they need?"

"Fifty cents a day and food. I need a dollar and a half a day and found."

"We ain't cooking for them." Guthrey wanted nothing to do with that.

"No, we can do that ourselves."

"Good."

"Where is this place?" Pete combed his silver hair back with his fingers.

"Congress Canyon. West side of the ranch. Noble can come back tomorrow and pack you and them boys' things up there. You have any firearms?"

"Sure," Pete said.

"Plenty of ammo, just in case?"

"I'll buy a box of cartridges in town. You expecting trouble?"

Guthrey shook his head. "Can't be too careful in this country. There isn't any law."

Pete agreed. Guthrey shook his hand.

"What all do you want to pack up there?"

"Two tents, bunch of my stuff. Take four packhorses. We've got burros to ride."

"I have three, but we'll bring five," Noble said, laughing as he turned to Guthrey. "He may have more to take than he thinks."

"Good. You two work that out. Pete, it's good to meet you. I'll look forward to having some success up there."

The older man squeezed his chin whiskers. "You can't ever tell about quartz outcroppings. Some are good sites, others nothing."

"I know that, but we have the blasting stick, caps, and cord. Don't blow yourselves up."

"I won't. Good to meet you," Pete said. "Now, I've got to get around to be ready in the morning."

Guthrey and Noble headed back to the ranch with their loaded horses. Noble spoke to him when they were out of sight. "Pete's good, if there's any silver or gold up there, he'll find it."

Guthrey nodded. He twisted in the saddle on the next high spot and looked over lots of desert country. Why did he feel spied upon? Was someone tracking them? He didn't usually have this feeling. Hell, it might be anything.

"Something bothering you?" Noble called out.

"Why do I think we're being watched?"

"Number of reasons. Whitmore may have someone watching us. The guy or guys who killed Harold Bridges may want us dead. Or some varmint like a big cat could be trailing us."

"I know that cougars do that. I was down on the border once, trying to catch some smugglers. It had been raining, and when I doubled back, I saw some tracks of a big cat that had been on my trail. His large footprint was in some soft soil and just filling up with water."

"What'cha do?"

"Got on my horse and went back to camp. Couple days later, some vaqueros with dogs treed and shot a two-hundred-pound cougar tom in the same country."

"You get them smugglers?" Noble asked.

"In time, but I wasn't going back in there alone again knowing there might be more of them big critters that could be interested in me for supper."

"Well, I ain't seen no sign of anything tracking us today."

"Good. I'm just edgy. Now we know that Whitmore may not be the only one to dodge."

Guthrey remembered to stop and talk to the funeral man in Steward's Crossing about Bridges. Mr. Jones was busy at his desk when Guthrey and Noble entered the open front door. The place smelled of fresh-cut pine lumber, and Jones stood up behind his paper-cluttered desk.

"Howdy, gents. How are you, Noble?"

"Fine. Mr. Jones, this is Captain Guthrey. He's helping the Bridges kids. We came to ask a few questions about their father's body."

"Nice to meet you. What can I tell you? He had two bullets in his body. Take a chair, gentlemen. They were, in my appraisal, shot from perhaps a hundred feet away. Both bullets came from the same gun. He had been shot in the back. Someone told me his wallet was missing and a gold watch."

"I did," Noble spoke up. "Or Hitch Caughman, who helped me bring the body in, told you. We'd looked for them up there 'cause Dan told us they were missing when he found him."

"I have the bullets right here." He opened his desk and took them out. "I suspect they're from a .44/40 rifle. One was in his heart. The other was in his lung. He was going to die from either, and I expect he didn't suffer long." He put the bullets on the table and Guthrey picked them up and inspected them. They both had similar rifling twists on their sides.

"Might be a new gun," Jones said. "That rifling looks new. From an older gun it ain't that easy to see the marks on the lead."

Guthrey nodded. He weighted the two bullets in his palm. "How many of these rifles are around?"

"Maybe a couple hundred."

Guthrey and Noble both nodded.

"You two have any idea who shot him?"

"Nope," Guthrey said, still thinking hard about who'd want to kill Dan and Cally's father. No telling in this lawless country. Gold, greed, and a range war all wrapped up together.

Jones walked them to the front door. "I've heard rumors that you might run for sheriff."

Guthrey nodded. "That's all they are."

"I'd sure donate some money to help you get in office." He lowered his voice. "You think on it. Bridges was a good man. Never wore a gun 'cause of his convictions about things. Shot in the back, and you two were the first to even ask me about his death."

"I may be back. Thanks." They went outside in the bright sunlight. Guthrey considered getting a drink across the street in one of the saloons. Instead he said, "Let's get back. Cally will think we left her and aren't coming back."

"Sure." Noble mounted up. "I've got to move Pete and them two boys up to Congress Canyon tomorrow."

"No, bring them to the ranch. Time you get back up here tomorrow it will be too late to go to the canyon."

"Whatever you say's fine with me."

"We can do it that way." Guthrey made his horse trot.

Noble caught up with him, leading the string. "You know, I ain't seen Shad Norman in a spell."

"Who's he?"

"A fellow I thought was real sweet on Cally. Oh, he ain't been around since before Bridges was shot. Kind of a cocky guy. He must have drifted on."

"Time is right, I'll ask her about him. What did he do?"

"Oh, his uncle Willy raised him and has a ranch up north of us. He helps out there."

"There's lots of folks I still need to meet if I stay here."

"I hope you do. Well, I ain't partnered with a guy I liked any better than you in years."

"It's mutual." Guthrey stood in the stirrups and looked back through their dust, but there was no one he could see.

Back at the ranch, Guthrey and Noble unloaded the packhorses. Cally helped them.

"We hired Pete Karnes and two helpers to work on the outcropping," Noble told her. "They're going to cook for themselves, but we furnish the grub."

She nodded, carrying the roll of cord toward the shed. "What did he think? Could there be gold up there?"

"He said they'd look for it. Noble, what did he say about it?"

"Quartz outcroppings were odd creatures. A few had gold, some didn't."

"What that means is, don't get your hopes too high and spend what you don't have yet."

Cally laughed, and when Noble had moved out of sight, she paused for Guthrey to kiss her. After, with a big smile, she continued to the shed to put the cord up.

Turning, she asked, "When will they get here?"

"Tomorrow. Noble's going to take some packhorses and get him up here, he hopes by sundown, then the next day he'll go set them up in the canyon."

"I need to go see Dan too this week. Doc may send him home."

"Be good to have him back?"

"Yes. Dan and I have been like twins all our life. I do miss him."

They finished putting the things up. Guthrey and Noble unsaddled the horses and turned them out. Cally went to the house and took supper out of the oven.

By the end of the meal it was dark, and Noble told them good night. Cally and Guthrey sat out on the bench and listened to the night critters. He told her all about the undertaker's comments. She bit her lip some but listened close. When he finished he leaned over and kissed her. She hung on his neck for a time and whispered, "I hope we find that person."

"We will. All those kind slip up somewhere and sometime. Right now I am doing all I can."

"No, you aren't. You haven't kissed me in thirty seconds."

"Cally, don't you have a suitor somewhere your own age?"

She shook her head.

"I think in the long run you should find one."

"Are you afraid of me?"

"I don't think so. I simply worry about

you being a young woman with an old man to take care of someday."

"That won't bother me one drop."

"Not today anyway —"

Her finger pressed to his mouth silenced him and she twisted around to kiss him hard on the mouth.

"All right, I lost that war."

"Good," she said. "Now, you go to thinking about other things besides trying to talk me out of —"

"Out of what?"

"Spoiling you to death."

They both laughed. But his stomach roiled. Could he really stand a wife? She was cute, young, and sweet — but he'd never more than visited that situation with some nice older widow women. Damn, life got complicated at times. Cally offered him a life with her. Family came next, but he had no paying job and the ranch was not large enough to support much more than her and Dan. And he also needed to check on selling some steers for them. . . . Maybe after Saturday night he'd have an idea of what to do next. People had offered him financial support to stay there. Cally turned toward him, and he kissed her again. He felt like he was losing his whole war to hold himself back from her, but damn, she was like honey.

Fourteen

Pete and company arrived the next evening. Estevan and Enrico had come with him. All three rode in on burros, which they must have had to beat a thousand times on the butt to keep up with Noble and his pack train. They could not have gotten any more "stuff" on the ranch horses. Noble'd borrowed four more packsaddles to move them.

The "boys" swept the ground with their sombreros when Guthrey introduced Cally to them. Pete, too, was impressed with her. They'd never met before. She served a spicy pork dish and the Mexicans thought they were at home. Guthrey was pleased. He had learned about the good, fresh-faced men from Mexico who came to work at any job they could find — very different from the hard-faced, lazy hombres that caused trouble and were really banditos.

The old man looked tired, but Noble never let on how weary he might be. They all slept out under the stars, and they were up when Guthrey went to milk the cow in the predawn. Enrico asked to milk the cow and Guthrey let him.

A short while after breakfast, they loaded up again, and Noble took Pete and the two Mexicans to the canyon. In the buckboard, Guthrey and Cally headed for Soda Springs to see about Dan. It was a cooler morning. The spring daytime heat had been warming more with each passing day. The northern breath was not cold, simply milder than the days before. The team even acted spirited. Lobo was saddled and tied on the back in case Guthrey needed a horse while they were in town. They made good time and were at Doc's a little past noon. Guthrey bought their lunch in the small café and they went back across the street to see about Dan.

They found him sitting at a table eating some of Kathryn's soup. She greeted them and made a fuss. "He's walking," Kathryn announced, like she had done the whole thing.

Dan was pleased and acted ready to go home. "How are things?"

"Fine, waiting for you to get back so Noble and I can sleep a few days," Guthrey told him. On the ride over, Cally and

Guthrey had decided not to say much about the rock outcropping and hiring Pete. The less that was out about that, the better, until they knew more. Gossip would get around fast enough.

Cally spoke to Kathryn about the doctor's bill they owed and she said the doctor would mail them one. Guthrey could tell the matter bothered Cally, but they would do something about it later. He excused himself and went over to the county offices to check on things. He slipped into the telegraph office and Tommy frowned at him. "You back with more prisoners?" he asked in a whisper.

Guthrey shook his head. "They all still here?"

"Yeah, and the sheriff has to have guards around the clock to watch and feed them. He really cussed you out over that the other day in the hall."

"Too bad. Just thought I'd check on them."

Tommy grinned. "There's a U.S. marshal here now too. He's checking on things. His name's Dobson."

"Good. Maybe he can really get them on the ball. I have to get back."

Tommy told him to wait; he had a message to take down but had news for him.

Guthrey remained standing at the high counter. When Tommy finished his message, Guthrey came back over to him. "I heard that yesterday someone wanted the paperwork for a petition to remove Killion from office. They were asking the land office for one. The office worker told them only the county clerk could issue one. He's hardly ever here. But that might be a put off to stall them. Killion ain't been in since they were here to get the petition."

"I didn't know about it. Thanks."

"Hey, would you run for sheriff if they get Killion out?"

"We'll see."

"The guys who came after it were two businessmen. I didn't know them, but they were serious about it."

"I'll try to find out. Thanks." Guthrey headed for the front doorway and crossed the street without being spotted by anyone in the jail.

"Can you drive?" he asked Dan, who was on the seat.

"I hope so."

"I can ride the horse just fine."

"Are those men still in jail?" Cally asked.

"Oh, yes." Guthrey looked around to be certain they were alone. "Two businessmen were here yesterday and tried to find the county clerk. They wanted to start a petition to remove Killion from office. No one knows where the clerk is at, they were told."

"Bet they get one," Cally said and winked at him.

"I will bet on that too." On Lobo, Guthrey short loped out ahead of the buckboard and they left Soda Springs.

They returned to the ranch late, but Noble had beans cooking on the stove and water ready for coffee when Cally came to relieve him.

Dan had lots of stories to tell about his stay at the doc's. There was a Mexican woman who delivered a blond-headed baby there, and when she first saw it, she screamed in Spanish that some ghost must have got her pregnant. They laughed at another story about a man with an infected foot who had gone to Tucson for treatment and the doctor there said he'd have to cut his foot off. Doc flat told him next time to come to him sooner and he might have saved it. But in this case Doc drained it and the foot healed after all. The man told him he'd never go to that bad doctor in Tucson again.

"Oh, I met a girl there. She's very pretty and she told me I could come and visit her."

"What is her name?" Cally asked.

216

"Cometa Valdez."

"She's Spanish?"

"Yes."

"She's Catholic?" Cally asked.

"I guess. Why does that matter?"

"You'd have to change your religion if you married her."

"Who cares? She is a lovely young lady."

"I don't doubt that she is. I'm only concerned that you've been a Methodist all your life. Now you're going to become a Catholic?"

"If I have to."

She nodded, then went for her cookie jar to share some of her oatmeal-raisin cookies to celebrate Dan's homecoming. Guthrey munched on one of the two that he took. Maybe he should tell her he was Catholic. No, no, only spoofing. But he wasn't so devoted to church as to worry about which one he sat in. Surely God was in all of them. Cally was damn sure upset at the very thought of her brother hitching up with a Catholic though.

Guthrey stayed when the others left, and dried dishes. "You were a little hard on Dan about that girl, weren't you?"

"I don't want him to make a mistake he might regret all his life." She plunged her hands down in the soapy water for more dishes.

He switched the towel in his hands and laid a palm on her back. Bent over close to her ear, he whispered, "He noticed a nice woman. He counts on you a lot. Think about it. He was sharing his most private business and you threw a wet blanket on the small flame inside of him."

She straightened and blinked at him. "You're a tough man, Guthrey. I just didn't —"

"Want to let him ruin his life." He kissed away her anger and then held her in his arms. "Tomorrow sit down and talk like equals with him."

She buried her face in his chest. "I will. I will, I promise."

"You may in the future have to share him with a Senora Bridges. But that's his choice, not yours."

"Boy, you can really pin me down."

"No, I love you and there are times in all our lives we need to step back from our own thoughts and look out for the other person."

"Love — me?"

He nodded. "That ain't any big surprise to you."

"But you've never said it before."

"Well, I said it now and I meant it." Her

closeness was eating him up inside, then she squeezed him and buried her face against his chest. "I am so glad you came and stayed here despite my sharp tongue that first day. I'd never have made it through all this without you."

When the dishes were completed, he kissed her softly and went to find his bedroll. He'd let the cat out of the bag. Damn, oh damn, if she'd been twenty-five years old he'd have no qualms about their match. But she was well short of that. He rolled over on his side in his bedding and went to sleep, still troubled.

FIFTEEN

Dan told them to go on to the dance. He was tired even though he'd done little since he came home. Cally was concerned about him, but Guthrey told her he'd be fine. Strength came back slower than one imagined.

They arrived at the schoolhouse mid-afternoon. They set up the shade and tied the team on the picket line. Cally wanted to stay all night and then attend church in the morning before they went home. That suited Guthrey and so they soon were set up.

A man in his thirties came around, stood back like he had something on his mind. When the sidewall tent was up, Guthrey walked over and spoke to him.

"Mr. Guthrey, my name's Reagan Worley and I wanted to talk to you."

They shook hands.

"What can I do for you?" Guthrey asked.

"I wanted to talk to you about Whitmore and his men," the man drawled. "Some of his men been coming by when I wasn't home and being plain disrespectful to my wife."

"What have they said to her?"

"Aw, things like they wanted to make love to her. She's been embarrassed and halfway scared of them. The men were drunk both times, she said. I ain't no gun hand, but I'd sure kill them if I was."

"Worley, do you know their names?" Guthrey's ire began rising.

"One was Jerry Keyes, another they called Soda, and the other guy she didn't know at all. I know Keyes and Soda because I used to work for Whitmore, but I don't ride for him anymore. Some folks might think she deserved that kinda thing. She worked in a house in Tombstone up till a few years ago. But I swear she's a good woman and she says she never was with any of those men. We've been living a Christian life since we got married and moved up here. The Bible says the Lord forgives you for your past, but some folks can't accept that. I'm about to go crazy over this and she sure is too."

"You try to speak to the sheriff about them?"

"No, sir. Besides, he ain't never in his office over there in the county seat."

"Where is your place?"

"It's downstream on the river past the crossing. I rent it and we make a garden, sell some produce, and I do day work. Have been since I quit Whitmore."

"Hold your peace. We may shortly straighten this whole mess out."

"I sure appreciate your listening to me. I'll get back home now."

"Next dance you bring her. You two belong here with us."

"I don't know —"

"I do. You bring her and hold your head high. If they come back, you tell me. I can make them believers, if I have to."

"You've made my day. Thanks." Worley shook Guthrey's hand and smiled. Then he went for his horse and swung aboard to ride away.

"What was wrong with him?" Cally asked.

"He and his wife are being run over by some of Whitmore's hands."

"Why?"

"Long story. His wife used to work in Tombstone in a house. They've became Christians and I suspect those cowboys got drunk. They insulted her and he's not a gunman. I told him that I'd help him if they came back."

She frowned. "Pretty bold of them."

"Oh, hell, they were fortified with whiskey. But it still goes along with their terrorizing folks. There are no lawmen in this county to protect the citizens. You can do all these kinds of things and still not expect to be punished."

She took his arm. "We better go inside and join the rest. I haven't seen Mr. McCall or the other man yet who wanted to talk to you."

"His name is Brown. I figure they'll be here. Let's go, Miss Bridges."

"Oh, Phil, I am so proud you're here with me."

"No problem. I wish I knew more about the petition and if they got it."

"You sound ready to sign it."

"For whatever good that would do."

A rancher stopped him with an apology. "I know you're here to enjoy the evening, but folks say you may be the next sheriff. I want to help you. Here's a hundred dollars to get you started."

Guthrey shook his head. "I can't accept that."

"Why not? You will need money to campaign."

"I'm sorry, I'm short your name. Mine's Guthrey."

"Fred Phillips." They shook hands.

"Fred, if and when I am a candidate, I'll accept your contribution."

The man nodded his head. "Folks said you were honest. We need a real sheriff. How can we get this going?"

"There are men coming here tonight who are supposed to bring the information with them."

"Ma'am, take good care of him." Fred patted Cally's shoulder.

"Oh, I will."

With Cally on his arm, Guthrey went up the porch steps and inside the schoolhouse. Plenty of greeters shook his hand and then hers. He felt the move of the wave he hoped was building among the citizens. People like Fred, anxious to be on Guthrey's wagon and back him with real money.

The grace was said and attendees lined up in the food line. The rich smell of the good food assailed Guthrey's nose. He looked at the assemblage: people with children in line, older couples, single men, widows in clusters. These were the voting citizens of this county. The Mexican people did not vote, except in areas predominately Hispanic. There was talk of giving Arizona women the right to vote, but it had not yet materialized.

That issue brought on all kinds of talk about proposed laws being considered to end prostitution and gambling and to bring on prohibition. When they had counties like Crook, where they didn't have the basics of law in place enough to even protect the citizens, why worry about the rest?

Guthrey and Cally ate supper with some other couples on the benches. Careful to watch his own movements toward her, he was enjoying his meal. And he was doing good, keeping things formal — until she fed him a bite off her fork of some dish she liked. They'd blown their cover again, he felt certain.

"Guthrey, you and Cally have such an easy way toward each other," Jane Briscoe said. "Can we expect to hear wedding bells soon?"

He smiled. "Do you have any wedding proposals on hand, Cally?"

"Who'd want me?" she said, shrugged, and sipped some tea. "Besides, I'm too busy gardening, canning, and feeding my crew. Now that Dan's home, I have three men to feed."

"How is he doing?" Jane asked, and Guthrey was glad she'd moved on to another subject.

"He tires easy," Callie said. "They say his

recovery may be slow. We're lucky he's alive, I guess."

"Can he walk?"

"Oh, yes," Cally said quickly. "He's not a cripple."

"That's good. My uncle could hardly walk after he had his horse wreck."

Guthrey was quiet. A musician struck up a fiddle to test it. The band was about to start playing and he could hardly wait to escape Jane's questions. This was all between him and Cally, and had nothing to do with Jane.

When the musicians started the waltz, Guthrey swept Cally up, excused them to their companions, and guided her across the floor. Time to move away from gossiping people and have Cally's company to himself.

"She obviously got your goat," Cally teased.

"I guess. I hate digging people who cross-examine us like our relationship is illegal or immoral."

Holding her in his arms, he swung Cally around and she chuckled at him. "I'll remember your response when I ask you something about us."

He looked down at her face. "You can ask me anything you want."

"Who was the woman who made you so resistant to accepting another woman?"

He mentally searched his past as they went across the dance floor. Who could she be talking about? The notion bothered him. He wanted to say no one, but his conscience dug him deep to be honest with her. The dance ended and he saw Carl Brown enter the schoolhouse in his brown suit and hand his hat to the lady hanging them on the wall for those who desired to check their hats.

Out of habit, Guthrey continued to wear his weathered one and removed it when he was introduced to women.

"He's here," Cally said as they waited for the next dance.

"I saw him. We'll have plenty of time to talk." The music stepped up the tempo with the next song, and they began to polka in a whirling path around the room. Guthrey loved Cally's smile and the excitement in her green eyes when they polkaed. He'd done that as a Texas teenager with girls his own age.

In those days his mind had been centered on courting Rebecca Carr. He'd almost forgotten her. The prettiest blond girl in the county. In the eyes of every young man who lived in Parker County, she was the big prize. He'd thought he had an inside track with her. Although he was just another teen-age boy, son of a poor Texas rancher, he rode as a Ranger. That drew him some respect as part of the semi-military organization that was the thin line of defense against the Comanche's vicious attacks and threat to the thin population west of Fort Worth at the time.

The discovery of a Comanche war party in the area sent all the Rangers on horseback to warn everyone they could reach. He was riding a well-spent horse down the Pease River road when he saw two saddled horses hitched in the mesquites alongside of the road. Who was there?

He reined in his huffing horse, which was dripping in sweat and had the breast strap on his chest frosted in foam. Pressed to warn everyone, he spurred his horse into the brush to find whoever was there. The branches swept Guthrey's bull-hide chaps as he drove through them to find the horse owners, his large Walker Colt in his fist, cocked and ready.

He busted into a grassy clearing. To his shock, he saw a couple on a blanket: a naked woman underneath a bare-butted, hard-pounding man. In a scramble, both of them broke off their actions. The naked man stood up, cursing Guthrey and shaking his fist, threatening his life. Guthrey only saw the blond girl, trying to hide her nakedness under a blanket — Rebecca Carr.

"You stupid people — a Comanche war party is roaming the whole countryside. Get your bare asses to a safe place."

He wheeled his horse, hardly able to swallow. With his spurs pounding hard into the horse's sides, he drove his mount out of the clearing. Brush tore at him and scratched his face as he drove harder. He had to escape that gut-wrenching ugly scene of betrayed hopes.

A knot behind his tongue threatened to rise and gag him. An urgency to upchuck everything from his churning stomach forced him to rein up the horse to vomit violently over the side. The episode left him nearly too weak to ride the next fifty miles of his assignment.

How could she have done that to him? He found no answer in his bewildered mind as he pondered his deep feeling about this discovery. Women had no conscience about betraying men who had dedicated themselves to them. Did that still remain as a part of his restraint concerning women in his life?

Was that episode with Rebecca Carr the source of his true resistance to committing himself to a woman? Was that, rather than her age, the reason he held himself back from Cally?

Damn, his life was crowded with memories of his part in the muddy hopeless battles he fought in Mississippi. Coming home afterward, barefoot, he'd lived hand to mouth until he began driving cattle to Kansas. Then he'd quit the drives after the tough loss of so many lives on that last drive up there and gone back to being a Ranger.

"Are you still with me?" Cally asked.

Her words broke into his deep recall. "Yes, sorry. I'll try to share something with you when we're alone."

Her elbow nudged him. "Brown is coming over."

The tall man nodded to her and shook hands with Guthrey. "How are you two this evening?"

"Very well."

"Will the young lady excuse you to talk with us?"

"What do you think, Cally?"

She nodded. "If it is what they desire, you're excused."

"No." Guthrey stepped in. "Cally is a part of my life. She knows lots about this situation and has had her own losses. I would like her to be there when we talk."

Brown shrugged. "Let's go outside, where we can speak more freely."

"We're coming. Lead the way." Guthrey squeezed Cally's hand and shared a confiding look with her.

Outside, they went around the bonfire crowd to the south end of the grounds. Six men waited for them in the lingering light of the bonfire past the parked rigs.

"He asked that Miss Bridges be here as well," Brown said.

Each man in the group nodded or doffed his hat to her.

"Glad to have you," McCall said.

"Thanks," Guthrey said.

McCall continued, "We have the petition to remove Killion from the office of sheriff. I believe in three weeks we can file enough signatures to call for an election. Are you in?"

"I'm ready to challenge him." Guthrey looked over the group. "I have no desire to become rich from this election, but it will cost me some money and my time."

"We have a money chest of four hundred dollars to start," Brown said. "And we can draw more from the people who want a new sheriff."

"We want to set up places around the county where you can speak and meet the people over this issue."

"Yes, that will be necessary." Guthrey nodded. "I understand the county clerk was not available at first?"

McCall nodded. "I guess we threaten them well."

"The county board president too?"

"Mr. Cameron says he has to be neutral on this matter."

"Anyone know what Killion thinks?" Guthrey shook his head, recalling his first morning meeting with the man and listening for any other response from the recall committee.

"You watch your back. This man has made a fortune doing his tax collection. I don't know if he'd kill you, but he's going to do all he can to discourage you before this comes to a vote." McCall sounded deeply concerned. "We don't expect you to risk being hurt or dying over this process. Do you want a guard unit?"

Guthrey shook his head. "If I can't manage my own business I don't deserve to be sheriff."

Cally frowned but let it go without another word about protecting him.

"We will be at the public meetings and back you. It's the going and coming that might expose you." Brown paused like he wanted a reply.

"I'll be fine."

"Our lawyer said we needed eight hundred voters to sign the recall papers to call for a special election." Brown dismissed it as no problem, then added, "We hope to find that many voters in the county."

"What if they've overcounted?"

"I think we will soon find that out."

"Good. Where do we start?"

"There are twenty-four schoolhouses in the county. That means we will need over thirty signatures at each one."

"That number sounds high," Guthrey said. "Have you tried here tonight?"

"We plan to do it when the musicians take a break."

"We're ready," Brown added.

"We can quickly see if folks want change," Guthrey said.

They went back inside the schoolhouse. McCall had Colonel Watson, an auctioneer, stand up and quiet the crowd. "Ladies and gentlemen, what I want to ask you for is your support in a big issue facing Crook County.

"Friends, we need a working sheriff to protect us and we don't have one. Do we?"

"No!" shouted a voice from the crowd.

"We have a paper we need you to sign

tonight so we can throw Killion out of office and put a man in his place who has been enforcing the laws of Arizona as a citizen. I want you to meet former Texas Ranger Captain Phillip Guthrey. Here is the man who is going to tame Crook County for all the God-fearing folks in our land. These terrorists have struck at many of you. They have driven away your neighbors and forced widows to sell out."

He waved his hat. "Here is Phillip Guthrey to tell you all about it."

"Thank you," Guthrey said to stop their applause when he stood on the low stage. "I'm a cattleman, and I've been a Ranger and enforced the law back home. I want to live here, but first we must put in place a state of law, controlling these bullies who have made life near impossible for so many of you. That's something I can do. Come up and put your John Hancock on these papers."

Men crowded in close to sign one of the petitions. Guthrey loudly thanked them and then joined Cally. "It must have been enough said, huh?"

She agreed. "I think everyone is signing it."

"Good. This is one of the larger communities. I bet some of those distant school-

234

houses won't have twenty signers."

"What will you have to do to get them signed up?"

"Take the paper to them."

Her eyes looked troubled by his answer. "I'm glad you're doing this. But I will be worried for your safety until it is settled."

"Naw, I'm a lot tougher than you think."

She gave him a sharp, disagreeing look. "Glad you think so."

"We better stick around and see how we did. I'll get a couple of petitions to take with us for folks to sign who want to support us."

She agreed and they exchanged pleasantries with the folks who stopped by to visit with them and thank them for doing this. The evening fled fast and after the dance, McCall announced they had collected fifty-two signatures. Guthrey thanked them, shook hands with his supporters, and made plans to attend more meetings.

After the dance, he and Cally returned to her tent under the stars. They spoke few words, lost in a whirl of all the excitement and dancing together until they became one. He'd not been this serious about any individual woman, not since his teen years. These teenage feelings were being smothered by the dark clouds of the petition hanging overhead like a thunderstorm ready to explode.

He stood and held her just to catch their balance after the whirlwind of events that evening. No need to worry or rush into anything. In the distance, a coyote yapped, and another joined in while the insects played a creaky symphony. But for now, they were just two people lost in their feelings for one another.

He cuddled her head to his chest and squeezed her. "Cally, someday we'll have all this behind us and we can live a much simpler life."

She pulled her head back and shook the fallen hair back from her face. "No, we won't. We'll have each other to lean on. But, Phillip Guthrey, I expect you will always be getting into something that you figure is unjust or wrong. And I'll love you more because of it."

They both laughed. She was probably right. He'd done it like that all his life, in the army, on the cattle drives, then as a Ranger; being a lawman would lead to more of the same. This new life he planned had one more element he thought he should add to it — Cally as his wife — someday soon.

Sixteen

Clearing his throat, Noble stood in the tent's doorway. He'd obviously ridden a horse hard to get there.

"What's wrong?" Guthrey asked.

"Sam Joyce came over this afternoon. Said about sundown yesterday a bunch of masked riders burned his haystacks. They told him to get out or they'd kill him. Joyce said his wife was near hysterical and the kids too. He has three small ones. Apaches killed his first wife and two kids back about the end of the war. He's a tough man but said he needed help. There were seven of them raiders and he said they were a tough lot. One of the raiders wore a ruby ring."

Guthrey looked at Cally, who he still held in his arms. "The woman you talked to who was assaulted — she said one of the rapists wore a ruby ring."

"Yes, she did. Does Whitmore wear one?" she asked when Guthrey set her on a cot.

Noble shook his head. "I never saw him wearing one the day I met him."

"It's the only lead we have. It's too late tonight to do anything. I'll ride over there and see what I can learn in the morning. Not much we can do in the dark."

Cally and Noble agreed.

Noble took a seat on one of the folding chairs. "How did it go up there?"

"We got fifty-two signatures. We need eight hundred to sign it."

"Whew, that's quite a few."

Guthrey agreed. "I thought the bar we had to jump was plenty high. But McCall and Brown and the rest, they think we can do it. I'm going to try to make it work. You may have to run the ranch though. Where's Dan?"

"I think he went courting after you all left."

"Oh, who is the girl?" Cally asked.

Noble shrugged in the dim light and shook his head. "Didn't tell me."

That was the first Guthrey'd heard about the boy's love interest, other than the Mexican girl in Soda Springs. Oh, well, Dan was at the same age Guthrey had been when he'd thought the first girl he kissed was an angel. And it turned out she was fickle as a gyp in heat. He'd like to put that part

238

behind him, but he wasn't really over it. Water went on by and downstream; so should bad memories.

In the morning Guthrey would need to check out the arsonists. He'd met Joyce somewhere and tried to envision the man's face. But he couldn't recall it, he'd met so many people lately. Must have been heartbreaking to see his summer work go up in flames. These bastards needed to be stopped.

At last in his bedroll, Guthrey tossed and turned a lot but finally fell asleep. Morning wasn't slow getting there. Noble nudged him with a boot toe. "I'll get back and milk the cow."

"Thanks," Guthrey said in a rusty, sleep-coated voice and sat up. Whew, his head hurt like he'd been drinking all night long — no such case this time. Been a long time since he threw a real drunk and his Rangers brought him home and put him to bed. That all happened after Judge Ivors in San Angelo found Henry Clay guilty of manslaughter and not murder. The killer got off with three years in Huntsville instead of being hung like he deserved to be.

Guthrey had felt like the decision was a slap in the face to all the Texas Rangers. Others did too and they joined together in a loud protest party at a local cantina, where Guthrey must have later passed out. Still angry. Still upset. But the next day he slept that off as well.

The cold water he splashed in his face at the washbasin did not particularly wake him up either. But the liquid that spilled on his shirt let him know quick-like that it was cool that morning. He dried his face and then his hands and Cally came over to kiss him.

"Sleep well?"

"No." Then he smiled and kissed her.

"Neither did I." Spatula in her hand, she went back to the campfire, where there were pancakes ready for her to flip over.

"I better go see Joyce and see what I can do for them."

She agreed. "Did Dan tell you where he was going last night?"

"No, ma'am. Noble thought he went courting."

She looked at the sky for help. "My brother's efforts at that are not too great. You never saw him dance inside the schoolhouse, did you?" She spun around to be certain that Noble wasn't in the area. "He probably went to a brothel in town last night to see a particular lady."

"Boys will be boys."

She shrugged her shoulder and blushed

some. "I guess. You better eat." She handed him the platter covered in pancakes, and he filled his plate.

"Has Dan done this before?"

"Yes, but I thought he was over her."

A nod to her and he busied himself fixing the cakes with butter and syrup. Most men seldom forgot the dove they slept with in bygone days. But Cally didn't need to know that bit of information. You didn't get over them. You simply rode on home with a pile of memories. Most of them were branded in the mind, comforting enough on a cold night alone to return and warm you. Enough of the ladies of the night business, he reflected. He better eat and get going.

He wiped his face on the cloth napkin.

"I hate to ask you, but would you go see that Dan is all right?" she asked.

"That would be a father's job."

"All I want to know is if he's all right. I don't care what he's done. I'm worried about him." She had her head bowed and he saw it as a sincere request.

"I will go see where he's at."

"Thanks."

"You go to church. I'll have Noble come back and haul you and the tent back while I go see about Dan and Sam Joyce."

"If I wasn't so worried . . ."

241

"Go to church. By then Noble will be here to get you and all this."

"Oh, Phil, all I have is you and Dan."

He handed her his neckerchief and shut his eyes. No time to waste. He had the team to hitch and then he had to get going. Take the team back, get Noble to come help her after church while he went to check on Dan and then over to try to soothe Sam Joyce. It would be a long day.

After sending Noble to move Cally and her camping gear back home, it was near noon when he reached Steward's Crossing. Noble had mentioned where he thought the boy might be at. When he'd located the house, he dismounted, hitched the bay horse at the rack, and walked through the open gate in the low picket fence and up the high stairs of the fancy house of pleasure.

A black maid answered the door and asked him what his business was. He almost snickered. What else was your business when you were knocking on a whorehouse door anyway?

"I'm looking for Dan Bridges."

"You sure he be here?"

"Yes I am. Where is he?"

"He may be with Steffany." Her brown

eyes narrowed. "That de boy that limps, huh?"

"Yes, he does some."

"I think he's eating brunch in the kitchen wid' de help."

"Please ask him if he'd join me out here."

She pointed her long, straight black finger down the hallway. "You's goes right back dere and talk to him youself."

"Thanks," he said and strode by her along the hardwood floor to the kitchen at the end of the hall. The door was open, but a wall blocked the entrance so he could not see who was in the room until he rounded the corner.

At the long table, several of the painted ladies in scanty clothing blinked in shock at the sight of him. Dan sat at the end beside a younger one of them and he jumped up. "Something wrong, Guthrey?"

He shook his head. "Just wondered if you were lost is all. No, just seeing that you're fine and taking nourishment is good enough."

"Join us," a tall blonde said, standing up and pouring more bubbly stuff in the others' tall glasses. She made some suggestive moves while refilling their glasses, then slipped in front of him with a sparkling glass and poured it half-full.

"It goes right up your nose. Try some. It's on the house, and you may want to climb in bed with me when you finish the glass, darling."

"Thanks," he said after downing the drink and handing back the empty glass. "Another time, maybe."

"Good for you. I live here." Her bare hand and arm snaked up toward the high ceiling to point at the upstairs.

"Dan, can you make it home all right?"

"Yes, sir. I'm fine."

"Where's the gawdamn whores?" a man out in the front hall shouted.

Every one of the girls quickly shared questioning glances with each other. Guthrey watched them.

Next he heard the black girl cry out for help. Sounds of a struggle came from the front hall. He spun on his heels and went to the kitchen door to see what was going on. Three men were standing there fighting with the maid. One was holding her arms pinned behind her back, the other two were busy ripping the clothes off her body. She was kicking and giving them hell like a wildcat.

Guthrey reached the one on the right and coldcocked him over the head with the pistol in his hand. The man's knees buckled, and he went down like a poleaxed steer. Then, before the other man with his hands full of the maid's black dress material could drop it, Guthrey shoved the muzzle of his cocked gun hard into his gut. Close to the men, he could smell the whiskey on their collective breath. "Tell that hombre holding her to stop or you're dead."

"Quit, Rattler. He's got a damn gun in my guts."

"Who the hell are you anyway?" the red-faced third man asked. When he let go of her arms, the maid whirled and gave the man her knee twice real hard in the crotch and he went down to his knees, oohing in pain and holding himself.

She fled down the hall, trying to gather up her torn clothes to cover her nudity. The man Guthrey had covered was backed to the wall, and Guthrey disarmed him.

"What in the hell is going on down here?" a fat-faced woman with smudged makeup demanded, halfway down the staircase.

The blond whore was there by then. "Those three crazy guys came in here shouting at Newby and went to stripping off all her clothes like they were crazy. This man here fought them all off."

"Who are you, sir?" The madam tightened up the fluffy white robe that had been exposing a good portion of her hefty breasts.

"My name's Guthrey. I came by to check on Dan and be sure he was all right. Minding my own business. I don't know any of these three and wanted them to leave the black girl alone."

"If we had some real law in this county, there might be some peace and quiet on Sunday mornings around here. My name's Ellen Foster."

"Yes, ma'am, I agree, and I'm the man who can deliver that."

"Guthrey, I believe you are that man. Girls, go eat your breakfast. Mr. Guthrey, what can we do with these men?"

"We can tie them up. Later this afternoon, I can take them to the county seat and have them put in jail for trial."

"Really?"

"Yes, ma'am." He waited for her answer.

She wrinkled her large nose at him. "I suppose they'd get off anyway."

"No, ma'am, the judge is tough and straight. They'll do time if we do it like I say."

"But Killion would send a boy around to collect more money from me if I did that."

"Have you heard that there's a petition going around to have him removed from office?"

"Well, no, but that's a good idea if anyone will dare sign it." She scowled at the three men.

"Over a hundred have already signed it. Folks are tired of being run over by bullies like these three." So he'd exaggerated the number some, but word would get out that the number was larger than that.

Hands on her hips, she nodded. "You girls go get some ropes and we'll tie them up."

"Lady, you do and I'll burn this damn whorehouse down," threatened the one called Rattler, who'd held the black girl.

"What's your name?" Guthrey asked.

"Burt, Burt Alson. What damn business is it of yours?"

"I think there's a reward for you in Texas. Kaufman County. I'll wire them when we get you over to the county seat and find out."

Alson's face went white, and Dan sharply warned Alson, "You go for that gun, mister, he'll kill you too."

"You all right, Dan?" Guthrey asked, not looking around at him.

"I'm fine. Sorry you had to come look for me."

"Aw, Cally just wanted to be sure you were still alive."

247

Dan frowned at him. "You tell her any-thing?"

Guthrey shook his head, busy disarming the men. He reached down, took a fistful of the groggy one's shirt collar, and dragged him on his butt over to prop him against the wall. "What's your name?" he asked the second one, a black-bearded man in his twenties.

"Roy Carlton."

"Address?"

"Tombstone."

"What's his name?" He indicated the one holding his sore head and seated on the floor.

"Deal Brant."

Guthrey had written their names on the back of a petition and put the stub lead pencil away along with the paper.

"What's your plan?" Dan asked.

"A bunch of masked riders raided Sam Joyce's place last night and burned his haystacks. I'm headed up there to look for evidence. You guard this riffraff here and I'll be back in a few hours. Then we can take them to jail."

"Joyce all right?"

"I guess so. Noble talked to him. Cally and I were at the dance."

The three outlaws were herded out on the

back porch. Their hands and feet tied, they were seated on the boards on the back porch. Guthrey told Dan to gag them if they became too noisy, and he agreed. Guthrey went out front and checked the contents of their saddlebags. They each had a money-bag mask in one side or the other. He glanced back at the two-story house. What he'd found pointed to them as being some of the Joyce place raiders he was looking for.

He hadn't seen a ruby ring on any of them. That must fit the leader of the bunch's finger. Someone else had to have noted that big ring besides Joyce and the ranch woman who had been assaulted. There was no money for them in burning down haystacks and terrorizing God-fearing folks. They were on someone's payroll. He noted that none of their horses wore a brand either.

Back inside the house he met Steffany, a black-haired girl in her teens with long eyelashes who drawled like she came from Dixie. A little on the chubby side, she acted very attentive to his and Dan's conversation about Dan guarding the three men until Guthrey got back.

Guthrey removed his hat to nod good-bye and told her he was pleased to have met her. Attached to Dan's arm, she smiled and said, "Thanks."

Then he promised the boss lady he'd be back and headed for the Joyce Ranch with all the crew of girls standing out on the porch waving hankies good-bye at him when he rode out.

It was hard for him not to laugh at the sight of them doing that as he rode on his way up East Mountain, headed for the Joyce place. Maybe he could pinpoint those three prisoners as the some of the night raiders. He certainly hoped so. A sun time check told him it was already midmorning and he hadn't even gotten to see the Joyce family. They probably thought he was not coming at all.

SEVENTEEN

The Joyce place was up a live water creek that fed into the San Pedro River. Guthrey could smell the burned alfalfa as he rode under some cottonwoods, the leaves overhead rustling in the rising wind. The narrow field of legumes was across the nearly dry streambed and under tight fencing to keep range cattle out. It wound up the way, and he could see how the man's flood irrigation system worked.

He must have been watering some of his crops. The killdeers were busy harvesting grasshoppers and other bugs set in flight at the advancing spread of water through the green stems. He saw the black rings of the once-tall stacks when the house and corrals became visible. A windmill creaked away, pumping well water into a huge tank.

Sam Joyce came to greet him, and a much younger woman who looked very pregnant came out of the house. Three small ones surrounded her, holding her apron and looking up to her for the answer about who this strange man on horseback was — friend or foe?

"Sorry I'm so slow getting over here," Guthrey said, dismounting and shaking Joyce's calloused hand. "But I had to check on some other things happening."

Joyce looked tired but he nodded his head. "Everyone's all right here now."

"Yes, I can see that this morning. You were real lucky. Obviously those people have no respect for families."

"I agree. Come on, the wife will make us some fresh coffee."

These folks were not Mormons if they were serving coffee. Guthrey led the pony over to the hitch rail, then followed Joyce inside the house.

Seated at the wooden table, Guthrey asked the man if he'd noticed the raiders' horses.

The man turned to his wife. "Henny, did you notice anything about them devils' horses?"

She looked pained walking across the room with the cups in her hand. "Not really. It was about sundown and the light was real red. I saw one had an army bridle with a U.S. button on it where the headstall was connected to the brow band."

"Thanks," Guthrey said. He didn't recall seeing the bridle headstall on any of the men's horses at the whorehouse, but there were supposed to be six men who rode in on the raid.

"This man with the ruby ring. Was there anything else about him that you can recall?"

"He was loud. Swore a lot. He rode a sorrel horse with a white blaze, and I felt sorry for the horse by the way he jerked him around." She came back with the coffeepot. "I've got milk. No sugar."

"Black's fine. Anything else?"

She looked at her husband as if she needed his approval, and he nodded. "Go ahead."

"If you repeat this to anyone, I'll swear I never told you. But Sally Landers and Jenny Samples both told me that a man with a ring like he wore had — had raped them both on two different occasions while their men were gone from the house."

Tears spilled down her red face.

"Did he ever assault you?"

She shook her head. "No, I never saw him before, but please don't tell anyone I told you about him." She buried her face in a rag, and her shoulders shook as she cried.

"Mrs. Joyce, I'll find him, and you won't ever be mentioned. And he'll pay for his crimes. But I need to know all I can about him. Is there anything else you can tell me?"

She shook her head and left the room.

Joyce made a wary face. "How will you stop him?"

"I'm not certain. I'll have to find him first. No one speaks about that ring, except a few people who saw it. I don't want him to take it off either, so we need to be quiet about it."

"I never thought about that," Joyce said at his comment. "All he has to do is take it off and we couldn't identify him, right?"

"Exactly. So let's keep this news to ourselves. And I have to wonder if the husbands know about those assaults."

Joyce set down his cup. "By gar, they might not know about it."

"Exactly. I don't want to make any trouble for those women. But I also want to know more identifying marks on the man that they might have seen."

Joyce went for the coffeepot on the stove to refill their cups. "I can see where this law business can be lots of work. I'm learning. Never thought before how hard it would be convicting them. In the old days, a man handled it himself. Like a bad cow-killing wolf or mountain lion, you hunted them down and shot them. Or hired hunters to do it for you."

Guthrey agreed. "That's why we need new law in Crook County."

"We sure ain't got none now."

"I better get back to town. I caught three men this morning having a rampage in a house and have them tied up over there. I'll take them to the county seat today and have them locked up. I suspect they were part of the raiders but I can't prove it. I'll let you know what I find out."

"Let me sign that petition now. I hope you win. We need a man like you as sheriff."

Guthrey shook his hand and thanked him. Then he told Joyce's wife good-bye and went for his horse. Still had lots to do before dark.

Back at Steward's Crossing, Dan helped Guthrey load each man on his own horse. The youth was still hobbling around, but he kept a straight face. With the hell-raisers on their horses, Guthrey stepped over to privately ask the madam if she'd ever seen the ruby ring.

"I have."

"Who wears one, Ellen?"

She wrinkled her nose. "Why do you need him anyway?"

"He's raped several ranch women and led

the raid last night."

"I have never heard about him doing that." Her blue eyes narrowed, and he saw her bulldog attitude set in.

"He may be one of your best customers, but the sumbitch has no business raping housewives or any women who aren't interested in him." His temperature started up. She knew damn good and well who wore that ring and wouldn't tell him. All he got from her was silence, and she looked the other way.

"Never mind, I'll find him — and don't you warn him either, 'cause I can make lots of trouble for you if you put him on the run. Raping honest women makes lots of problems for them that they don't deserve. Think on that. I'll be back, and I want his name."

"I think you're a tough man, Guthrey. Crook County needs a tough lawman. I hope they elect you after the vote. But you don't know the problems I might have either."

He left her, mad as a hornet that she wouldn't tell him the son of a bitch's name.

"Something wrong?" Dan asked when he joined him.

"No. Let's get these things straight. Are you feeling good enough to ride over there with me to deliver these three?"

"Yes, I can stand the ride."

"I hate for you to make it. You're still limping."

"Get on your horse, Dad, I'm riding along," Dan said. When Guthrey looked at him with raised eyebrows, Dan continued, "You sound like my father."

Guthrey shook his head, recalling that he'd told Cally that this business of checking on Dan was a father's job, and smiled. "Let's go deliver them."

He swung up on the ranch horse and told Dan to lead the prisoners. He jerked the Winchester out of its scabbard, looked around to be sure they were not being threatened, and they left in a trot.

Soda Springs blazed in the setting sun when they pulled up at the county jail.

"Stay here," Guthrey said to Dan and went inside.

"That you, Guthrey?" Tommy asked from behind his high desk at the key. He raised the green celluloid visor and smiled. "You got more prisoners?"

Guthrey nodded and turned to look in the jail office. The grizzly faced jailer behind the desk looked sour as he discovered who was out there. He rose and stretched. "What the hell do you need?"

"I have three men who are suspects in a

257

raid on a rancher and his family last night."

"I don't have any room in this jail, I can tell you right now."

"I am swearing out a warrant for their arrest and for you to hold them."

"You got any evidence?"

"Yes. Three new masks they wore last night in the raid."

"That ain't nothing."

"I don't know any normal folks who go around with masks in their saddlebags. Do you?"

The man held out his hands. "I ain't accepting no more prisoners."

"I can go get the judge —"

"Gawdamnit, we had a peaceful county here until you got here. What are all these arrests going to do?"

"Make this county a damn sight better place to live for honest folks. Get ready. I've got three of them to lock up and hold."

The grumbling of the prisoners back in the cells almost caused Guthrey to smile as he strode back down the hallway to get his new ones. The three were listed on the sheet, searched, and then pushed in the already crowded cells. The wounded one, from the house of ill repute, was in one of the cells lying on a lower bunk.

Then Guthrey filed the three masks as

evidence and made the deputy sign for them along with the arrest papers. He made an X on the paper.

Dan visited with Tommy across the hall at the telegraph key while Guthrey finished his paperwork in the sheriff's office. Guthrey could see that the deputy, called Drummonds, was illiterate and made it clear by marking the tops of the papers with signs so he could identify them for whoever needed to look at them.

After all the time it took they finally left the courthouse. Guthrey decided they better find some food. It would be long past midnight before they reached the ranch, and his belly told him he needed to eat something.

The café was empty, but the waitress came out and smiled at them. She promised them she could feed them something, though it was Sunday and closing time.

"We'd eat about anything," Guthrey assured her and she went back to discuss the matter with the cook.

She stuck her head out of the kitchen. "How about breakfast?"

"Suits us fine," he said to her and Dan agreed.

She and the unseen cook provided scrambled eggs with chopped ham, German fried potatoes, a pile of toast with grape jam, and fresh coffee. After the great meal, Guthrey paid her fifty cents and thanked her for being so kind to them.

"No problem. Glad you two came by."

Guthrey waved at her before closing the front door and he and Dan stepped out into the twilight. Side by side, they headed east on the main road. Heat from the day began evaporating and the stars started to peek out in the vast sky over them. Night insects chirped and a few desert owls hooted for their mates. Then the coyotes began to howl to each other. The desert night woke up, and Guthrey and Dan trotted their mounts to make as much time as they could. Cally would be worried about them taking so long to get back, and there was no way to allay her concern but push to get back there.

Guthrey knew he had lots of riding ahead of him to collect the number of signatures they had to have on the petition. No doubt there'd be lots of turns and twists for him in the road to the election that he had not even imagined. And he needed to find out who the man with the ruby ring was.

EIGHTEEN

Dawn was peeking over the Chiricahua Mountains at their backs when Guthrey and Dan finally reached the ranch. A light was on in the house and Cally ran to the doorway.

"Are you two all right?" she asked, holding her skirt up and heading for Guthrey's arms. He kissed her, and she shook her head.

"Why, I've been praying and crying and worrying about you two all day and the night. What took you so long to get home?"

"We've been busy," Dan said. "Wait till he tells you the whole story."

Oh, fine — Dan wasn't going to mention a thing about his part and leave Guthrey to tell her about their activities in some cleaned-up form. Noble brought in the milk pail. Looking them over, Noble nodded. "Why, they ain't got a scratch on 'em that I can see, missy. I told you they'd be fine."

Guthrey started his recitation. "I went to see about Dan. Then there was an altercation at a house of ill repute and I stopped it. I arrested those three troublemakers and tied them up. Dan guarded them while I went to see Sam Joyce, and he told me a few things about the raiders from the night before. But his wife also told me this mystery man who wears the ruby ring was the leader. Also, he had repeatedly raped some other wives —"

Cally's loud inhale and pale face scared him. Fingers pressed to her mouth, she said brokenly, "I told you — he did that before. There were even more than the woman I knew about?"

"Yes, there were more. I'm sorry this bunch is so mean. Yes, she named others."

"Did they harm her?"

"No, she's about to have another baby."

"That's why I asked."

"She's fine. Nice young lady."

Chewing on her lower lip, Cally agreed. "Go ahead. I'm sorry I interrupted."

Then she went to get the coffee for them that he could smell boiling on the range.

"To make things short, I found new masks in the saddlebags of each one of those men who I had held for causing the ruckus. So they will be charged as terrorists in the Joyce matter.

"After all that we took them to Soda Springs, where the jail is full and the jailer complained he couldn't take any more, but he did take them and I filed charges on them. We had supper late over there and have been riding ever since."

Coffee poured, she kissed him on the cheek and put the pot back. Then she brought them each a large platter of food for breakfast from the oven. "It's still hot. I imagine you two need to rest all day."

"Half a day anyway. You have any trouble, Noble?"

"Nope, doctored a few cattle. But we seem to be doing all right."

"No sign of that branded calf?" Dan asked.

"Nope, he's vanished."

Dan, between bites, promised him they'd find it while Guthrey was off politicking.

After breakfast, Guthrey had a cold wash in the sheepherder's shower, shaved, and went back to the house. Cally had given him some fresh clothes to dress in afterward and wanted his other clothing for her to mend and wash.

"You can sleep on my bed today," she said when he came inside with the dirty clothes in his arms. "You look real nice all cleaned up. You have any money? We need to buy some better clothes for a sheriff candidate."

"I have enough. I also need to ride into Tucson and see about selling those cattle you wanted sold."

"It can wait. Sleep in your britches on my bed and get some rest today. Your eyes look drawn in the sockets. My, you are a tough man." Then she dropped her voice to a whisper, "Who is this dove my brother is seeing?"

"Steffany. I'd say she's close to his age. Dark hair and dark eyes. She acted pleasant enough. I don't think she's mouthy."

She nodded. "I don't want to run him off, but does he realize most of those girls don't stay married long and that he doesn't have a lot of money as she might think he does, being a rancher?"

"Whatever." He was about to laugh.

"You go sleep. It is not funny." She shooed him off, but not before he kissed her lightly on the cheek.

On the bed, he sank into the goose-down mattress. To him it felt like sleeping on a cloud. He closed his eyes and, before he fell asleep, the faint aroma of Cally's lilac perfume went up his nose. That smelled lots better than the thick aroma of heavy-duty scent he'd encountered in the kitchen yesterday morning at the big house. Whew, that about made him dizzy. . . .

He awoke in midafternoon, swung his bare feet over the bed, and combed his too long hair back with his fingers, then he headed for the kitchen. Maybe he had found his own piece of heaven in the spiny desert outside. For once, he really hoped so as the creosote aroma of the desert came on the breeze. Since he'd greased its gears, the windmill outside only clacked as it spun more water up from the depths.

A couple of chickens squawked in the yard, and Cally came back in with a basket full of produce from the garden. She spent hours working out there: weeding, watering, and making it work. Guthrey needed to pay more attention to her operation of it. Then she had rows and rows of canned jars in the cellar a few steps outside the back door. Dan and Cally's father must have been quite a detail man — all the things he fixed and built to provide for them on the ranch amazed Guthrey.

"You sure slept hard."

He laughed. "I felt you watching me."

"Good. How are you doing after the short nap?"

"Ready to do some work."

"Why don't you simply rest this afternoon?"

"Hard for me to do."

She took the ears of corn out of the basket and put them on top of her dry sink. "You know what it's hard for me not to do?"

"What's that?"

"Not sit on your lap and kiss you till the sun goes down."

He rubbed his knees under his pants and shook his head. "That's mutual, darling. We need to do something about that."

She washed her hands in the pan on the counter, then threw the water out the front door. When she turned around, she looked hard at him. "I knew one day a knight would come riding up that road from King Arthur's Court, and when he finally did come, I damn near ran him off with my snappy mouth."

"Naw, I don't run away easy."

She repeated his words. "We need to do something about what?"

"You and me."

She chewed on her lip. "I'm going to ask you a question — and it's a hard one for me to ask. Did I drive you to use that place where you found Dan?"

"Lord, no, girl." He swept her up in his

266

arms. "I went there to find him, not some woman dipped in loud perfume. No, you haven't done anything. But —"

She began humming a waltz. He held her close in his arms and they danced slow-like around the table. He forgot about the ears of corn, the girls in the whorehouse kitchen yesterday morning, the terrorists, Whitmore, and all his problems with the law business. His world became simply him and her, and he'd never felt anything in his life like their being there together that afternoon, dancing slow in each other's arms. *Dear God, I'm grateful you sent me here. . . .*

NINETEEN

Tuesday night, Guthrey and Noble were at the Alkali Hills Schoolhouse for a meeting with folks, asking them to sign the petition. Guthrey shook hands with the men, dipped his hat to the ladies introduced to him.

After she was introduced to him, one sharp-eyed woman in her late thirties asked if he was married.

"No, ma'am. I'm not."

"Lucille, get over here," she demanded, and a gangly teenager about fourteen came over.

"This is Mr. Guthrey. Stand up straight and show him what a nice-looking girl you are. Mr. Guthrey is single and he will need a wife when he becomes sheriff."

"Nice to meet you, Lucille," he said to be friendly.

She nodded. "Nice to meet you too. You got any good horses to ride?"

"One of my own."

"You going to get any more?"

"I don't need any more. Why?"

"Well, if I was going to marry you, I'd expect a nice paint mare and saddle for me to ride."

Mother swallowed hard. "Lucille, why, that ain't a nice thing to say."

Guthrey agreed with the girl. "Looks like I'm out of the running, then."

He and Noble shared grins as the mother took her daughter away by the arm, scolding her all the way outside the front doors about killing her chances to marry the next sheriff.

One man named O'Riley waited till after the petition signing to speak to Guthrey. They were standing aside and Guthrey was waving and saying good night to people, fixing to leave.

"I heard something today," O'Riley said. "I heard that Whitmore told a man he'd pay him two hundred dollars gold to get you out of this country."

"Did he tell you the name of the man Whitmore told that to?"

"No. Guess the guy he talked to must have been tough 'cause he wouldn't tell me that either."

"Did he say if the man took the money?"

"No, sir, he said that guy wanted five

hundred to kill you. The man who told me all that said Whitmore acted mad and walked off, told him he could get it done a lot cheaper than that."

"No names mentioned?"

"Nope," O'Riley said. "But you better keep your head down."

"I appreciate the news. I'll watch closer."

Satisfied, O'Riley moved on.

Noble asked under his breath. "You believe that?"

"Maybe Whitmore paid him ten bucks to give me that warning. What do you think?"

"More than likely you just hit the nail on the head."

"Did O'Riley sign the petition?" Guthrey asked.

Noble laughed aloud. "Hey, we can check on that, can't we?"

"Yes," Guthrey answered, then said good night to more folks who were leaving.

After everyone left, Guthrey checked and they'd gathered forty-six signatures. He didn't find O'Riley's name among the signers. Glad he'd checked, he blew out the candles and they rode up to the place of a rancher friend, Mike Thorp, and spent the night at his house. Mike's wife, Melda, cooked them a big breakfast in the morning and they had an interesting talk at the table afterward. When Guthrey asked him about O'Riley, Mike told them he didn't trust the man. Then Guthrey told him about the supposed threat.

"I doubt he knows anything at all about any plans to plant you. He's just sizing you up for a silver deputy badge when you get elected," Mike said.

"Why do that?" Noble asked.

"Hey, there's lots of guys would like to walk around as deputies."

Guthrey nodded. He'd forgotten about those men who did that back in Texas. Good point. He'd watch who he deputized if he ever got elected. Guthrey and Noble left Thorp's place and rode back home.

Guthrey had down in his small notebook that on Saturday night he was to attend the social at Farnam Schoolhouse. The person who set it up was Earl Southern, a man he could not recall, but perhaps the organizers had made the appointment. Carl Brown and Lester McCall were a big help to the campaign, and he was anxious to learn how many signatures they had gathered that week. Maybe getting eight hundred signers was actually feasible. He hoped so; spending all his days going here and there had proved time-consuming for him.

Cally came out from the house when they

rode in. "How did you do?"

"Near fifty signed up."

"Wow, you two did good."

"Anything happen here?"

She shook her head. "Just same old stuff. Dan went to check on water holes. He promised not to be out too long."

"He'll be fine. What are you doing?" he asked.

"Canning corn and more green beans. I need some beets harvested so I can put them in jars tomorrow."

"Noble and I can do that, soon as we put up these horses."

"I hate to bother you politicians. But I better get back and watch that cooker."

He kissed her and she hurried back inside.

"She's a busy girl," Noble said. "Don't forget to tell her about that girl that rejected you."

"Oh, the one who wanted a paint horse to marry me." Guthrey chuckled.

The two men pulled up the red beets and hauled them to the house in a wheelbarrow. Then they busied themselves washing them down by the big tank and separating the beets from the tops. Cally had told them she'd can the beet tops too.

Dan rode in and laughed when he came up to the site where they worked.

"She's got you working, I see. Did you do any good up there last night?"

"Near fifty signatures," Guthrey said, straightening his sore back. "Water holes working?"

"Yeah, but we need rain." He looked with concern at the blue sky.

"Part of being a rancher, always looking for one more rain."

"I used to let Dad worry about that. Now he ain't here, I figure I have to worry about it."

"Well, don't just sit that horse," Noble said. "We've got beets to wash."

"Yes, sir. I'll put Snorty up and be right back." He rode off, laughing.

With the beets finally washed and separated from the tops, Cally came out to inspect their work. "You three do good work. Thanks."

Noble had to tell them the story about the girl and her mother along with the paint horse. They all got a good laugh out of how he told the story.

Cally shook her head afterward. "Maybe I better go along with him on his trips and protect my interests."

"Who'd do the canning?" Dan asked.

She laughed and invited them up to the house for coffee and the fresh dried-apple pie she'd just taken from the oven.

The next day, her three ranch hands rode hard, looking for the Whitmore-branded calf. No sign of him or his momma. Guthrey was beginning to believe that he'd been taken from the range, along with the momma. The whole thing about the branding made little sense, but there was no reason for lots of things these raiders did, except someone wanted them crowded out. Whitmore wore that cap.

By the third day back at the ranch, he began to wonder about his main opponent. Since the day he saw Whitmore standing by and watching the aborted gunfight between his gun hands and Dan, Guthrey had not had a peep out of the man. These days, Guthrey did not frequent as many saloons as he used to do in Texas, with a Ranger camp close by them. Still, in all his trips to the county seat, arresting men, he'd not noticed Whitmore once. Maybe Guthrey needed to find out more about the man and what else he was up to.

"Anyone seen Whitmore lately?" he asked at breakfast.

"Not me," Cally said.

Dan shook his head.

Noble looked up before spooning some

oatmeal in his mouth. "Not seen hide or hair of him."

"Odd, isn't it? He sent Hampton after me at the first dance I attended. Hired some men to shoot at me here, and has been sending raiders out to harass folks."

"He don't like his own hands to get dirty," Noble said between bites.

Dan agreed. "Why do anything when you can hire idiots to do it for you?"

Guthrey agreed and changed the subject. "I'm going to ride into Tucson and try to find a good cattle trader to buy some steers before the heat gets worse and they lose their fleshy condition."

"Do you have the time to take off now?" she asked.

"We're doing all right on the campaign. I'll tell Brown and McCall what I must do and then go over there next week."

"We really should have some more money," Cally said.

"We can do this," Guthrey said. "Gathering and moving the cattle may be a bigger challenge. You two keep your eyes open for the big steers and each day push the ones you find over this way. That way gathering them won't be such a problem. Three dozen do?" he asked Cally.

"That should tide us over," she said. "But

how do we send them all at one time?"

"I'll try to figure that out. Let's get busy. I'm going to ride in and see McCall today. Maybe he has more ideas."

The other two men left the room and Guthrey kissed Cally good-bye before he left her with the dishes.

Two hours later, he dismounted at McCall's yard gate. His place was set under some big cottonwoods above the river. Guthrey felt certain the man was busy farming at this time of day. A woman came out and welcomed him. A full-figured woman, she smiled big at him.

"You must be Mr. Guthrey. Lester's around at the barn shoeing a horse. How have you been, sir?"

"Fine, nice to see you," he said, tipping his hat to her, and started around the yard, leading his horse.

McCall was in the shade of one of the big cottonwoods. Bent over, busy nailing a plate on a nice-looking bay horse, he looked up as he finished and dropped the hoof. "How are you today, Guthrey?"

"Better. We collected forty-six signatures up at Alkali the other night."

Taking off his leather apron, McCall nodded. "With the ones Brown and I've collected, that makes over two hundred. In the short time we've been working on this. I think it's going good. Any more news? I heard you helped fill the county jail some more."

"Those three men I think were in on a raid at Sam Joyce's place and burned his haystacks. I found new masks in their saddlebags."

"Good. That business needs to be stopped. I heard the sheriff was complaining about our campaign against him."

"What was that?"

"Oh, he told someone over at Soda Springs that the Mormons and the outlaws over east were getting a petition up to oust him from office, but he had enough gentile friends to hold it."

"What's your handle on that?"

"That we will get him ousted. Us Mormons and the outlaws. If there were outlaws over here, why isn't he patrolling it, then?" McCall shook his head. "Someone stole two good horses from one of the brethren this past week. He hasn't done one thing about that either."

"What did the horses look like?"

"One's a single-footing bay horse with a stripe down his face, and the other's a nice work mare about twelve hands. Well broke to work or ride. She's their kid's horse."

"I'll put the word out up there. But I bet that they're gone to New Mexico. Out of the country anyway."

"No doubt, but the law should take notice and attempt to catch them."

"I need to get moving. Next week I have to ride over to Tucson on business. So I'll do Farnam Schoolhouse this weekend, then not be back for a few days."

"Have a safe trip. I'll tell Brown how we're getting along and your plans. Let's eat lunch before you ride back."

Guthrey agreed.

The large woman was named Betty. She laughed a lot and served them hot corn bread and brown beans for lunch.

"If only Lester'd told me you was a-coming, I'd'a caught a chicken and fried it."

"Aw, don't be too hard on him. My trip was simply to bring the petitions I'd gotten signed and kinda check on things."

"I am simply embarrassed all I had was brown beans ready."

"No problem. I've ate my share of them. And these are good. I've ate lots that were as gritty as the riverbank sand."

"Don't you hate that sand on your molars?" She laughed some more.

Guthrey reckoned that Lester had her at

this house to keep him happy. No doubt like most of the leading men in his religion, Lester had more than one wife and Betty shared him with some "sisters." Guthrey didn't even have one woman as his wife, and McCall probably had three or more of them. How did a man satisfy that many wives? Beyond him how they did it. After the meal, Guthrey thanked them and headed back to Steward's Crossing and home.

Guthrey stopped and drank a draft beer in the Texas Saloon. The place was near empty save for a few men playing a small card game in the corner. He nursed the brew and the bartender polished glasses on the other end. Not a very talkative man for his profession. Made no difference.

When Guthrey left and went out to unhitch his horse, a man came down the boardwalk and spoke to him.

"You're the one going to oust Killion, ain't'cha?"

"My name's Guthrey, sir." He offered his hand. "What can I do for you?"

The man checked around, then shook it. "You going to oust Killion from office?"

"That's the plan. Why?"

"I been a-hearing about you arresting folks. You know he'll be counting the votes, so there's no way you're going to win."

Guthrey nodded. "Thanks for the tip."

Searching around again before he spoke, the man said, "That's how he beat the last guy. You heard about that?"

Guthrey nodded to get him to continue.

"I better not talk no more out here. They just didn't count all those ballots for the other man. My place is down the road from Noble's on the right."

The man, in his forties, unshaven, shabbily dressed, hurried off down the boardwalk. Guthrey stepped aboard the gelding, considering another obstacle in the road to him becoming the sheriff of Crook County. Who counted the ballots? Was that guy just a rabble-rouser or the real thing? Noble would know him.

He reigned the pony around. Time to get back to the ranch. Still no sign of Whitmore or any of his hands in town. Guthrey short loped the bay most of the way home. When he halted him at the corral, Cally came from the house, hem in hand, wearing an apron.

"How did it go?" she asked after he kissed her.

"Fine. A man in town told me that in the last election, Killion counted himself in and discarded the votes against him. You hear anything about that?"

"They do some bad things to win is all I know."

"Maybe a U.S. marshal can help count the next election?"

"We may need one to do that." She swung on his arm and headed for the house.

"You'd cheer up a sour lemon," he said, amazed at her ability to free him of his worries.

"You're easy to cheer up. I hope selling the cattle doesn't interfere with your plans too much. I really believe you will get the signatures."

"You need to sell those steers. We won't be that distracted by doing that."

"I bet I can find you some lunch."

"Good."

Saturday morning, he left by himself for the Farnam Schoolhouse gathering. He knew the ride up to the northeast settlement in the county was far away. Rather than going to Steward's Crossing and turning east, then back north, he cut across country, following a map that Noble had drawn for him. Noble made sure he had a complete map for the trip. Guthrey kissed Cally goodbye, satisfied he'd be there in plenty of time.

He used Lobo, who was well rested and the toughest horse on the place. He set out in a hard trot to the river crossing and then took the mountain range trail. It was mostly unpopulated desert country, and he caught sightings of several cattle bunches but could not see their brands. He pushed the tough horse hard to reach the summit and dropped off the top into a canyon. The scent of a fire made him sniff the air. The narrow cut he rode down through must be working as a chimney for the country that opened ahead. He hoped it wasn't a range fire he was smelling. Then he could hear cattle bawling loud like they were being worked. When he topped the next stair step, he reined up and could see the dust made by several head of cattle being worked far down country. The crew down there was branding, and they had lots of stock gathered. Something was wrong here.

He was outnumbered twelve to one, by his count of various riders. Somehow he needed to cross through them and get out the other side. The smart thing for him to do at the moment might be to ride back over the mountain and find a new route. But he had no map to a new way, and he could easily get lost for a day without any supplies. This was to have been an easy ride to a social event, not riding up on what he suspected was a large, wholesale rustling deal in broad daylight.

If he could stay to the juniper brush that grew at this elevation and sidle his way down the mountainside before he was discovered, he might get by them. He pushed Lobo into the brush, which would take more time but might make the difference between life and death for him. This had been a well-planned deal to have this many cattle bunched and that number of men working the brands over. Might be the largest rustling operation ever handled.

Finding himself facing a sharp drop-off, Guthrey was forced to retreat to find another way off the mountainside with his horse. Not taking any chances, he jerked the .44/40 out of the scabbard. He didn't carry much ammo for the long gun. He had plenty of the Texas legislature's free .45 ammo in his saddlebags, but that was not long-range ammo. Damn, this could be a pickle of a place to be if they spotted him coming through.

All the way down the mountainside, the juniper made good cover and unless some puncher stopped and saw him, his approach was working. On the flats they'd be hard-pressed to chase down his tough horse. Besides, from what he could see their horses were lathered from working the stock and would not stand a long chase. In the brush, he could hear a lot of their swearing and shouting over the cattle's complaining.

At last, undiscovered, he reached the bottom of the grade. The sun began bearing down on him, and ahead of him he saw open country save for two hands driving some breakaway cattle back to the herd.

This pair of men, who he didn't know, looked tired. Good — their horses were breathing hard and were lathered. His own was barely breaking a sweat. If they didn't manage to shoot him, they'd never catch him.

Guthrey broke out of the junipers and headed for what looked like open country ahead and away from all the herd activity. This was his break for freedom and he set spurs hard in Lobo's sides.

Shocked at the sight of him and his horse breaking out of the cover, the two riders tried to rein up and draw their pistols. That was a big mistake. The rider on the sorrel found his horse went to bucking like a high-lifed mule. The second man accidently fired his pistol in the ground next to his horse. That pony started bucking as well, and last that Guthrey saw, the rider was out of his stirrups. The cattle ran bawling away from the herd. And behind him he heard the entire herd make a familiar thundering sound — stampede.

Whether they were headed after him he wasn't certain, but he was racing Lobo as hard as he could eastward across the greasewood flats for the next range of hills. Pursuit or no pursuit made no difference; he'd done enough to distract the rustlers and was actually fleeing them at a fast pace.

In a short while as he came to the top of a rise, he reined Lobo in and turned him around. There was lots of dust boiling up in the sky in the south, obviously the direction the spooked cattle had taken. No sign of anyone coming after him. Good news.

He turned Lobo northeast and short loped him. Whew, that had been close. He'd have to investigate that operation and somehow stop them from selling those cattle. That was all he needed — one more job. Looking back and seeing nothing, he felt some more of the hype that had built up in him melt away.

Midafternoon, he reached the schoolhouse and mingled among the early arrivals. Womenfolk fed him apple and cherry cobbler. Men visited with him about their problems with rustlers and the pressure from Whitmore to sell out. Guthrey told them they needed serious law enforcement and protection. They agreed, and before the dinner even started, he had twenty-two signatures.

He felt better about his narrow escape by the time he sat eating his supper with two widow women on the wall bench. They both were in their twenties and nice-looking ladies. Both had young families and would suit any eligible man, besides the fact that they owned small ranches.

"Guthrey, have you ever been married?" Laura asked, seated on his right.

Both women waited for his reply.

"No, ladies. First the war came along, then the cattle drive business to Kansas, and I rejoined the Rangers."

"Well, if you become sheriff, will you have time for a wife then?"

He acted pained. "Being a sheriff's wife is not good. He's so busy."

"I could manage," Laura said, and Candace added that she felt the same.

There would be no beating those two, so he listened to the advantages of marrying either one and felt like he always did in these cases — he had to escape them. Not because they had any bad deals about them — they just were not what he wanted. Cally beat them all to death for his part.

Later he talked to two ranchers, Kelly

Brightwater and Ute Gleason. The three men squatted on their boot heels out where the tall shadows from the bonfire started petering out. Guthrey told them about the suspected rustling operation he had come across on his way here.

Brightwater twisted the end of his mustache and nodded. "Cobberly Flats."

His buddy Ute agreed, then he asked Guthrey, "You recognize any of them?"

"No, I was trying to slip by them. I figured I'd be dead if I wasn't careful."

"Good idea." Ute scowled. "How many cattle did they have?"

"Maybe a hundred and fifty head."

"That was real rustling, wasn't it?" Brightwater shook his head. "Those bold bastards."

"If you two can get some evidence we can give to a grand jury, we might get them rounded up."

"How?"

"I have a half dozen or so in jail now waiting for trial. Jailer has to hold them until the judge says they can go."

"How did you do that?" Ute asked.

"It wasn't hard. I found the judge after they let one get away, and he told them they could pay the reward on the escaped ones. They've held them all in jail since then."

"We can take several men and ride up there, can't we, Kelly?"

"Damn right. They may have several head of our own stock in the ones they got up there."

"Go easy. That jail is about full."

All three men laughed. "We'll get all the evidence and get someone who wants to talk a lot about it."

"Good. All we need is some evidence to get them arrested and tried."

In the morning, he rode back with sixty-two names on his petitions all told. He stopped and rode across the ground where the re-branding had been held. No sign of much but cattle tracks. He hoped maybe his new friends could find answers for him, and he hurried up over the mountain. It had been a great gathering of his supporters to attend despite the close call with the rustlers. By noontime, he was back at the ranch, though if he'd had to go around the area the rustlers had been, it would have taken all day.

"So you made it back," Cally said, coming out in the sunshine when he dismounted at her doorstep. Before she even realized it, he had swept her up in his arms and kissed her.

"What are you doing in June?" he asked her.

"Why? What does that matter?" She looked shaken, being held in his arms.

" 'Cause I want to get married then."

"Who — oh my God. . . ." She pressed her fingers to cover her mouth. "You're asking me?"

He looked around and mildly shook his head. "Is someone else here?" Then he let her down to stand against his body. "I want to marry you, and I don't have a paint mare for you to ride."

"You crazy man. When you rode off yesterday, I said to myself, 'He's a going over there and find him a real woman for sure.' "

"I don't need a so-called real woman. I need you."

"Why, any day you want you can have me."

"No, the bride sets the right day for her to be married on."

"Oh, I never knew that." She began counting on her fingers. "June third will be a good day."

"Then that's the day we'll get married. I think it may rain today." He looked at the gathering clouds.

"Noble and Dan went way west today. I hope they are already headed back." She pressed herself hard against him. "You know, I can hardly wait. When you were sleeping on my bed the other day. I wanted to just sleep in your arms, but I behaved, didn't I?"

"Yes, you sure did not misbehave. But you are as tempting to me as a fresh-cut layer cake."

She swung her head from side to side like a clock pendulum. "Now I've got to wait even longer."

"Now you need to see if my grandmother's ring will fit you."

"Fit me?" She threw her hands to her chest and looked ready to faint.

"She'd be proud of me today." He reached into his pocket and took out the ring, which was wrapped in cloth, and used his knife to reveal it. He held it up in the sunlight; it glinted brightly.

"I can't believe you have her ring. I better sit down. It's my knees. They feel awful weak." She reached around behind her to find a chair, and he caught her so she didn't fall down. At last with her seated on the chair, he slipped the ring on her finger.

She swallowed so hard, he thought she'd choke. Then she looked up, her face all drained out. "Phil Guthrey, I love you with all my might."

Thunder rolled across the sky, and they were united kissing each other. Soaking wet, Dan and Noble soon came stumbling in.

Her brother, sounding peeved, asked them if all they had to do all day was stand around and kiss each other.

Cally finally perched her face on Guthrey's shoulder to look at them. "We're getting married June third."

"Well, hell, let's dance," Dan shouted. "Good for you two."

Let's dance. . . . That was what Guthrey thought as well.

TWENTY

They took her measurements for the wedding dress Guthrey was going to order in Tucson. She gave them the directions on what to measure, Dan used the tape, and Guthrey wrote the numbers down. It was a trying deal, but they finally finished taking the measurements. Guthrey planned to leave early the next morning and when they were done, Cally ran the other two men off so she had some time alone with him.

"How will we pay for the dress?" she asked, wringing her hands.

"I have some money. I can buy it."

"But, but — later you may need that money."

"Let me buy the dress."

She looked at him for some sympathy. "The girl's family usually does that."

"It will be fine. The guys say we can easily get forty head up to sell. I'll find a market for them."

"What will they bring?"

"That depends on the market. The army and the Indian agents buy beef all the time."

She made a sour face at him. "Whitmore has those markets tied up with Ike Clanton."

He agreed. "Half of it is stolen too. I'm going to get a handle on those rustlers I almost ran into and lock a bunch of those thieves up one day."

"Good, just don't get yourself killed doing it."

He rounded her up in his arms and kissed her. "Listen, Miss Bridges, you can't go through life married to a law officer and tell him that all the time. I won't do anything to get myself shot, but I want you to know I won't let anything illegal happen that I can stop."

"I know. I know, but I don't know what I'd do if anything happened to you."

He hugged and kissed her some more. "Three to four days and I'll be back. Now buck up. We are going to have fun in this world. You and me, we can whip anyone."

"I will try to be brighter."

"Be yourself."

"I will."

There was little sign of the day before's

shower when Guthrey rode away long before the sky lightened the next morning. Tucson was forty miles away on a hot, dusty road and no shortcuts. He used Lobo again and by evening that day he had him in a stable rubbed down and eating grain.

After a Mexican woman on Tucson Street fixed him some spicy beef wrapped in a flour tortilla for his supper, he took a bed in the Congress Hotel. At dawn, he was up, he had a street-side breakfast, and then he went looking for a butcher to sell his steers to. After several tries, he met a burly man named Michaels with a small slaughter-house at the south edge of town and explained his business. He had forty half long-horn–shorthorn cross steers, fat and ready for the butcher. They weighted close to nine hundred pounds apiece.

The man nodded. "I would like them better than those straight longhorns I get all the time. But I can't hold half that many at my ranch. Usually with good beef I can slaughter and sell two a day. Maybe three if they're fat. That means, say, fifteen a week."

"It is a two, three day drive in here. Is there any pasture I can rent while you work through them?"

"Maybe we can find such a place today. I

really want those cattle, if they're like you say."

"No problem, I know cattle. These are good ones."

They hurried out of his office, caught a ride across the shallow Santa Cruz River, and went to see a man that Michaels called Gar. The man's property was under new steel barbed wire fencing strung on stout posts. Many blacksmith shops were making this wire and it worked, once experience with it taught cattle to stay behind it.

Gar sat in an old stuffed chair on the porch of his jacal and greeted them, rising to shake their hands. After Michaels introduced Guthrey, he went on to explain that they needed a pasture to hold forty head for not more than four weeks.

Gar considered the matter and said, "I'd take forty dollars."

"How about thirty?" Guthrey asked.

"All right, thirty dollars. When will they be here?"

"Inside of a week," Michaels said, looking at Guthrey for his approval.

"There's plenty of grass in there for them to eat," Gar assured them.

From viewing it, Guthrey was sure there was. Michaels nodded and they left.

"If those steers are as good as I said they

were, how much can you pay a pound?"

"Twelve cents a pound on the hoof." They kept walking.

"I think you are the most honest man I have met in the beef business," Guthrey said. They shook hands again, then they hailed down a man driving a buckboard for a lift across the river.

Seated on the tailgate, Michaels asked Guthrey what he was going to do next.

"Go buy a dress for my wedding in June."

The big man looked over at him. "You're getting married?"

They both slipped to the ground and thanked the man for their dry crossing.

"I thought it was about time."

Michaels laughed. "I guess it is."

The beef deal completed, Guthrey walked to the business district. He found a nicely dressed Mexican woman coming back from shopping with her baskets full. He tipped his hat to stop her and asked her in Spanish where the best dress store in town was.

"What do you need to buy?" she asked, looking him over critically.

"A wedding dress for my bride."

"Hmm," she snuffed and made a face. "The Paris Shop is expensive but very good. I would have liked them to have done mine. They are very good."

"But high priced, huh?"

"*Sí,* but Louise is just five doors down. They are very good but —" She dropped to a whisper and he leaned over. "They will dicker with you."

She leaned back and looked pleased at him.

"Just what I needed to know. I am very grateful for your generous help."

"You are most welcome. She must really trust you to order her dress."

He agreed and thanked her again.

First place he found was the Paris Shop. A stiff-backed woman in her thirties met him when the small bell rang as the door closed.

"May I help you, sir?"

"I need a wedding dress for my bride."

"Oh, is she here?" The woman tried to see if she was outside in a buggy.

"No, but I have her measurements."

"Well — I guess we could fill that."

"Do you have some dresses to choose from?"

"Yes, will you have a chair? I will have the ladies bring you some dresses to examine."

He pushed his hat back on his head. "Ma'am, bring me three or four and tell me the price on each one and we can close this deal."

"Yes, sir."

Three ladies brought out dresses. He couldn't see Cally in any of them. But the fifth dress looked more like her. The girl held it up and he studied it.

"That dress is priced at sixty dollars," the saleswoman said.

"How about forty-five?" he asked.

She frowned at him. "What did you say?"

"I offered you forty-five dollars for that dress made to fit my bride."

"The price is sixty dollars, sir."

"I've been in here about twenty minutes. Not another customer has come in. I offered you forty-five dollars for a dress you asked me sixty dollars for."

She squared her shoulders and said, "The price is sixty dollars."

"I bet your competition will take my money."

She folded her hands together in front of her and looked at him very hard. "Sir, this is not an auction. We are the finest dress shop in this city. We sell that dress for sixty dollars every day."

"I see you don't want to sell me a dress. If I want a sixty dollar one, I'll be back. Thanks." He tipped his hat to her.

In the second dress shop, Louise's, he found a dark-eyed lady who was older than the woman at the last shop.

"I am looking to buy my future bride's dress today. I have every measurement you need. Will you show me the dresses you have?"

"Certainly." She clapped her hands and two young Mexican girls appeared. "This Mr. — ah?"

"Guthrey."

"Mr. Guthrey would like us to model some of our wedding dresses." She showed him to a chair and sat down beside him. As the girls went in back, she offered him a glass of champagne.

"No, I simply need a nice dress."

"Certainly."

"How does this dress look?" she asked as one of the girls modeled a dress with a long train. That wasn't Cally's style.

He shook his head.

Dress number four was his choice, and he turned to ask her the price.

"Sixty dollars."

"Would you take forty-five dollars for it?"

"Would you tell anyone what you paid for it?"

"No, ma'am. You've got my word on it."

"You have her measurements?"

He handed them to her.

After she looked at them, she nodded. "I

can have this ready in two days."

"I'm bringing cattle back in a few days, oh, maybe a week. I'll pick it up then."

She smiled. "It will be ready, Mr. Guthrey. And thank you again for shopping with us."

He tipped his hat to her. More grateful than anything else to finally have his dress buying ordeal over, he could only hope that Cally liked the one he'd chosen. On his way to the livery he passed the first dress store and went on by, whistling. They didn't look like they'd had any business since he left them.

He checked Lobo out of the livery and rode out of Tucson before noontime. The journey would be a long ride home, but he had his bedroll if the way was too far. He'd sold up to forty head of big steers at a good price. That should solve Cally's money worries for the ranch for the time being. Over four thousand dollars would help anyone's needs. He short loped the stout horse. The afternoon was not real hot and he made good time. When the night cooled, he loped him more until by nine he came up the road to the 87T Ranch. A light went on in the house when he passed under the bar, and Cally stood in the doorway in her nightgown.

"I knew you were coming home. I could

feel you coming." She ran to hug him. They kissed and embraced for a long while, savoring each other.

"How did you do?" she asked, out of breath and close to trembling in his arms.

"I sold forty steers at twelve cents a pound. Had to rent some fenced, irrigated pasture so we could take them all in one trip."

"What did that cost?"

"Thirty dollars, which is cheaper than hiring some more hands for another trip."

"Good. What about my dress?"

"Doggone, I knew I forgot something — no, no, it will be ready when we go back to Tucson in three days."

"Oh, you worried me to death. Will all of us go there?"

"No, I'm hiring two men to ride with you, me, and the cattle, and we'll leave our two men here to watch the place. You can be the camp cook for the drive. I'm sure Noble can find me two good cowboys, cost us thirty bucks and food for them."

She quickly agreed. "I think it's a good idea to leave Dan and Noble here to watch things."

"Yes. No telling what Whitmore's bunch might try to do with no one here. Any other word?"

"No, but a few folks stopped by and signed the petition for you. Said they wanted to thank you for doing this for them."

He hugged her neck. "Girl, after we get these cattle delivered, we're going to swoop this country and get that petition drive over."

"I'm ready."

"I hope you going along don't ruin —"

She frowned at him. "Stop worrying about my reputation. I don't give a damn about it. Let's see, this is the fourteenth of May. In three weeks I'll be your wife and they can all lump it."

He stopped and gently hugged her. "Cally, someday I'll tell you about some parts of my life that you need to know. They aren't bad things I did. They were situations that happened, and they may explain why I am like I am."

"Don't change one bit for me. I like you as you are."

"Good, 'cause you ain't getting much more, girl."

"Yes, I am." She drove a soft fist into his iron-muscled gut.

After eating some of her apple-raisin pie, he kissed her and left the house. In his own bedroll at last, he decided it would be nice to have someone to share his bed. In no time he fell asleep, stiff from all his hours in the saddle.

In the morning after breakfast, Noble rode out to find two day workers to help Guthrey drive the steers to Tucson. Dan promised he could locate the other five steers they needed and have them in with the bunch they had gathered. He set out to drive them in.

Guthrey wanted the shoes reset on Lobo. So everyone was busy. Cally watered her garden and came by between changing sets while he worked on new shoes for Lobo. He was disappointed when he found the old ones were worn too thin to reset. That meant he would need to heat up the coal-fired forge and reshape new ones.

He looked up from shaping the first shoe during Cally's second stopover. "If you want to, tell me about the money situation for you and Dan on this place, since I'll soon be family."

She blushed. "Heck, you are now. We owe the bank five hundred dollars that Dad borrowed to fix the water development on the ranch before — well, you know that story. Then we owe two hundred for our food, other things, and salt for the cows, all things we got at the store in town. Plus your wages."

"You don't owe me anything."

"I feel we do. You've done lots of work here since you came. I'd never have made it without you after Dan's wreck."

Finished with forming the shoe, Guthrey rested it in on the anvil and came over to her, removing his gloves. "That's all going to be family, ain't it?"

She shrugged. "I guess so."

"We'll have to pay Noble. He's been a lifesaver."

"Oh, I know that," she said. "But we will be all right for quite a while if we sell these steers like you said."

"Good. I simply wondered. We may need to find a place of our own someday."

"Leave here?" She blinked her lashes at him.

"I said someday."

She tackled him around the waist. "Someday I'm going to wrestle you to the ground."

"Someday," he said, lifting her up to kiss her.

When she left him to go back to watering the garden, he went back to work on hoof number one. His back ached by mid-afternoon, but Lobo was shod all around and ready for the drive. He had two more horses to shoe so that he would have adequately shod horses to drive the small herd to Tucson. Ranch horses being shod was not so important if they were rotated. But on any drive a man needed sure-footed, ready mounts, and Guthrey was pleased to have Lobo done with. He'd need to get another horse shod before dinner.

"When can we leave?" Cally's words broke his concentration on the bay horse's hoof and what he needed to trim. He released the leg easy, let the horse lower his limb, straightened, and walked over to the corral fence to take a break.

"When do you want to leave?" He put his hand on the top rail.

"Now."

"My, my. I have that horse to shoe and one more. We'll get there. I'm not magic."

She wrinkled her nose at him. "Oh, I guess I want to rush it all."

"Don't worry. It will all happen."

She raised her face to kiss him. "I have no shame, Phil Guthrey. I can hardly wait to be your wife."

"It is hard, isn't it? The waiting. You get your watering done?"

"Oh, yes. I'll be fine. I'm going to make a couple of pies. I'm just getting anxious."

"So am I." He laughed when she held her

hem up and went to the house.

He settled in using the rasp to shape the horse's hooves. Noble came in about then and dismounted. "I got your two riders. Julio Contras and Jim Phelps. Jim's got two tough herd dogs. Contras can throw a rope a hundred feet, and they'll be glad to go for fifteen bucks apiece."

"You did good. Give me a hand shaping the shoes for this horse so I can get done."

"You look a little stiff."

"I don't do this every day. I already did Lobo."

Noble laughed. "I can shape some shoes, but my old back won't hold up a horse hoof to shoe him."

"I can do that. You hear anything else in town?"

"You must be stepping on their toes. I didn't hear much but some griping about how many outlaws there were in the county jail."

His saddle and pads off his horse, Noble put his rig on its horn so the fleece under the seat could dry. Then he took the horse to the gate and turned him out. Noble was no stranger to shoeing. When he joined Guthrey, he went to examining a new shoe.

"What else did you hear today?"

"It ain't what I heard, it's what I didn't.

Bartender in the Texas Saloon I know said he hasn't heard one word in two weeks. That tells me they have sealed all talk."

Bent over tacking on the second shoe, Guthrey agreed. "He have any idea what they planned to do?"

"No. But he'll send me word if he learns anything. That bunch that works for Whitmore have run off all his local customers by coming in and threatening them. Really hurting his business. No way he can get them to stop, and folks aren't coming back. I can't blame them."

"I hope we know what they'll try next. He's moved on families and of course most of them won't fight back. But if we have an advantage on any trick they try against us, it would help."

"Best shot we have so far."

"I'm not complaining, we just need to have our ear to the ground."

"I'll do what I can. Dan's coming in."

Guthrey was anxious to know about his success. "I hope he found us the rest of the steers we need."

"I saw a bunch up on the north end last week."

"We may have to all ride up there and drive some of them down."

Guthrey still had two more hooves to

shoe. Noble's hammering to shape the shoes to fit was helping him get done. Dan dismounted and limped over to the corral.

"Quit worrying, guys, I found some more steers and drove them in with the big bunch."

"Hurrah for you," Guthrey said. That was the best news he could hope to hear at this point.

"That ain't bad at all." Noble clapped his hands. "I was sure dreading riding up there to the Tucker Flats to bring some of them back here."

"These won't be hard to drive either. They were no problem for me to round up."

"Did you get the extra steers?" Cally asked, entering the barn.

"Yeah, they're down here now."

"Good."

"Don't ask," Guthrey said, shaking his head at her. "We can head for Tucson day after tomorrow."

Later that day they loaded Cally's tent and camping gear in the buckboard. Guthrey planned to get some horse grain on the way. They also loaded firewood in case there was none where they camped. Three small kegs of drinking water were loaded too, and she fussed about what food she should take.

Guthrey decided he'd gone to Abilene or

Newton, Kansas, with two thousand head easier than this, but made no mention out loud. The big steers all looked fine the next morning when he rode through them. Michaels wouldn't complain about them. How many more did they have to sell? Better buy that boy a tally book and make him keep track of the herd. No way to do business without a good count on your own stock. His father must have done that.

Noble went and found the two men, Julio Contras and Jim Phelps, and brought them out to the ranch. Contras was about thirty, had a dark complexion and white teeth, and looked like a vaquero. He rode a tough-looking dun mustang and carried two reatas on his big horn saddle. When he met Cally, he bowed and swept off his sombrero. His English wasn't bad and he acted proud to have the work.

Jim Phelps was close to Guthrey's own age. He rode deep in the saddle, he was short and broadly built, his hair on top was thin, and he smiled big, meeting Cally. He had two well-trained stock dogs; one had a white eye, and they both minded him. Jim called the gray one Dog, and the one with more white he'd named Gyp. Easy enough to remember, and these two were no strangers to the chaparral or cactus.

At supper, Jim asked whether they'd been lately run over by Whitmore and his outfit.

Dan told them about the loss of their father and his near run-in with two of his gun hands. Jim nodded.

"I'm hoping you get the job of sheriff," he said to Guthrey. "Maybe we can go back to living like ordinary folks again."

"I guess Noble told you we might have trouble taking these cattle to Tucson."

"Bring 'em on. Right, Julio?"

"Right, hombre. They've tried before."

"I personally hope we can go sell our cattle and come home without incident. But it's their choice if they want to die."

The men all nodded in agreement as Cally jumped up and began to refill their coffee cups. Guthrey could tell she was upset as the trip drew closer but hid most of it.

The next morning, all the hands gathered the steers and counted them in the first light. Then, planning to get the herd well on its way, all four men rode south to get them on the main road.

Cally drove the buckboard ahead of the file. The steers, doing lots of bawling, came on behind her. The dogs nipped at the heels of a few errant ones and they soon lined out like they'd done it all their lives. Things were going all right for Guthrey's part when

Noble and Dan shook his hand and parted with them.

They were soon over West Mountain and headed west. Conveyances, wagons, and even some people hiking on foot got back some from the main road to let the cattle go by. Their presence did not bother the herd.

The first day they made good time. Mid-afternoon at the Bar 8, the foreman, Curly Bradley, let them put the herd in a large fenced pasture with graze in it and water in a tank. By dark the steers were lying down, chewing on their cud, and settled.

Cally fixed a big meal, and Curly came down to eat with them. After the meal, he sat on his butt on the ground and hugged his knees. He wanted to know more about Guthrey's plans when he became sheriff.

"I have to get elected first."

"Aw, you'll do that. Killion ain't got a friend left in this county. I've had cattle and horses stolen from me, and he ain't turned a tap to help me. Of course, up here on the road it's lots worse than back in the hills. But he simply won't do anything."

"I'm going to try to stop that. I'm going to get a force of good men to be my deputies and we will worry more about crime than how many cows you have."

"They told me that the county courthouse bunch don't want to spend much money on deputies."

"They better get ready to," Guthrey said. "I left the Texas Rangers 'cause we weren't being paid. They've got money to pay him a big commission for tax collecting, we'll use that."

Bradley smiled. "I'll back you all the way."

After a while, Cally excused herself and went to her tent to sleep on a cot. Guthrey tossed his bedroll on the ground nearby to keep close in case anything happened. The night was uneventful. The next morning they had breakfast and headed out again.

Bradley rode a few miles with them and quizzed Guthrey about his cattle deal.

"I need to make some sales like this. I usually let Ike Clanton have my big steers to fill his army and Apache contracts. But I've never got that much for them." Guthrey nodded and they shook hands.

That day they passed the halfway point to Tucson, and in the afternoon Guthrey started looking for a good place to stop for the night. They found water for the herd in a wash, some good holes, and plenty of grazing. They planned on taking turns at riding herd through the night.

When the tent was up, Cally cooked them

supper. She made a big pot of coffee for the night herders and turned in. Guthrey watched her go in the tent and nodded to himself. It had been a long, hot day for her. He felt good that they were selling while the cattle had plenty of flesh. Without rain, the summer would be a tough one.

By midafternoon of the next day, they were probably ten miles out of Tucson. They found another good camping spot and settled in for the night, the routine from the previous night running just as smoothly tonight.

In the morning they moved on to the pasture. They reached it by the time the sun was overhead. When they reached his place, Gar came down and inspected the cattle, which were watering beside his windmill.

"Good-looking cattle. You never lied about them. Michaels will sell lots of that kinda beef."

"They'll do," Guthrey said. "In two weeks or so I'll be back here, or I'll send someone, to pay you the rent and collect my money for them."

"Fine with me, Guthrey," Gar said and went back to sit on his porch.

After paying the two hands for their work, he drove Cally on to the dress shop. He noticed she wrinkled her nose a lot going into the city.

"Sanitation isn't too big a deal around here, is it?"

"Whew," she said. "I forgot how this place stinks so much. I have already seen two dead pigs lying beside the boardwalk, and one dead burro on an empty lot feeding the buzzards. And their outhouses smell like they're cooking them."

He laughed. "Nice to live out in the country, isn't it?"

"Yes, very nice."

The dress took her breath away when the girls showed it to her. She looked close to tears. When she came out in the front room dressed in it to show him how well it fit, she was crying and sniffing. "Oh, Phil, you spent too much."

He shook his head. "You only go around once in these deals."

"But where will I ever wear it again?"

"Any damn place that you want to."

That evening they camped on the river by themselves. She still wasn't over the shock of the dress. In the morning, she made them breakfast and they headed home early. Halfway home, a tall bank of clouds showed on the southern horizon. They were dark, forbidding thunderstorms coming up from the Gulf of California. Monsoons were about to begin. Guthrey made the team trot and kept a wary eye on the storm.

He decided they should stop at the next stage station and wait the weather out. The wind had picked up, and dust and sharp bits of sand were pelting them by the time they reached the outpost and he hurried her inside. The man who ran it stood on the porch and told them they were welcome. By then visibility was down to ten feet or so. Guthrey secured the horses with thunder making rapid-fire booms close by.

The man who ran the station was a tall, thin man who wore a white shirt. He had an enlarged Adam's apple and it bobbed up and down when he talked. "We sure needed rain, but not all this."

He was talking about the reddish mud that ran off the porch eaves. His short squaw wife held her hands over her ears and looked bug-eyed at him in the candlelight as heavy winds and driving rain rattled the small windows and the very building they were in. Guthrey and Cally sat in the back of the room and held hands. Hail pounded on the shake roof, and drips began to leak in the room. The woman went for empty tin cans to arrange under them. Then some men began stomping on the porch. They were cussing when they pushed open the door.

In the dim light, Guthrey watched the big man come in first and sling the water off his sodden hat. Then two more half-drowned, unshaven men followed him in, still cussing.

"Hush up," the big man said curtly to his companions. "There's a white woman in here."

"Aw, hell, Curt, who gives a big damn? That damn rainstorm blew away my good hat that I paid ten bucks for."

Then Guthrey saw the ring on the leader's left hand. A large ruby stone glinted in the candlelight when the man they called Curt sat down. Guthrey hoped that Cally had not seen it. But who were the other two? Hired guns, he guessed. But the raider and rapist was in the room not twenty feet from him. What backup would those others give him?

"You got any whiskey?" The hatless one pounded his fist on the tabletop.

The station man said he did.

"By damn get us some cups. We're thirsty, ain't we, Curt?"

"Yeah," he said and turned his attention to Guthrey and Cally. "You two get caught here too?"

Guthrey nodded. "We only beat it by a

few minutes."

"I've seen her before, but I don't know you."

"Guthrey's my name."

The other two's eyes flew open.

"Why, he's the —" Hatless said.

"Shut up." Curt cut him off.

"But —"

"I said shut up."

The protestor swallowed hard and nodded.

"Get up," Curt said to his men, holding his hands out from the table. He said something else to them. Guthrey decided it was "Keep your hands clear." Both men took on a wide-eyed look as they obeyed the big man.

"Go get our horses," he ordered. His blue eyes in a hard stare never left Guthrey.

"Aw, hell, it's still raining out there."

"You heard what I said. Get them." His voice still even, he eased himself up and slipped toward the door after the two wary men.

He closed the door after their retreat and Guthrey heard one ask aloud, "Who was the sumbitch in there?"

"That gawdamn Texas Ranger."

"Oh, hell —"

"Oh my God, I thought we were both

dead," Cally whispered.

"Easy. They ain't gone yet." Guthrey patted her leg for reassurance.

"Mister, I don't know who you are, but you put the God-fearing hell into them three," the station man said, coming out of the kitchen with a shotgun in his hands. "You know them?"

Guthrey shook his head and stood up. "I think he heard you break open that shotgun breech back there."

"I don't know a thing about that. When I heard your name back there, I knew then you were the reformer, and I knew good and well them three sided with the crooked ring that runs this county."

"What's Curt's last name?"

"Slegal."

"What does he do?"

"Good question. He has a ranch south of Steward's Crossing, but most of us think he holds up stages and burns people out for guys like Whitmore." The man smiled, showing he was missing a tooth in the top row, and shook his head as if he still did not believe how the three men had left. "That bugger was sure not wanting any part of a shootout with you."

"That was the good part." Guthrey worried more about how upset Cally was.

At last he had a name for the ruby ring wearer: Curt Slegal.

"You all right?" Guthrey asked Cally.

"Yes, I'll be fine."

But he could tell she had been taken aback by the entire episode. For his part he was glad they'd had no gunfight in the small station. A damn close call but while Slegal might rape women, he wanted no part of a gunfight in such close quarters with a man of reputation. It could have been a blood-bath. The situation had come within inches of exploding into that sort of thing.

The sun was soon out and the storm had passed over them. Everything looked crystal clear when they came outside. The purple mountains showed every detail. Once dusty, the desert brush and cactus looked freshly washed. A pungent smell of creosote filled the cleared air. Cally dried the wagon seat with a towel while Guthrey checked the harness. Satisfied, he climbed on, winked at her, and drove off with his unsaddled horses tied on behind. She clung to his arm.

"Now you know who he is, what will you do?" she asked.

"I will need witnesses that will testify to a grand jury. They will not be easy to find. I am more interested in what the stage man said back there. He called these outlaws part of a crooked ring. How many others are involved?"

"Yes, before I blamed it all on Whitmore. Now it sounds like there may be more to it."

"So did I. I thought Killion was out to make the most money. Use his deputies to find taxable cattle. But if all this is planned to allow the others to break the law for their purposes, then there is a ring involved. With all that talk about the county board not wanting to hire more lawmen, we are seeing others involved that run the list of the county administrators and others."

"I think you are getting close to exposing the whole lot of them."

He slapped the horses to make them hurry. "Could you quietly speak to some of his victims? I know the shock of asking an honest woman to testify about the fact they've been raped is going to be really hard. But we have to stop him."

She agreed. "I'll try."

"I know someone who would not tell me his name. I'm going to confront her, find out why she wouldn't tell it to me."

Cally frowned at him in disbelief. "And she knew it."

He nodded and still could not figure her reason. Curt might be more powerful than he thought.

They reached the ranch long after sundown. He could see the signs that they'd had some rain there as well. Sometimes it only rained on the just and left the unjust without any. Not this time.

Noble met them and after Guthrey and Cally had some food, the men left her to go to bed. Noble and Guthrey went down by the corral to talk more about the confrontation.

"You know this man Slegal?" Guthrey asked him.

"Not well."

"He's the one who wears the ruby ring."

"I'll be damned. I never saw him when he didn't have gloves on."

"It's damn sure chilling to see him wearing it and knowing what all the sumbitch has done."

"What are we going to do?"

"If I had the whole thing in my mind and knew how to stop it, I'd set out to do it. I was warned that even if we got more votes in the election they'd not count the ballots right. There's a whole group of them that runs things around here."

"Whew, all this sounds damn complicated as hell to me."

"You ain't alone, pard. Better get some sleep."

Noble agreed.

Guthrey nodded to him as he stared at the North Star and Big Dipper. There had to be something he could do to expose the crooked ring. One big program to take over the county government and get this entire organization closed down. By himself that was impossible. He needed to talk to Judge Collier. But even he did not have the power to do all this, and if something did not happen, all this petition work would go down in flames and the so-called ring would remain in power.

He'd also need to go talk to McCall and Brown in the morning about that very matter. Start there and work up. All the things that were happening needed to be taken in and considered. Maybe they had some ideas on handling things. In the morning he'd go down there. Knowing that Slegal was still on the loose made him more upset than all the rest of it.

In less than two weeks, he and Cally would be married. All in the midst of this tornado of crime and underhanded activity sweeping the chaparral country. He found sleeping in his bedroll evaded him that night. Too many loose ends in his life.

TWENTY-ONE

Around midmorning, Guthrey found Carl Brown at his farm, busy repairing a place in the corral that his Jersey bull had smashed apart. Brown was busy nailing up rough lumber. Guthrey stepped in and held up the other end of the board.

"I can't believe a two-year-old, seven-hundred-pound calf could do this much damage," Brown said as he straightened to examine his work.

"They can kill you too," Guthrey added, recalling others' past experiences with dairy bulls.

"I know. They're very dangerous. What can I do for you?"

"Do you know a man named Slegal?"

"He has a ranch east of here. He's been spoken about as a troublemaker, but I know of no incidents with him in our community."

"The man, besides his terrorism activities, has raped a half dozen ranch wives and probably more."

"Oh no. How do you know that?"

"He does it masked but wears a large ruby ring."

"What can we do about him?"

"It will be hard to get many of these women to testify, but I am trying to find some who will."

Brown pushed his straw hat back on his head. "It will be hard to get them to do that. Testify in open court about a man raping them."

"In my investigating, a man who might know told me that Killion will count his votes and not our people."

"No, we will have plenty of witnesses there. And be sure the ballot boxes are not stuffed between the polling place and the county courthouse."

"It is beginning to look to me like there is a ring of officials besides Whitmore and Killion who are in on this deal."

"Sounds serious. Maybe we have not looked at the real depth of this?"

"What if we interrogate some sub-officials about this business and tell them that if they don't testify against the leaders they will be charged too?"

"It might work. But there are so few workers in those county offices to get to." Brown backed his butt to the fence and shook his head in disgust. "Any more ideas?"

"I've been thinking. We could make up a posse, say of eight men, then we begin arresting all those we know are in on this deal and the rats will jump off the ship when word leaks out. I think if they face long sentences, they will turn state's evidence and talk."

Brown agreed. "McCall and I will get all the evidence and information on this Slegal we can get for you."

"How many signers do we have?"

"Over five hundred now, and our people are working it hard to get the holdouts."

"We keep adding names at these gatherings. I hope, by the election, we have the ballot-counting thing under control."

"We can handle that. Thanks. I can see you are doing lots of self-examination about this matter. Don't worry, the people of Crook County are behind you."

Guthrey nodded and headed back for the ranch, still not certain their plan would work. Lots of these co-conspirators had control of many things that still stood in their path.

Noble was at the ranch alone when he returned. "Cally and Dan went to see some people about this ring guy."

Guthrey leaned over. "Don't tell anyone. All he has to do is throw that ring away."

Noble shook his head in disgust. "He needs to be strung up."

"I know, but that is not the way we need to straighten out the wrongdoing around us."

"All right, I won't hang him, but he still needs it."

Guthrey laughed. "I wonder if Slegal has any detractors. People mad enough to testify against him."

"I don't know."

"Let's think about our business for a while. I want to ride up and talk to Pete Karnes and see what he's found out about the outcropping."

"Sure. I'm ready. Let's go."

They reached the operation midday and the crew was eating lunch. Pete set down his tin plate, rose, and shook their hands.

"Go ahead and eat," Guthrey told him. "We simply wanted to see how things were going up here."

"We've been blasting and are down about ten feet in the shaft."

"Any more gold?"

"Some, but it's spotty." He handed Guthrey some white quartz pieces with larger streaks in them. "Not much. But it's worth looking deeper."

Guthrey handed the rocks to Noble. "There's a little more in them."

With a nod of approval, Noble agreed. "Sure hope you can find something."

"We might," Pete said. "We're going to blast some more today."

"Have you seen anyone around up here?"

"Funny you ask. We had someone here a few nights ago. It was dark, and I had a toothache so I was sitting up. Someone on a horse rode up here, and when I challenged him he rode off."

"No idea who he was?"

"No, but now we're taking turns guarding at night."

"Be careful. They shot Bridges in the back up here."

"Oh, we will. You can tell those kids that I don't know, but there might be gold down there. We do have a few more signs."

Guthrey nodded and they rode back looking for any tracks of an invader in the canyon. Leaning over in the saddle to read faded tracks, Guthrey wished he had an identity for this person. Too many things needed to be found to advance all his causes. This mine deal had him more convinced there was something up in that canyon. No one had any business in the box canyon but a person involved in Harold Bridges's death and the gold deal.

Cally and Dan were back when Guthrey and Noble returned. Cally rushed out to hug and kiss Guthrey.

"You learn anything?" he asked her.

"We may have a woman who will testify. She wants to talk it over with her husband some more. She's a strong individual and hates that man riding around free to rape others."

"You may have done some good, then. Thanks."

"What did you learn?"

"Brown says they are going to be prepared to really oversee the election."

"Do we need to postpone our wedding?"

"Not unless you want to."

"Oh, I'd marry you today, but I don't want you worrying about me in the midst of all this other stuff happening."

"Let's just proceed. If I see any problems ahead we'll talk about it."

"Thanks," she said, standing on her toes and kissing his cheek.

"What next?"

"East Fork meeting Saturday night, three days from now. Want me to go over there with you?"

He quickly nodded. "I'm always pleased

to show you off."

She blushed. "I'll go, then."

A boy delivered a letter from Judge Collier in the midst of all their activity. Everyone crowded around while Guthrey read it.

Dear Guthrey,

I have spoken to the governor twice this week. He plans to immediately appoint you as sheriff and Chief County official for Crook County if the election issue passes. Which is wonderful news.

Deputy U.S. marshals will be in charge of all ballot boxes and counting the ballots so there will be no chance to steal the election. Be prepared to swear in enough lawmen to enforce the law and handle the jail, as well as preserving the peace, should there be a show of force as a result of the election.

Judge A. Collier

A cheer went up.

"That means that you will be the acting sheriff after the ballots are counted," Cally said, excited at the news.

"Well, it sounds to me like we'll be busier than a beaver in a flood," Noble said.

Guthrey agreed.

■ ■ ■ ■

Guthrey and Cally drove over to East Fork, arriving midafternoon on Saturday. Prepared to camp overnight and drive home in the morning, he was amazed at all the assistance he got in raising her tent. Men were full of questions about what he planned to do first after the election.

"If and when I can, I'll get warrants and arrest the people who have been terrorizing the citizens, and any other law violators."

"Will you have enough help?"

Guthrey nodded. "I think enough citizens will come to my aid."

"Count me and my brothers in for those volunteers. My name's Hanson."

"I will keep you in mind, sir."

"I know you are going to clean them all out."

Guthrey nodded again. "Crook County will be a much better place to live."

"I'm glad you came here. We've needed you for a long time as our lawman."

Volunteers came by all day, and Guthrey felt much better when he escorted Cally to the event that evening. They entered the schoolhouse and were welcomed with applause. He made a short speech asking for their help and for them to go get more signatures so they could close the drive.

Invited to the head of the line, Guthrey and Cally moved in to fill their plates at the food-crowded tables. He could see how happy she was, teasing him some, quietly, about his new fame. He shook his head. "Simple enough, they want to be rid of this ring of outlaws."

They ate seated on benches at the north wall with a friendly crowd around them. Questions about their pending wedding came around.

"June third," Cally said, and the women in the crowd nodded in approval among themselves. Soon the band started playing and they danced.

"Are you feeling better?" Cally asked as they spun across the floor.

"Yes, I think we may make a showing."

"And what about the governor's promise that marshals will oversee the election?"

"Judge Collier's letter said they will watch over everything done that day and will count the ballots themselves."

She beamed and said, "Oh, Phil, I am so relieved for you."

He hugged her shoulders a little tighter. "I am very grateful for all this effort, darling."

In the morning they headed home. When they rounded a bend in the road, they came upon a man dressed in a suit sitting on a bay horse in the middle of the dusty road that wound off the mountain they'd crossed.

"Trouble?" she asked.

"Trade sides. I'll stand up and you slide over to my left."

"I'm ready." They changed sides. She rearranged her skirt and sat up. He put his reins in his left hand, then set the revolver in his lap.

"Do you know him?" she hissed.

"No."

Upset with what might happen and having her along, Guthrey shook his head. "If he goes for a gun, you get off and run for cover. Damn them anyway."

The intensity of the situation fell on his shoulders. Though he saw no one else, the chaparral cover beside the road made him suspicious that there might be a backup force along with this stranger.

He reined up way short.

The man opened his coat. "I am unarmed. I want to talk with you, Guthrey."

"Who in the hell are you?" Guthrey asked, still suspicious of this well-dressed man and his purpose.

"Charles Bentson. I'm a lawyer and I have

an offer for you. I am offering you a ranch up on the Verde River in exchange for the Bridges place. This ranch is well watered, and you can move your cattle up there."

"That is not my ranch to trade, sir."

"Come on, you will own your wife's share in a few weeks. I am sorry we had to meet like this, ma'am."

She never answered him.

Guthrey shook his head. "I am not going to be bought off."

"Don't be foolish. You stand no chance, by yourself, of changing things around here. And you have no partners in law enforcement to back you up. I know you aren't dumb enough to try and take over this county by yourself. They'll have a fast funeral for you."

"Bentson, you tell your people they'd better saddle up and start riding like hell for the border. My law will be a swift sword when it comes after them."

"Miss Bridges, talk some sense into him. You want a wedding or a funeral for him?"

"Bentson, tell your clients what I said. They'd better ride for the border or they'll be sweating in Yuma Prison."

The man openly scoffed at him. "You'd better reconsider, Guthrey. You can't win your struggle here."

Tired of having to listen to the man, Guthrey, with the Colt in his fist, waved Bentson aside, keeping his eyes open for any movement. Cally took the reins and clucked to the team. The anger Guthrey saw in her eyes told him the lawyer was lucky she didn't have a six-gun.

"Save your breath," he said to the man as they drove by him.

Bentson shouted at him, "You will rue this day."

"I'll lock you up with them if you like their ways so well."

Out of hearing range, Guthrey holstered the Colt. "I'm sorry."

"It isn't your fault. They've tried it all now, haven't they?"

"I guess so. Hampton came for a show of force, now their attorney offers us a bribe."

"What will you do now?"

"When we get the go-ahead, I have plans that will secure us."

"I know you know lots more than I do about all this. But it smells kinda bad to me."

He clapped her on the leg. "The smell is obvious to me. Let's get the horses trotting. But we, you and I, will have to be more careful coming and going."

"Damn that bunch," she said in disgust

under her breath.

"Yes, I'd do that too."

She laughed. He patted her on the shoulder. "This will all be gone someday. Have patience."

"I'll try," she promised him.

He heard her words and knew things were opening up. It was time for him to call in some cards he'd held back on. When the situation broke, he had some aces he'd held in reserve. But it wasn't time yet to show them. Time would tell him when to move and how.

TWENTY-TWO

Noble rode in early in the afternoon and came immediately to the house. Standing in the doorway, Guthrey greeted him.

"What's happening?"

"They say Whitmore has put out the word he's hiring more gunmen."

"Let him. What else is happening?"

"I think Killion must be working on a deal to turn all the prisoners loose."

"How in hell's he doing that?"

"He's pushing for bond hearing for all those prisoners you brought in."

"Where at?"

"Preskit."

"You mean haul them up there and let them out on bond?"

"Yeah, it sounds like that."

"It will cost the county big bucks to transport them."

"Yeah, but once they're bonded out they can run. No more food bills and jail guards help costs."

"I'll see what Judge Collier has to say about that."

"How close are we to having the number of signatures we need?"

"I think we're there. I'm meeting the other two in town tomorrow. You learn anything more about Curt Slegal?"

Noble lowered his voice. "Ain't heard nothing about him. None of the women have come forward? Thought there was one that might talk, but we haven't heard back from her, have we?"

"No." Guthrey shook his head. "I doubt that we will either."

"Damn shame that bastard is still out running around."

"I agree, Noble. Get some rest today. We've got plenty to do next week."

It was late afternoon when a couple drove up to the house. Guthrey went to the door and Cally was behind him.

"That's Wilma Maples and her husband, Claude."

The couple looked in their early forties. The man helped his wife down from the wagon. "Good afternoon. You must be Guthrey, the man everybody's talking about."

"Cally says your name is Claude and she's Wilma. Glad you came by. What can I do for you?"

"We want to talk with you about — the ruby ring man."

Guthrey nodded that he understood. "Come in. We want to talk with both of you."

Cally made fresh coffee, and they all took seats around the table.

"I'm not sure where to begin," Guthrey said. "But it is terribly important we apprehend and prosecute this man. But it will only come about if someone will agree to testify against him. He has hurt several families."

Wilma put her hands on the table, rubbing them together. "I didn't want anyone to know about this. Claude and I have talked long hours about our own situation. I know some people will scoff at my denial of ever having any relations with another man besides my husband except for both of the times that man raped me.

"I talked Claude out of going over there and calling him out. My husband is not a gunman, Mr. Guthrey. I want you to know that he wanted to go kill the man. But I feared for his life at the hands of such a violent person. I begged him not to. Now we've talked and we don't care what folks think or say. Twice that man raped me in my own house and my own bed." She began to cry. Her husband gave her his handkerchief and put his arm around her shoulder.

"He rode up the first time with two men. He told them to strip me naked and tie me on the bed inside. They did as he ordered and he came in when they had me tied to the bedposts, dropped his pants, climbed on the bed, and raped me."

She shook her head. "I wanted to die. Never in my life had I ever considered suicide. Claude came home that evening and found me there. Still tied. We knew there was no law in this county to punish him. Slegal swore to me he'd take his gun and kill my husband if he came after him. I could not afford to lose him. We told ourselves that he wouldn't be back." She shook her head as if lost. "But he returned. This time not only him but his two henchmen raped me as well when he was done."

"Do you know these men's names?"

"Yes, one is Hardy Clayton and the other's a man named Seviers."

"You realize you may have to sit in a witness chair in court and tell a jury this story?"

She blew her nose hard and then agreed. "I know the whole business. We have talked for hours about it. I am ready to swear out a warrant for his arrest."

"What if I asked you to wait until the referendum is passed to do this?"

"I could wait. You mean until you're in office?"

"I'm sorry, but yes, until then, when I have the sheriff's job."

She looked at her husband. "Claude, do you understand what we must do?"

"Yes, and I am certain he knows better than we do how to handle this."

"When the time comes, I'll ride out to your place and get a precise report for the prosecuting attorney."

Cally rose to pour the new coffee. "Now we have this business in hand. Let's have some coffee. God bless you, Wilma, for coming forward."

"I'll do anything to have him put away and punished." She turned her palms up.

Guthrey reached over and squeezed her hands. "Yes, you have done a brave thing. You will get your rewards when that bag of wind is behind bars."

The couple went home shortly after, and Noble came to the house.

Guthrey looked up and said, "We have a witness. Keep it quiet, but she will swear out a warrant for him for rape."

"That's good news, by doggy. This damn country may be rid of them all before we know it."

"Amen," Guthrey added.

The next day Guthrey held a council with the judge, Brown, and McCall over in Soda Springs. Petitions were still coming in and they had the necessary number of signatures with them at the judge's house that morning. The next problem they had was that the county clerk had to certify them.

"We don't necessarily trust them," Guthrey said to Collier. "They could take all day to count the signatures or even destroy enough to make the election void."

"Then," Brown began, "what can we do about that?"

"The governor promised me deputy U.S. marshals would be in charge of every box," Collier said.

"Good. Guthrey showed us your letter," McCall said and they all nodded.

"Now how do we get by the county clerk?" Guthrey asked.

They all laughed. They were back to the first problem again.

"I'll handle that," Collier said. "Leave me the petitions. I'll get this taken care of in the next hour."

"How soon can we have elections?" Guthrey asked.

"Twenty-one days."

Good, Guthrey decided. He would be married in a week and that matter would be done with, leaving clear time for the election. Now they needed to get out the votes. No end to the details in this business.

"As soon as this referendum is passed by the voters, the governor will appoint you sheriff and in charge of the county until new people are appointed. Elections for offices will be held in the fall."

It was time he sent telegrams. If three of his former Ranger buddies would come and help him, he'd have things handled in a minimum number of days. But the only man he trusted to send even a coded wire to them was Tommy. Perhaps he needed to send someone besides himself over to wire them so no one got suspicious about his actions.

Where would he start? Wire Todd Bowles in Denton. He could be the team leader for one team he planned to gather. Then Chuck Magio, the wild Italian stallion. He should be in San Angelo at this time. And then Gus Agnew in Fredericksburg. He used the judge's desk and writing implements to pen three telegrams.

I'm in Stewart's Crossing, Arizona Territory, and need your professional help to clean up an entire county. I will be in charge June 19 and will have horses and deputies ready to ride with plenty of warrants and good men to go along to back you. If you can come out here and help me, I'll have you home in two weeks or less. Wire me at P. Guthrey, Soda Springs, Az T.

"Brown, to keep things quiet, I need you to take these three wires over to Tommy. Have him wire them and not let out a word about them."

"How will he connect with you with responses?"

"He can find a boy on a fast horse to bring their answers to the ranch, and we'll pay him a dollar when he hurries over."

Brown nodded and went off to send them. Guthrey would need to talk to Dan when he got back. He spoke to the group. "We're going to need about sixty freshly shod horses at the ranch to use around the morning of the twentieth. I'll get Dan to line them up and have them ready. We may need to buy a load of good hay and some grain out of our fund. Can we do that?"

McCall nodded. "We can handle the hay."

"I will need you and Brown to invite the toughest ranchers you know to be there on the nineteenth and ready to ride that night."

"Ride at night?"

"Yeah, Rangers always like to wake the ones they go to arrest at sunup. They are the least organized at that time."

"I'm learning," McCall said. "Will those guys you send the wire to drop everything and come help you?"

"I think at least two of the three will do that. Maybe all of them, though there is also the chance that maybe none will come. If they don't come, I'll have to go to plan B."

"What's that?" McCall asked

"I ain't got it figured yet but I will if I have to. Dan will borrow sixty-some horses and we need to find some tough men to back us on the sixteenth. We'll need some tents to put folks in. Any ideas?"

McCall said, "There's enough around that folks use for camping or even staying over for church at the schoolhouses. I can get some of them and have them set up at the ranch."

"Great. What am I leaving out?"

"A jail big enough to hold all of them. A cook to feed them, and the guards," Collier said. "Along with handcuffs."

"We can use locks and chains if we need

to, maybe build a temporary prison out of barbed wire."

"This might be a real big job to house and feed them. You have a jail full now here at Soda Springs."

"I'll have the deputy U.S. marshals handle the jail for a few days," Collier said.

Good enough. They'd have enough things lined up to handle matters.

Guthrey rode home with his head full of ideas for things that needed to be done. Dan, Noble, and Cally all rushed out to greet him.

"We have lots settled," he said, dismounting and pulling his latigos loose. "The Mormons are going to set up tents here to house the deputies overnight. Dan needs to borrow about sixty shod horses to use on our raids. I wired for three of my old Ranger cohorts to come help us."

"Will they come?" Noble asked.

"I think all or some of them will come if they can. That means we can get married as planned," he said turning to face Cally.

"Can we have the wedding at the school-house this Saturday?" she asked.

"I don't know why not. That nice young minister from Clawson might do it."

"I'll find out. That will predate my date by two days, but it's still in June."

He went and hugged her. "And you've got it two days closer." Then he kissed her.

Her laughter rang out and he walked Dan outside. "I know we can't totally surprise them, but we can try."

"We've got more company coming." Dan frowned at the three young men coming up the ranch road. Dressed in suits and string ties, they looked like businessmen under their simple felt hats.

"I'll see what they want." Guthrey had no idea, but they looked important. He greeted them. "How are you and what may I do for you?"

"My name is Wisdom, Jory Wisdom. I am a law clerk, so are these other two. Judge Collier sent us up here to ready the arrest warrants for you. This is Christy Halman and the last man is Glen Heffner. The judge said for us to get up here, find us shelter, and get ready."

"We have a wall tent that you three can pitch to stay in. Dismount and I will introduce my wife-to-be, Cally Bridges."

She fixed them some late lunch. Jory explained how they'd build a list of the suspected raiders and make warrants out for them. When those subjects were arrested and brought in, each of the prisoners would be offered one of two choices. If the only charge was terrorizing folks, they could stand trial and, if found guilty, serve three years in Yuma. Or they could plead guilty, answer all the questions put to them, and get off serving one year down there. He added that they would have two of the jail wagons ready to haul the prisoners down there when that day came.

Judge Collier was certainly thinking well ahead. Guthrey personally needed more information about how to run the county offices. How did the county pay bills? How much money was in the county treasury anyway? Judge Collier could learn that from the town banker. Guthrey scratched that on his notes. They'd need a treasurer and a set of supervisors. A citizens council might help in solving all of his questions.

He'd need a list of honest folks to head up those operations and give him help appointing folks. It was like they pushed a landslide over on top of him. If he'd lived there for years he'd know them, but he didn't. Well, in six months' time he'd know them all better.

When he leaned back in the chair, Cally came by and asked, "Will our wedding mess up all your business?"

He tipped back the hat he still wore and grinned at her. "No, it will work in fine."

"I feel like some small spoiled little girl about this marriage business."

"I was only teasing you. Don't worry."

She rubbed his stiff shoulders from behind. Her fingers began gouging deep into his stiff muscles. "I'm glad you put up with me."

"Keep rubbing. I can stand a lot of that." He had never realized how tied up his back was. Must be the tension of the job ahead that had him in knots.

"This marriage is for you and me anyway," she said.

He agreed. Then he made some more notes before he swung around and caught her waist. "You are the neatest and finest thing that ever walked into my life."

"I wondered about a place for us to . . . well, hide after the ceremony. A friend of Dad's has a mountain cabin up on Mount Graham. Maybe we can borrow it — or is that too far away?"

"No, that's fine. That's north of here, right?"

"Yes. Could we go there for a few days, maybe a week, for our honeymoon?"

"Sure."

"I'll get hold of him. It is pretty up there, and it will even be cool."

He had done enough bookwork for the

348

time being and rose. With a hug and kiss for her, he went outside. Noble had gone to Soda Springs with the rest of the petitions for Judge Collier that they'd rounded up. Dan was off to borrow tents and horses. Now Guthrey had to check on his law clerks. He discovered when he rounded the house they must be campers. The first tent was set up and looked good.

He spoke with the three young men lounging around the tent. "I guess you need to talk to folks about who they've seen riding on the raids. We need the names of individuals who have been riding with those raiders. Many were unmasked and known by name. Maybe people are ready to spill about them now that it appears we may succeed in getting them out of the country. When Noble gets back, he could take you out to meet many of these folks and you could get names from them."

"There is a murder warrant too," Jory said.

"Yes, there was a shooting that eventually killed Ted Rawlings. One of the shooters is in the Soda Springs jail. He was wounded but still alive last I checked. A second man is one who has been raping any woman he wanted to. Before, no one came forward to report his crimes, but there is a woman coming forward now, and I say more will join her in her effort to get him put away."

"Was the other man you arrested at the same time as the murderer an accomplice to that gang?" Heffner asked.

Guthrey nodded. "I believe he was. He threatened us when we tried to get past him to the doctor. Also another man involved was wounded during the murder and I hear he's over in the Chiricahuas. His name is Kyle."

"There's a lot to straighten out for us to charge these men," Heffner said.

"You know any more about this Kyle? We don't have him down on our list," Jory said.

"When you are trying to get rid of widespread corruption in power, there are bound to be some vague things. I had no deputies to help me run him down."

"Oh, Mr. Guthrey, we think what you have done here is amazing, but now we need to finish the job. Put the guilty ones away and clean up this mess following the referendum election."

"It still has to pass," he reminded them.

The clerks laughed, and Jory spoke up. "Those petitions contained eighty percent of the people who are even eligible to vote. You didn't need that many, so already we know you will win."

Amused, Guthrey chuckled. "I knew those

officials had asked for a lot of signatures."

"It's a wonder they didn't tell you that you needed everyone to sign," Heffner said, as if he could not believe the situation had even occurred.

"According to what has been going on here, if you're shot dead today, there is not a chance that an officer of the law will investigate your murder, so don't make anyone mad today."

They laughed, and he considered what he should do next. People were coming by and offering to help to be sure the election sites had ample protection. He encouraged them to do that. They would look like an armed camp on election day, with deputy U.S. marshals transporting the lockboxes back to Soda Springs, where they would stand over the counting.

He wondered if those people in Boston that threw the English tea in the harbor had been this mad. In his short time spent in the territory, he had seen the quiet people being run over by the barons. Those same people were well-armed these days, and their memory began to find the names of those thugs who rode with the terrorists. He recalled his early questions. Who were they? They were all masked.

In the early morning of the twentieth, with

the Texas Ranger–style raids that he planned, they were going to cover the prime troublemakers — Whitmore's headquarters and the rapist Slegal with the ruby ring, as well as his gang, plus Killion, who he aimed to arrest himself and have charged with dereliction of his duties regarding the murder of Cally's father, Harold Bridges. He could still see the lawman in his expensive suit that morning sitting on his horse acting like Guthrey was less than welcome in the Arizona Territory.

The next morning, two men in a buckboard arrived, and he recognized them as ranchers from the eastern part of Crook County. He met them in the yard and shook hands with Ute Gleason and Kelly Brightwater.

"Congratulations, Guthrey, we heard you had most folks in the county signed up to vote for you."

"It sounds good. We still need to hold the election. What brings you two over here today?"

Kelly nodded. "We investigated that cattle rustling deal you got mixed up in. Found out that a guy called Hampton who works for Whitmore was involved. According to what we could find out, they sold those worked-over cattle to Clanton and they were delivered the next week to the Apache agency."

Guthrey nodded. "And of course no chance to find the hides and arrest anyone. Those squaws use those hides. Not like a slaughter operation where a check of the hide pile would point a finger at the thieves."

"Right," Gleason said and shook his head in disgust over the matter.

"We wanted to tell you that several of us will help guard the ballot box sent to Farnam Schoolhouse and the deputy marshal who comes with them."

"That's good. I'm sorry I didn't get back to you again. There's been lots to do. I want you two to tell your story today to the law clerks down here taking depositions. They are lining up the arrests we plan to make with real names. We will make a huge sweep when we have that appointment, but let's make it a surprise."

They both agreed to his terms, shook hands with him, and then he took them to find Jory. With the two ranchers lined up to talk to the young men, Guthrey told them one day after the election, he'd need some posse men. They were invited.

"We'll damn sure be here that day," Ute said and his partner agreed.

There were so many details, Guthrey

needed a secretary or something. Back in the house he went over all his notes and the timeline he planned. Word was bound to get out about his proposed raids. But if the three Rangers answered his call, he'd have three more professional lawmen to head up the parts of his plan that would swoop up the bad guys altogether in less than forty-eight hours.

By midday, he realized that all the business about their wedding was also being planned. Several women dropped by. There was hugging, and Cally was busy saying thank you all day.

Dan came by and told Guthrey he had two loads of hay donated and plenty of good ranch horses promised. The hay would come the following week. Horses the day after the election.

Cally and one of the other women who was on hand somehow managed to feed them all their meals. Noble rode back after lunch. He and Guthrey talked at the corral where he unsaddled.

"Tommy sent you word, but there is something afoot," Noble began. "Three men in suits came and met with the sheriff in a closed meeting in the courthouse for several hours early today. He thinks they are part of the Tucson ring. Says they sent telegrams to the governor protesting the election and seeking writs to stop it."

"Any replies to their tries?"

"Tommy said the governor sent the sheriff a direct telegram saying anyone attempting to stop or disrupt the elections was to be stopped and arrested. Helluva lot of good that would be, huh? That said, we'll need some level heads in Soda Springs the days before and after the election. They ain't going to take this business lying down. Tommy also sent word he's got a boy with a fast horse can bring you any answer to your wires."

"Talk to Dan. He's got hay donated and the horses we may or may not need."

"We'd better check the cattle again this week."

Guthrey agreed. "Locate some good men to ride through the herd for you and Dan this week and next. You both need to be available if anything breaks loose."

"I can do that."

"Cally has got some lunch for you to go eat," Guthrey told Noble.

"Thanks. I'm amazed how this is all happening."

"Yes. You recall me telling you about the rustlers I had to dodge going to Farnam?"

"Sure do."

"Two ranchers from over there told me just an hour or so ago that it was Hampton's deal and they sold those cattle to the Clantons for a San Carlos Apache delivery."

"Those sonsabitches. Can we ever stop them?"

"Damn right we can, and we will."

"You know, I even believe we're going to do it."

Guthrey clapped him on the shoulder. "You take good care of yourself. We're going to be busy as hell around here."

A smile peeled back Noble's sun-bleached lips and he asked, "You and Cally getting hitched this Saturday night?"

"Yes."

"I'll be looking forward to that event. She's done asked me to walk her up the aisle." Noble looked ready to burst over it.

Guthrey thanked him and watched him limp for the bunkhouse Cally had cleaned up for them to sleep in. That old man was a treasure and a good one besides. What else? He realized Cally had joined him and hugged his arm.

"You getting concerned about the wedding?"

"No. But I don't want anyone hurt or left out from this cleanup of lawbreakers."

"Will your buddies from Texas come help you?"

"If they can get away." He was watching a distant eagle soar on the wind drafts. Then he turned and wrapped her in his arms. "I won't forget you. Don't worry. You're the light in my life."

TWENTY-THREE

When Saturday arrived, Noble drove Cally to the dance with her white wedding dress packed carefully in a box in back. Dressed up, the old man was going to give her away. Guthrey's best man, Dan, rode on horseback with him.

The law clerks were guarding the ranch. Guthrey hoped they weren't challenged. He doubted they were really tough enough to withstand an attack, and his roiling guts warned him it would be a bad situation if they did have to defend the place.

The sky was deep blue and the summer temperature was raising waves of heat off the ground, making the mountains to the west look fuzzy. A few buzzards, searching for something dead to feast upon, coasted across them on the wind.

There had been no answer to his wires for help so far. But the Rangers were all busy men and the messages may not have reached them if they were off chasing down criminals. And Guthrey had asked Noble to ride to Tucson while he and Cally were gone and take care of paying the rent on the pasture and collecting the money for the cattle they'd sold to Michaels.

The main thing on Guthrey's mind was his bride. For the next week or so he intended to forget about everything but her. A man who had waited this long to pick a bride had many things to fret about.

Would he please her? Be the partner she expected? Would the honeymoon evening when they were finally alone shock her? Damn, things got so complicated.

The schoolhouse looked like a grand ball was about to begin. There were hordes of campers and folks set up all around the yard who must have come from miles away. They spilled out into the desert and set up their tents down near the dry creek. He hoped the yard pump had plenty of good rubbers in it. They might burn them out trying to get adequate water up from the depths. He needed to stop worrying about every damn little thing. He couldn't fix them all anyway.

"You look nice," Dan said softly.

Guthrey dropped his chin and shook his head. "Nice isn't good enough. I hope I'm not dragging your sister down with me."

"Hey, you've worked your butt off to help all of us and it is still unfolding. I'm proud to have you in the family. She's a big girl. She can take licks and wants to be your wife. Just enjoy yourself. You deserve her."

"Thanks. We'll have a good life, I am certain."

"You will. There's some people outside who want to volunteer to help you."

"I'll speak to them."

He stepped out of the tent set up for him. Cally had her own tent across the grounds. He glanced up there and saw she was having lots of company and probably getting more friendly advice.

When he came out, a cheer from all the folks spread out before him went all the way up to the schoolhouse. He stood and nodded, saying thanks. "I want all of you to be involved in our election and use your vote to send the bad officials out of office." They cheered. "We plan to take charge immediately after you vote them out, and those lawbreakers better get on a fast horse or catch it from us. We will get all of them. You must support all the deputy U.S. marshals in charge of those ballot boxes and be sure they aren't bothered."

Someone handed him a telegram. He frowned, reading it.

I am on my way. Stand your ground.
C. Magio.

A smile swept Guthrey's face. Number one was coming. It was all going to work.

Think about your bride, he told himself. He reminisced about those sparkling dances with his princess at the various times they'd gone to socials. Time to dedicate a new life for both of them.

Finally it was time for the wedding ceremony to begin. There was not room enough for everyone there to fit inside the schoolhouse. Guthrey wore his new starched white shirt and britches Cally had acquired for him. Noble, like a handsome prince, brought Guthrey's bride to him at the altar. The vows they repeated were like fat snowflakes falling to earth on soft pillows. He kissed the bride and then they went through at the head of the food line. They ate a few bites of the enormous amount of dishes set on the tables, then Cally cut the great cake and they fed each other a piece.

He saw the sparkling pride in her eyes. In a few minutes after the cake cutting, they rushed out to the waiting team and buckboard. Guthrey swept her up on the rig in the snowy dress and drew some loud cheering. Joining her, he waved at the crowd ahead to make room for the horses to pass through them. The people backed up and he clucked to the excited team. They danced away, and she squeezed his arm.

"This is the biggest day of my life, Phil. Oh, my heavens, I think I can fly, I am so high. I'm glad you have so much patience for me."

He leaned toward her as they reached the end of the lines of well-wishers on both sides. "This is really the first day of our lives together and they will all be this rich or richer."

She leaned her head on his shoulder as they hit the river road and headed north. They camped their first night off the road at a watering hole that Noble had told him about. The topknot quail flocks came cautiously in for water. The two of them ate some packed food and sat on a blanket to watch the small soldiers come in at double time to seek water and then dust in the loose dirt.

They soon melted into each other's arms upon the blanket and the sunset on their first exciting honeymoon evening.

The second morning the honeymooners woke up on top of the summit of Mount Graham in the tall pines as the cool air flowed over one of the highest ranges in southern Arizona. They had set aside a little over a week for their honeymoon. Noble and Dan could keep an eye on the ranch that long, and McCall and Brown would be monitoring events in the county seat to make sure that no one succeeded in putting a halt to the election that would take place in two weeks. For the next week, Guthrey and Cally had nothing more pressing to do than cook their meals and spend time in each other's arms.

After a week of bliss, Monday morning Cally was busy making them breakfast with the front and back door of the small cabin wide open to usher through the soft coolness.

"We have one more day of this peaceful world."

She looked up at him from her cooking and quietly asked, "I hope you are pleased with me. I have no experience at pleasing a husband as his wife."

"Don't change a thing you do. I am very pleased with the entire experience of becoming your husband. Does that answer all your concerns? I want us to go on day after day living our life so we please each other."

"It is so unbelievable. I'll try." She spun around, then laughed. "I am still light-headed."

He wrapped his arms around her and kissed her. "You're not alone, darling."

"We better go home today . . . or tomorrow?" she asked.

"One more day up here in heaven, then we better get back to work."

"Someday we need to get us a cabin up here to get away from it all."

"Yes, we will."

TWENTY-FOUR

The newlyweds drove home. Their descent off Mount Graham was a steep, narrow road that wound down from the pine-forested mountaintop, through the juniper pinions' section, until they reached the hotter chaparral desert floor, billowing dust churning up in their wake.

"What will you do first?" Cally asked, holding Guthrey's arm in both hands as they rocked on the spring seat of the buckboard.

"I'll need to check and see how many of my Ranger pals are coming."

"How long have you known them?"

"I've known Todd Bowles since I was a kid. We grew up together in northeast Texas. We got into lots of things as boys, but if you were going to fight, you had to fight both of us. He was a Ranger last time I talked to him. Chuck Magio is the craziest guy I know, but when things get serious he'd be the toughest one. He's a big lover and flirt, so you be sure to avoid him. Gus Agnew is another tough Ranger. He doesn't talk much, but when he does, men listen. All three know the law and how to handle lawbreakers."

"You're going to send out four teams to arrest all these guys?"

"For starters. One team will be at Whitmore's headquarters that second morning after the election and arrest him, Hampton, and everyone on his payroll. Second team will arrest the man who wears the ruby ring, Curt Slegal, and his bunch. There's at least two of those raiders over in the Chiricahuas, and we'll have a group get them. My group is going over to arrest Killion at his ranch for malfeasance of his office."

"What does that mean?"

"Means he didn't do his job properly."

"He didn't do it at all." Cally shook her head in disgust.

"Well, you're right about that. Backed by some solid men, we should have every outlaw in the county in jail or on their way to prison in a very short time."

"Will my father's killer be with them?"

"Cally, I am hoping someone will slip and tell us who killed him. I'm going to coach the law clerks to listen for any reference to his death. Criminals will do anything to save their own necks, like testify against each other to get a shorter term or even to get released. We'll use it as a carrot."

"I know you're doing all you can. But I don't think I'll ever really put that to rest in my mind until we find the one who did it."

"I agree."

They reached the ranch in late afternoon. Among all the people standing in the yard he saw Pete and his two Mexican boys. Was something wrong? Had something happened?

They looked at each other as Dan came on the run to meet them. Out of breath he gasped, "You won't ever believe what's happened!"

Guthrey stepped to the ground, then turned and reached out to lift Cally off the buckboard.

"They've found gold!"

Guthrey whirled around. "Who — Pete?"

"Damn right."

He turned and asked Cally, "Did you hear that?"

"Oh, yeah, big man. I heard him very well." She beamed down at him.

Someone said, "Lots of it. Maybe a fortune."

Guthrey lifted Cally off the buckboard,

and she kissed him hard as he set her down. "I can't believe it. How did they do that?"

"He said they've been blasting and finally found it today."

"I trusted he'd find it if it was there," Guthrey said, but he still felt taken aback by the news. "Anyone know how much?"

Pete held up two fingers. "We brought out two buckets of nuggets to show you."

Guthrey backed into the wagon wheel, still half-overwhelmed by the news. "You know what that means, Mrs. Guthrey?"

"Kinda."

"Kinda?" He broke out laughing and then he hugged her. "You're rich."

"Oh, Phil, I wish Dad was here. He'd have loved this day, and he'd sure have loved you."

"Hey, you two, come inside," Dan said. "Kinda wild out here right now."

"I have to ask Pete one question," Guthrey said to Dan. "Go ahead, Cally. I'll be right there."

He drew Pete aside. "Do you think there was any way that someone knew there was gold in that outcropping before you opened it up?"

"I don't think so. Unless he found some richer samples that were on the surface and removed them. I bet over the past number of years several prospectors poked around that outcropping. Those types of formations intrigue people who are looking for sources of gold. Why do you ask?"

"Dan and Cally's father was killed right there. Some think it was the big ranchers trying to run the small ones out who shot him. But I wondered if someone wanted him dead to own that mine someday 'cause the kids couldn't handle it alone."

Pete nodded. "Sorry I'm not any help. We didn't find anything until we were close to twelve feet down in this shaft."

"Thanks." He talked a few minutes to others in the yard and then excused himself.

"Whew." Cally hugged him when he came into the house and whispered, "When are all these people going to leave?"

"I don't know, darling. A real gold strike like this is rare anymore, they say."

"We should have stayed on the mountain."

The crowd did not thin fast, but finally the folks outside dispersed and Guthrey blew out the lights. Undressed, he slipped into the bed and found Cally's warm, silky body there. He rolled over and hugged her. Damn, he was one lucky guy. The gold would be nice, but Cally's subtle form and having her was worth lots more to him than any gold treasure.

TWENTY-FIVE

Guthrey took the gold to town in the morning. Chuck Magio was supposed to be coming by stage any day. Dan had received telegrams from both of the others too. Todd Bowles was catching the train from Fort Worth to El Paso and then coming on by coach. Gus Agnew would be here later, but told Guthrey he'd be here before he was needed as well.

The stocky Italian had already arrived, but Guthrey didn't know it when he rode into town with a packhorse carrying the gold. He dismounted at the bank, hitched the horses, and took the first pannier inside.

"Mr. Guthrey. What can we do for you, sir?" the teller asked.

"You can watch this bag. I have another."

"What's in them, sir?"

He leaned over and told the man, "They're full of raw gold."

"Oh my —" He looked bug-eyed but said,

"Oh, I will watch it."

Guthrey delivered the second one and found the banker and the teller on their knees, looking in the pannier.

The banker, named Mitchem, rose to his feet and shook his head, dusting off his hands. "My heavens, where did all this gold come from?"

"The Bridges Ranch." He shushed the man's response, then in a low voice asked if they could speak privately in the banker's office. Once safely inside, Guthrey asked him, "Anyone mention to you that they wanted to buy that place recently?"

"A couple months ago, maybe longer, Jim Burroughs mentioned that to me. How he really liked the place and how with the way things were going, Harold and his kids might sell out, and he wanted it worse than Whitmore did."

"Thanks. Don't mention we talked about this to anyone. Especially to Burroughs."

"May I ask why?"

"I think that's who murdered Harold Bridges. I believe he knew that the gold was up there."

"Oh my. All I ever heard was that it was the masked night raiders who killed him."

"I'll let you know. Not a peep to anyone." They took the gold nuggets and dust into the back room and put all of it into cloth bags to be sent in two strongboxes to the smelter over in Silver City.

"Is there more?" Mitchem asked.

"Pete says it's a rich find. It could be only a pocket, but he thinks there's more."

The banker shook his head. "Tell Dan and your new wife, Cally, that we can handle all this transfer, have it melted into bars, and do everything else for them."

"I will do that." He excused himself and walked the block to Ellen's house of ill repute. He was in the front yard when someone appeared in the upstairs window. "That you, Phil?"

He looked up at the man in the snowy white shirt and smiled. "No, I'm not him. When did you get here, Chuck?"

"Last night. They don't have a good hotel in this place so they put me up here."

"I bet they did." Guthrey chuckled.

"See you downstairs."

The black girl opened the door. "I sure never did thank you that day for arresting them bullies. Land sakes, they was plum crazy. You know's this man that done come in last night? He's sure funny. He said he knows you." She shook her head and offered to take his hat.

"I'm not staying long. Is the boss lady up?"

"She's in the kitchen."

"I'll go see her for a minute. You go up and tell that wild man we need to ride to the ranch."

She agreed, and he went down the hall. He found Ellen busy counting the bottles of wine in her pantry, dressed in the same white robe she'd been wearing the last time he was here.

"I only have one question. Now, I want to know why didn't you tell me that man's name when I asked you."

She looked askance at him. "I've got my reasons."

"In a few days I am going to be sheriff of this county. I don't want to start my term in office and you not level with me about things I need to know about."

"Damn, the only reason I didn't tell you —"

"Hey," Chuck said, "am I breaking up a private conversation?"

"I'll be right with you, Chuck. Well?" he asked, glaring at the madam directly.

"I owed him money."

"Go to the bank and refinance the loan."

"I . . . all right, I will."

"Good. Next time don't tie in with those kinda people." He frowned hard at her.

"I won't — sorry if I caused problems,

but I had no choice."

He spun around and shook the hard hand of his friend. "Good to see you. This outfit will feed you, then we'll go out to the ranch and you can meet my bride."

"Your bride? I can't believe that you're married, but it's sure good to see you. All that I've heard about since I got here is you and all you've been doing to make this place livable."

"There's an election next Tuesday and after that we're gonna use a broom on this place."

"I'm a great sweeper. I'm proud to be here to help you. I ain't never forgot when we went after Red Carson and his gang. You saved my bacon. I sure owed you one more round."

"What do you do in San Angelo these days?"

"Chief deputy for the sheriff. I told him I had to go get you out of the ditch. You recall Hank Shiver? That's the sheriff I work for, and the county pays me every month. Can you believe that?"

"Not really."

The tall blonde Guthrey recalled from the last trip came into the kitchen in a fluffy robe and shouted, "Hi!" to him. The cook brought Chuck a big breakfast of eggs, biscuits, and ham on a platter and offered Guthrey some. He declined. They sipped coffee and talked in general terms.

His future operations did not need any more publicity. Blondie asked about Dan, and Guthrey told her he was working the boy too hard.

She laughed and never mentioned Steffany.

They left the house, took the horse to the livery, and left the packsaddle and panniers there. Chuck threw his own saddle on the bay and they rode back to the ranch.

As they rode away, Guthrey told Chuck about the gold find. It sent Chuck to whistling. Then he explained how Cally and Dan's father was killed and how he'd gotten involved. They were back to the ranch by then.

When they rode up, Cally came out smiling and Chuck threw his hat in the air. Dismounted, he ran over to hug her and swung her around. Then he kissed her on the forehead and went to talking a hundred miles an hour about how she should have waited for him before she got married. She was in stitches and bent over laughing.

"Tell him some lies," Guthrey said to her and took both horses to the corral. Noble joined him.

"Who was doing all the whooping down there?"

"My man Chuck. He's wild and a big tease. I need to ask you all about Jim Burroughs."

"Mining man. Not out in town much. He used to be an engineer for the big mine at Tombstone. I don't know much, but he lives like he has some money. He lives here in town. Pretty much keeps to himself. Why?"

"Would their father have known him?"

"Yeah, I'm certain he would have."

"Don't say a word, but Burroughs just made my A-list of suspects for the killer of Harold Bridges."

"My lands, why him?"

"He talked to Mitchem at the bank about how, if the Bridgeses wanted to sell out, Burroughs wanted that place more than Whitmore."

"I'll be doggone."

"Not a word to anyone, but we need to keep an eye on him."

"I guess anyone can kill someone, but he would have been low on my list. But I see how he could have done it. He's rode all over these hills looking for signs of minerals. No one would even think about his coming or going. How do you prove it?"

"Trick him. I don't know how, but I'll find a way."

"I learn anything, I'll sure tell you. Damn, how did you think to ask Mitchem about it?"

"It came to my mind right there in the bank with the gold. I got to thinking, if someone wanted to buy a place and needed a loan or inside track, why not talk to a banker about it?"

"You got an inquiring mind, you know that?"

"I need one. Thanks, Noble." He headed for the house to stop Magio from stealing his wife. Chuckling to himself, he had just now thought of a plan to test his suspect. But it would keep until their roundup of all the bad guys was over.

Chuck was drinking Cally's coffee and sitting across the table from her, telling her Ranger stories about Guthrey. Oh, man, Chuck was a great storyteller and was obviously enjoying every minute of Cally's company.

"Don't believe a word he tells you." Guthrey sat down, and she shook her head as she got up to pour him a cup.

"Oh, I'm learning a lot about your past."

"That Phil was an ornery guy back then," Chuck said. "I bet he whirled you around polkaing and made you so dizzy he asked you to marry him and you said yes."

"That was it." She laughed and refilled cups.

"Pard, you are one lucky guy. You've got a beautiful wife and a nice ranch with a gold mine."

"What did the banker say?" Cally asked. "Maybe you could finally pay off your loan now."

"He didn't say that."

Guthrey shook his head. "No, but he was very excited for the two of you."

She raised her eyebrows at him. "And my husband as well."

He nodded at her. "Where's Dan?"

"He and those two day men we hired are checking cattle and will finish that up today. He told Noble to guard the place."

"Fine, no problems. The three of us are going to ride around the next few days. I want Chuck to get a feel for this country before we do our thing."

"Good idea," she said. "I'll feed you some lunch. He said he had a big breakfast this morning."

Things were going smoothly. When his other two Rangers arrived he'd be in great shape.

After lunch he took Chuck up to the mine.

The men were getting ready to blast some more and Chuck was impressed. "There's lots of gold showing." Guthrey also told him where Bridges was found shot and all about the unrecorded murder.

"You have a suspect?" Chuck asked as they squatted on the ground.

"I found one this morning," he said and explained how he did it.

"You're too lucky these days. As I said earlier, your wife is wonderful, you have a great ranch, and now gold."

"And an election for change I must win next Tuesday."

That evening Todd Bowles arrived. A rancher in a buckboard brought him out to the Bridges Ranch. Guthrey thanked the man for delivering him.

"I'll be here Wednesday afternoon with a stout horse and my long rifle to help you all. Nice to meet you, Mr. Bowles."

"It's good to see you, Phil. Sounds like you have this entire country behind you. He was telling me all that you've done so far." Bowles shook his head.

They went through the wife introduction. Chuck hugged Bowles. It had been a long time since they'd seen each other. They played poker, dime limit, and went over the whole business in Arizona until Guthrey showed them their beds in the bunkhouse.

Back at the house, Guthrey undressed and was soon snuggling in bed with his sensuous wife. Oh, he was glad he'd found her. Whew, he couldn't believe all the great things that had happened in his life since the near shoot-out. Damn!

TWENTY-SIX

Gus Agnew, under a bushy mustache, arrived the next day. A short man in his forties, he wore a brown business suit, white shirt, and tie. He hardly looked like a lawman, but of the four of them, Guthrey considered him the toughest of them all. He was a few years older than the other three, and they'd served under him as their captain.

They went through lengthy meetings with the three law clerks about who would be where and how they would arrest them. Whitmore's was the prime site. Guthrey wanted Chuck to lead that posse, and Noble was going with him. He wanted Gus to get the two raiders hiding in the Chiricahuas, and those ranchers from Farnam were his choice to help him. Noble said he knew a breed tracker who had been up there a lot with the army and could find them easy.

"What in the hell are you going to do while we're all out working?" Chuck finally asked him.

"I'm going to ride up to the ranch of the former sheriff, Killion, north of Soda Springs and arrest him for malfeasance of his duties. And Todd will be leading another group going after the rapist and his gang."

They all nodded. The plan was set.

On Saturday, they attended the supper and dance at the Cane Springs School-house, and there was a beehive of talk about things. Folks visited with Guthrey's new bride and many talked privately to him about helping his efforts.

He reminded everyone, "Be sure to vote Tuesday or we can't do anything."

It sounded to him like they'd have plenty of help. He wasn't saying much that would forewarn them, but the raiders weren't dumb and might be better prepared than he imagined. He hoped that loss of lives would be very small or none. That worry niggled at him.

When he danced with Cally and she looked so happy, he was bursting proud of her. Her presence was enough to make him satisfied. He'd done the best thing in his life, marrying her. If things held together for an election, his appointment went through with no problems, and the roundup all worked, he'd be in tall cotton. That wouldn't make much sense to a non-farmer, but tall cotton had lots more bolls on it than bumblebee cotton. Those were the plants the bumblebee had to bend over to pollinate the blooms. Amused with himself to be recalling that old saying, Guthrey led Cally outside into the yard with the bonfire.

"Guthrey," someone on horseback shouted from back in the shadows at the edge of the grounds. Without a thought, Guthrey shoved Cally aside and drew his gun in one swift move, trying to locate the challenger. The fire's glint off the barrel of the shooter's weapon gave him a target, but another gun barked twice before Guthrey or the challenger could fire a shot, and the shooter was pitched forward off his shying horse.

"I seed him all evening kinda slinking around," Todd said, holstering his gun. "Sorry your missus had to get in on it."

Guthrey pulled her up to her feet. "I didn't see him in time. You all right?" he asked his wife.

"I'm fine. Is he dead?" She brushed off her dress with her hand.

"I'll be surprised if he ain't, or at least halfway there," Guthrey said as they joined the onlookers around the still body.

A man stood up from checking the fallen form and shook his head. "He's dead."

Guthrey made Cally stay back and stepped over among them. "Anyone know him?"

"Called himself Denver something. He worked for Whitmore," a rancher said, pointing at the dead man. Another man nodded.

"He sure ain't going to tell us much," Bowles said. "Sorry, Miss Cally."

"I'm fine, and so is Phil. That's all that matters. Glad you were so attentive."

"Yes, ma'am."

Guthrey said, "I want his body taken to the funeral parlor in Steward's Crossing and a justice of the peace hearing held on his death."

"Don't worry, Bowles. What you did was necessary," a man said. "And we'll all testify for you."

"Todd understands," Guthrey said. "It's the way the law should work."

If there were any more raiders in the crowd that evening, they didn't show themselves. Though Guthrey had had nothing to drink, the danger that exposed Cally concerned him and it felt like it sobered him up. He also needed this matter of the shooting to be settled in a legal way.

Guthrey drove her home instead of staying the night. He felt a lot more comfortable being back at the ranch. Chuck Magio, Guthrey decided, must have found a generous widow woman since he wasn't around.

Chuck didn't make it back till midmorning Sunday, and the rest of the Rangers chided Magio pretty hard about him getting lost. The day passed with the crew busy feeding the spare horses that folks had delivered and setting up tents for those coming from a long distance.

Monday passed uneventfully. Guthrey expected no problems. But the day went by slowly. The hands on his gold watch seemed to turn slowly as well. There would be some tough problems for him to solve in the coming days, but he wanted all that behind him. The thing that concerned him most after the try on his life Saturday night was thinking of how Cally might have gotten hurt in his company. He needed to minimize the chance of that happening altogether. It would be a hard thing to do.

The Rangers played cards. Low limits and lots of fun, card tossing and storytelling. Todd recalled a time when they were chasing a couple of horse thieves and had run into a hornets' nest.

"Why, Guthrey's eyes were so swollen from the wasp stings, he couldn't even see them when we rounded those two up."

"Or the time," Guthrey said, "when we were sneaking up on the guy's house to make an arrest and Chuck fell in the old outhouse hole."

"Yeah, and you guys wouldn't pull me out by your hands. Gus went and got someone else's rope to do that. I'll raise."

"Well, you did stink pretty bad."

"What about the time we charged the barn we thought that guy was hiding in and ran into that skunk? He sprayed us all. That was almost as bad as the dunking Chuck took."

"I ruined a damn new pair of boots the day we arrested that skunk," Gus complained. "Texas didn't pay me for them either. That pencil pusher said, 'Aw, it'll wear out,' but it never did."

Guthrey spoke to most of the arrivals coming early to his place. They'd butchered a fat yearling and put him on a spit to cook. He hired a young Mexican boy to turn it and keep the fire built up. Cally told Guthrey that she hoped the meat held out.

"We can always kill another one," Guthrey decided.

"I just didn't want to be short," she said

to him privately. Three ranch wives were helping her make pies, cobbler, and bread. Her range was getting a workout and so were the Dutch ovens outside the house. All in all he felt they were doing a great job.

Election day came. The ranch looked like a military base, buzzing with activity. Guthrey prepared to go to Soda Springs that afternoon and be there for the counting of the ballots. He had not been in the territory long enough to be considered a voter, so he had to abstain.

Reports came in all day: Things were quiet, and the deputy U.S. marshals had things well in hand at all the election sites. Cally and Dan were staying behind to handle things at the ranch. Guthrey and Noble were going to ride over to Soda Springs, and Gus planned to go along. Chuck and Todd had gone to Steward's Crossing for something.

Guthrey kissed Cally good-bye, and the three left for the county seat. The summer heat was settling in on the long days of June. The ride into Soda Springs was hot, hot enough that they had to mop their faces a lot. A large crowd had formed around the courthouse. The bars were doing a good business. There was no room to hitch another horse at the racks.

Folks spoke to Guthrey when he rode up to the courthouse. He asked a man on the street who he recognized whether the sheriff was there.

"Why, hell no. He's rarely here, so why be here today?"

Guthrey nodded and rode on. No sign either of the big ox of a deputy he'd tangled with. He handed Noble the reins to his horse and went inside the courthouse to see if Tommy was working the key. He found him busy taking down messages and held back so as not to disturb him. The halls were full of people, and he could hear the prisoners bitching back in the jail.

"Be right with you," Tommy said, busy writing out an incoming telegram message.

From the way Tommy sounded, Guthrey thought the man wanted to talk to him. Guthrey stood with his back to the wall, nodding to people he recognized who came by in the congested halls. The note that Tommy handed him read, *Watch your back, they plan to shoot you down today.*

With a slow nod of his head, he thanked Tommy and stuck the note in his vest pocket. He eased outside and moved between Gus and Noble's horses.

"Tommy gave me a note in there," he said

in a soft voice. "Says they plan to kill me today."

Gus frowned and Noble swore under his breath, "Them bastards better not try."

Standing in the rising heat, Guthrey moved to mount his horse. They'd better have gotten up early and dressed nice. He wanted them to look good on their way to hell.

"Where're we going?" Noble asked him when he was mounted.

"Doc's office. He won't mind. We can put our horses in his corral, water and feed them."

Gus looked over the crowd and then he nodded in agreement. "Lots of folks here. We'll need to pick our ground to stand on."

"It may be another bluff. Killion looks like he's avoiding town so far." Then Guthrey spoke to a man who told him, "Good luck."

"Thanks. We'll need it." He tipped his hat to a farmwife who waved at him.

At Doc's house-office, he dismounted and handed Noble the reins.

Doc's wife, Kathryn, answered the door. "How are you, sir?"

"Good. We'd like to stay around town for the election results and not be too obvious."

"Fine. How is your wife?"

"Doing well, ma'am. The two men with

me are Noble, who you've met, and Gus Agnew, a friend from Texas."

"I think you are a shoo-in," she said. "You have aroused the public against all these raiders."

"Yes, ma'am. We hope so anyway."

"Make yourself at home."

"We may simply stay on the porch."

"You're welcome to the entire house."

"Thank you." He went to tell his associates.

"Noble, put the horses out back and we'll stay here. I'd leave them saddled."

Gus asked Noble if he needed any help with them and the man shook his head. Gus thanked him and went to join Guthrey. They found seats on the old furniture on the porch, which was shaded from the hot afternoon sun.

"There is no law in this place?" Gus asked, taking a seat on the old couch.

"There's that big clown who tried to arrest me. But he does little of anything except drink."

"How will you handle this?"

"I'll need some real deputies."

Gus frowned at him. "Do they have the money to hire them?"

"They paid Killion twenty thousand for ten percent of his tax collection last year."

"Whew, that would hire several deputies."

Guthrey simply nodded. "We will need them."

They spent the rest of the morning watching traffic for any signs of trouble. Things were quiet. Kathryn served them lunch. She brushed aside Guthrey's polite attempt to stop her. Not to be denied, she brought trays of food for them and smiled.

After lunch, they continued their watch. By sun down, they thanked Kathryn for her hospitality, took their horses, and went to the courthouse. Horses hitched, they moved through the throng of onlookers as marshals with ballot boxes came in from the far corners of the county. Most parties with ballot books brought a large group of concerned citizens making sure no one messed with the election results.

McCall met Guthrey at the door. He acted as an overseer for the recall vote. He told Guthrey in the hallway that they had so far received eighty percent of the votes in favor of the recall.

"Sounds good. I'm going back to the ranch. Things have been peaceful enough here. Send me word when the governor puts us in charge. We are ready to close the doors."

"It should be in the morning. I understand

an assassin tried to kill you Saturday night?"

"He didn't manage it."

McCall frowned hard at him. "Be careful."

Guthrey nodded. "I want you and Brown to watch the jail too. So no one escapes. We will make our sweep and bring everyone in on Thursday morning."

When they got back to the ranch, Cally had food waiting in her warming oven for them. Pleased that Guthrey was unscathed, she hugged him.

The messenger from McCall arrived on a hot horse at dawn. An out-of-breath youth said, "The governor's appointed you as the man in charge by executive order, sir."

"Thanks. Get down and have some breakfast. Rest your horse."

"Yes, sir."

Considerable numbers of men filtered into the ranch all day on Wednesday. Things were made ready, especially the wagons to haul their prisoners back to the county jail.

"What do you think now?" Cally asked during a slow moment.

Guthrey hugged her and threw his head back. "I'll be glad when it's over."

"I imagine you will. But you know I love you and I'm proud of all this. It's an effort my father would have really enjoyed."

He closed his eyes and savored their closeness. One more day.

TWENTY-SEVEN

Noble had gone to Whitmore's with Chuck Magio and that posse, since the old man knew that place well enough to keep the team leader informed.

In the predawn, Guthrey sat quietly on Lobo and studied the dark buildings of the Killion Ranch headquarters in the clearing. Juniper rangeland surrounded the place, and it was cooler there than in the chaparral country lower down in elevation. His posse members ringing the ranch were in place. He kicked Lobo off the slope, and he and his second in command, rancher Mike Thorp, got closer to the house.

"Killion," Guthrey shouted. "We have this place surrounded. I am here to arrest you."

Half-dressed men came out of the bunkhouse only to face the rifles of Guthrey's posse. His crew searched the corrals and buildings. Waiting for the ex-sheriff's response, Guthrey dried his right hand, sweaty from holding the rifle, on his pants leg.

A woman came to the door. "He's dressing."

"Very well, ma'am," he said and dismounted. "Watch for him," he told Thorp and walked to the men being held at the bunkhouse.

"Are any of you men deputies?"

"No, sir."

"Have any of you participated in a raid on anyone's place?"

Heads shook. One man motioned to him. "Yes?"

"Sir, we're only ranch hands."

"I understand." At the sound of the front door opening, Guthrey turned to see Killion in his suit coming out of the house in the predawn's low light. He held his coat open to show them he was unarmed. Guthrey left the ranch hands and hurried over to face the man.

"Why in the hell are you here?" Killion asked.

"I am arresting you for malfeasance of office. You may ride unhandcuffed if we have your word that you will not try to escape. The governor has appointed me as the chief law enforcement officer of this county."

"You have my word." Killion turned to speak to his distraught wife and reassured her. One of his men went to saddle him a horse.

With the tension defused, Guthrey spoke to his posse members. "All we need is a small patrol to take him to Soda Springs. I thank all of you for coming to make this arrest go so smoothly. I want you to report any future infractions of the law. Crook County has a new law enforcement agency working for everyone."

He went down the line shaking hands with each man.

Then he excused himself, and they left in a hard ride back to Soda Springs. How the rest of the groups were doing concerned him, but his best men were handling those situations.

When they got to Soda Springs, Guthrey took control of the crowded jail from McCall and Brown, who looked like they had gone two days without sleep.

"When do you expect to hear from the others?" McCall asked.

"Chuck Magio and Noble, with a large posse, are at the Whitmore Ranch this morning. Noble knows that bunch and he can separate the plain workers from the gun hands. They better not try Chuck. He's quick with a gun. Then Ranger Todd Bowles

and more good men have gone to arrest
Curt Slegal and his bunch. Gus Agnew,
along with Ute and Kelly as lead men and
with an Apache scout, have gone to the
Chiricahuas to arrest a couple more men.
One is at the sawmill and the other one was
wounded in the Rawlings murder and is
recovering around there somewhere, hiding
out. A dozen volunteers are with them. They
may be a day or two getting back."

"I figured Whitmore would have a lawyer
here already."

"I met a guy named Bentson, who said he
was a lawyer and offered me a ranch up on
the Verde for Cally's place and to simply
ride off and turn my back on this job."

McCall shook his head. "That's pretty
country up there. You missed a good deal."
He laughed. "I doubt a trade for the King
Ranch would have suited you."

"He didn't offer me that place."

Brown said, "There are ten men out back
going to build a barbed wire compound for
you to hold the rest of the prisoners."

"Thanks." Guthrey nodded his approval.

Late afternoon, Noble rode in on a frothy-
shouldered, spent horse. From a distance
Guthrey saw the old man and rushed to see
what had gone wrong up there. When he
reached close to his man he had to clear

back the crowd of bystanders who closed in around him.

"Let me in. Give him some room." Guthrey could see that though Noble had dismounted, he still clutched the horn to hold himself up. "Everyone get back now."

They finally backed up, but not before they'd put an edge on Guthrey's temper.

"You all right?" he asked Noble.

"Yeah. Yeah." But he still clutched the horn. "Things went good. Chuck's got it under control —" He gasped for his breath.

"Sit down."

Noble shook his head. "That damn Whitmore ran off — maybe he got word last night . . . we was coming . . . Chuck got someone . . . to spill the beans where he's gone. My God, that man can get tough."

"I know him. He can do that when you won't answer him. Noble, sit down."

"I may not get up. You ain't never been to that canyon — I'm going with you."

Damn. That hardheaded old man was going to die, he was so worn out already and still insisting. Guthrey turned to the crowd. "Someone get him a chair and find my horse."

"Get me a fresh one too." Noble's shoulders gave a shudder.

Guthrey shook his head, looking hard at

Noble. There was no talking sense to him. He'd probably fall off his horse when he did get one and break his neck.

A chair arrived, and Noble looked over his shoulder at it and nodded. Guthrey caught him and set him down. "Did the man say how many were with him?"

"Two of his gunmen rode out with him," Noble said. "We got Hampton and the rest. Chuck's coming with them."

Someone handed Noble an open canteen and he took it in both hands. "I'll be fine in a minute. Just hold your horses; we'll get 'em. I'm damn sure going along for all them folks that the sumbitch ran off and hurt. You know, it's harder than hell to get a toehold in ranching. Takes years to get one going, and not many folks do it. Those people he ran off, they had a toehold and he broke it off for them. All that bullshit we been hearing about how he was going to have you kilt — it was just that, bullshit. That bastard hurt women and kids — but he wouldn't buck a real man."

"Noble, I appreciate your concern. My concern is that you are completely worn out."

Someone brought two fresh horses and they began to unsaddle the worn-out ones.

"Hold it, don't saddle him one. Can't you

see he's done in? Sit there, Noble. I can get a guide to show me this canyon," Guthrey said.

Noble took off his hat. "No way, I'm going along with you, even if I have to crawl on my belly and back you up. Now saddle me a damn horse."

"All right, but you tell these folks what you want on your tombstone when I bring your carcass back belly down over that horse."

Several folks in the crowd offered to go along and help Guthrey. There must have been twenty or more ready to join a posse. Guthrey took off his hat, scratched the hair and an itch in the middle of his skull. "Boys, boys. Since I can't talk sense into this ole man, I'll take him along. I don't want any innocent citizens shot by these three. So I'll handle arresting them."

Someone in the crowd shouted, "One problem, send one Ranger." The crowd shouted, "Yeah, they do it that way in Texas."

"And we got one of them right here in Crook County. Made more arrests today than Killion did in four years."

Another roar went up.

"Give us a little room, folks. Back up, please. This old man's going with me. He's one of the best friends I have —"

The applause was loud, and they did back up.

"Noble, you all right?" Guthrey's mouth was close to the man's ear when he spoke.

"I'm getting there. I'll be ready in a few minutes."

"Good, take your time. I know what getting Whitmore means to you. I won't deprive you of that. I am real concerned about your condition. You are plumb tuckered out." He glanced up at the crowd of people, who probably couldn't hear his conversation. This grand old man had been his steady partner since Guthrey'd hired him. Noble wanted to see Whitmore arrested and put behind bars before the sun set. Guthrey's own lovely wife would be on pins and needles if she knew he'd given in to Noble by letting him go along when he was so worn out. But he trusted she'd understand in the end. He could just ride slower up there and maybe Noble would recover some from the pressure of the hard ride to tell him that Whitmore had run.

They helped Noble onto his horse. He looked better in the saddle and forced a smile, then he nodded thanks for their help. When he reined the horse around, they gave him a cheer, and the two set out with many words of encouragement from the crowd.

One old woman with an age-wrinkled face under her sunbonnet turned back, stepped out of the bunch, and spat tobacco in the dust. "I hope you wring that damn bastard's neck. He kilt my husband, John."

"We'll get him, lady," Noble said and they rode on.

About to laugh at the woman's defiance, Guthrey kept a straight face and looked over at Noble. "Can you stand to trot these horses?"

"Hell, yes. That canyon is in the Red Tanks," Noble said as their ponies hit a trot. "He must have a place up there. In the past, when things got hot on some of his men for beating up someone, I think he'd send them up there until things cooled off."

Guthrey had lots of time on his hands while riding through the mesquite, catclaw, and desert vegetation scattered across a strip of bare caliche-exposed surface that grew little forage on it, and he did a lot of wondering about what their man might do when cornered. All those so-called plots Whitmore had taken on to have him killed had evaporated like a mud hole from a summer rain.

"How much farther?" Guthrey asked.

"It's a good ways up there. There's a big

spring up close to the top, but the water goes underground pretty fast after that. A former resident built a large stone mortar tank, but you can see there isn't much forage in the country, so who needed the water up here?"

Guthrey nodded. "Funny, ain't it? Where you don't have grass there can be water and vice versa."

Noble agreed. "It's sure like that. Those kids' daddy was a real hand at finding and capturing water. That's why their cattle do so good up there."

They entered Gregory Canyon on a wagon track between the towering black rock walls that closed in on them. With an itch between his shoulder blades, Guthrey kept an eye on the rims above them for sight of a sharpshooter. It would be an easy place to dry gulch them if Whitmore and his men were wary of pursuit.

"It's not far from here," Noble said at a wide place in the road. They dismounted and hitched their horses to some spindly mesquite.

On the ground, Guthrey slipped off his spurs and hung them on the saddle horn. Then he slid the .44//40 Winchester out of the scabbard and opened the lever halfway. The chamber was loaded. From a box in his saddlebags he filled his vest pockets with the long cartridges.

"You up to hiking?"

Noble nodded. He looked tired but determined as well.

The way grew steeper. Noble made him get to the right where it looked like there was some cover for them. Stopped, Guthrey could see a shake roof and then the rock house. No one was in sight, but three horses stood hipshot in the rail pen.

Where were they at?

Guthrey had no big hankering to be out and exposed when he challenged he house. The hundred or so feet from where they stood to the front door was open ground — no cover. Just some gravelly ground.

Guthrey and Noble were backed up and on their bellies where they should be able to duck any bullets when Guthrey cupped his hands and called out, "This is Sheriff Guthrey. Get your hands up and come out unarmed. I have a posse with me, and you won't escape alive."

He saw a gun muzzle as the door cracked open. He took aim and shot. Someone screamed and another cussed.

"I'm not kidding. Surrender or die." He shot out the window to the left of the door to punctuate his order.

"All right, all right. We're coming out. Dave can't raise his left arm. He's shot."

His finger on the trigger, Guthrey closely watched the two men come out. One of them was wounded in the arm, and it dripped blood off the end of his finger. There were only two.

"Where's Whitmore?" Guthrey asked as he scrambled to his feet.

"He ain't here."

"You damn liars, tell him to get his ass out here." Guthrey turned to Noble and said, "Stay here, this may be a trick. Keep your gun on them and shoot them if necessary. He may be escaping, and I owe him."

"Be careful, he's a snake."

"I will."

Jumping to his feet, Guthrey rushed the house, and then he saw someone climbing the steep mountain. A hatless man, it had to be Whitmore. Guthrey rested his rifle on the corral fence. "Stop and throw up your hands."

He saw Whitmore look back and then return to scrambling upward. Guthrey's first shot was to the right of the man and must have sprayed his eyes full of grit. He screamed and his hands went to his face. He slid downhill a ways on his belly when he lost his grip on the boulder.

"You can die up there and the damn buzzards will eat you, or you can come down careful and surrender. Your choice."

Guthrey's rifle was reloaded. Whitmore seemed to be considering his chances of reaching the top safely or being shot while trying.

"Better give up. There's no horse up there. No water either. Dying of thirst is lots worse than going to jail, I can guarantee you that."

"Damn you, Guthrey. I should have had you shot that day in Steward's Crossing. If I hadn't had such sorry help, I could have done that."

"You tried to hire several men to kill me, didn't you? What happened to those guys?"

"No nerve, no damn nerve at all. Somehow the legend of you being an ex–Texas Ranger scared them all."

"They were right to be scared. Rangers are a tough bunch. Now start coming down or I'm finishing you off for all those God-fearing folks that you and your grubby bunch hurt and ran off. I don't really care if I shoot you or not. Right now my trigger finger is kinda itching to send you directly to hell."

"I'm coming."

Guthrey went to meet him, and when they got back to the house, Noble had the disarmed outlaws handcuffed. Both men sat on the ground. Whitmore came with his suit coat and pants floured in light-colored dirt. His hands held high, he shook his head when he finally arrived at the side of the house. Guthrey cuffed his wrists behind his back and shoved him to the ground beside the others.

"Now, why don't you snap your fingers," Guthrey said to him, "and have me killed."

TWENTY-EIGHT

When they were back at the jail at last, Doc had looked at the wounded man. The other prisoner and Whitmore had joined the rest in the barbed wire cell.

Noble, who had recovered remarkably in Guthrey's eyes, was telling his part of the capture at the Whitmore Ranch.

"No one got shot. But Whitmore wasn't there at his ranch. We couldn't find him. Best we know, he'd gone to Mexico. We've got that blustering Hampton and over a dozen prisoners that the law clerk said were to be charged as felons."

"They offer any resistance?" Guthrey asked, busy listening to him.

Noble smiled. "Your Ranger Chuck went in there, fired off a few shots in the air, and told them the Crook County sheriff's officers had them surrounded. And we did."

"Todd coming?" someone asked.

One of the posse men said, "Yeah, he's

got that raping bastard too. They have maybe a dozen prisoners with them."

Guthrey said to Noble, "Why don't you go down to Doc's and get some sleep. Kathryn will give you a bed to sleep in, and you can get some rest. You look plumb tuckered out."

"I'll do that," Noble agreed.

Guthrey paced the office. The only ones left not accounted for were the crew with Gus and his rancher friends Kelly and Ute plus a dozen more over in the Chiricahuas. They might cross the county bounds, but Guthrey didn't care. The men on that list were wanted for committing crimes.

Jory and the other law clerks came by with a list. "We have seven men willing to turn over evidence for shortened sentences already. I think we will have to go out and look for others they have named."

"Do you know a fancy lawyer named Bentson?" he asked the young law clerk.

"Oh, he's high priced. Where did you meet him?"

"He offered me a large ranch up on the Verde if I'd leave this part of Arizona."

"They couldn't scare you, so they tried to bribe you?"

"Yes. Who does he represent?" Guthrey asked.

"He does lots of law work for a larger Tucson group. I imagine he will represent Whitmore and that rapist Curt Slegal." The other law clerks nodded in agreement.

"I wanted Whitmore to answer for all this raiding that he ordered done." Guthrey could never have stood for Whitmore to have gotten away from his sweep. He was glad they had brought justice to Whitmore so swiftly. That, and he missed Cally, who'd become so much a part of his life in such a comparatively short time.

"Your raids will break down this bunch," McCall said. He was still there despite Guthrey's suggestion to him earlier that he go to bed. "We're all beholden to you for all that you've done for every one of us. Your bride was in the middle of that assassination attempt at the dance. You stopped and challenged them at a community gathering and disarmed them. Arresting people when there was no backup from the ones in charge. You sure need to be proud of this recall and today's efforts to wind this reign of terror down."

The men lingering around the office murmured agreement. "Oh, I am grateful one of the main leaders is behind bars tonight as well," Guthrey said to them. Then he turned to McCall, who had led the ef-

410

fort. "These three men I asked to come will need to be paid."

"How much do we owe them?"

"I'd say five hundred apiece for their expenses and all."

"I'm certain we can pay them that amount. It was good to have such experienced men in charge of these widespread raids. When will you go home and file for what you need for all your work?"

"I won't take money for that. I'll meet with the county committee and see that my extra jailers who have been working around the clock are paid."

"I'll be back and help you." McCall rose wearily.

Guthrey clapped him on the shoulder. "You and Brown have sure helped me. Let me know what I can do for either of you."

"Nice to be a winner for once in this town," McCall said as he started to go home.

With everything winding down, Guthrey considered that he might go find another bed at the doc's for himself. Everyone acted like they were stoned from all the lack of sleep and the events of the day. It was the end of the terrorizing ring. Jory came by looking equally worn down. "Two of us talked to the man with the ruby ring. Todd made him give it up as evidence."

"Good. I have some women who I think will identify that he was their attacker. Did Todd turn it in as evidence? He won't steal it."

Jory quickly agreed. "I know that. But I heard you talk about this man. I hope the women will testify against him. Your man Noble said they needed to castrate him."

Amused, Guthrey laughed. "How is your offer for lower sentences if they give up information working?"

"Quite well."

"Can you find a place to sleep?"

"Don't worry about me. You've done a helluva big job here. I never thought you could do this whole thing in one sweep. You proved me wrong." Jory shook his hand. "Oh, one more thing. I have a pocket watch taken from one of the raiders." He reached in his pocket and gave him the watch. "It says To Harold Bridges."

"Who had this?" He looked at the inscription in the cover.

"A guy in the barbed wire prison named Horace Woodward. We made them empty their pockets when we arrested them. Each man's things were in a bag with his name on it. One of us found his bag before we interviewed him and discovered the watch.

When we interrogated him, we asked him how he had a dead man's stolen watch. He said he won it from another guy in a card game. The man told him to hold it and he'd pay him fifty dollars to get it back in two days."

"You believe him?"

Jory nodded. "He was really scared; I think he told us the truth."

"Did he describe the seller?"

"Said he had not seen him but the once. Past forty, tall, and he wore knee-high hiking boots. Woodward thought the guy was a prospector."

"I have been investigating this matter."

Jory nodded. "That was Miss Cally's father's watch, wasn't it?"

"Yes. How much did you say he paid for it?"

Jory repeated his story. "He won it in a card game last week and the man was to buy it back for fifty."

"Since the gold strike, I've been working on finding someone who had wanted to buy the Bridges Ranch. I asked the local banker if anyone had talked to him about buying the ranch, and he told me there was a man who wanted to buy it. Guess he slipped up pawning the watch and our roundup cut him off from recovering it. His name is Jim

Burroughs. A former mine superintendent. Noble and I will go arrest him in the morning. Thank you. My wife and her brother will be very grateful for your help in finding the watch and apprehending their father's killer."

"This guy will swear in court against the one who gave him the watch, once you get him."

"Don't say a word. He will get to meet Burroughs when he joins him in jail."

"I'd sure like to work with you some when you get settled. You're a helluva lawman."

Early the next morning, Guthrey and Noble rode back to Steward's Crossing. They came through the chaparral to a frame house under the small elm trees on the side of West Mountain. They left their horses and came up from behind an adobe barn. His Colt in his fist, Guthrey could hear someone grunting while lifting things and then hooking them on packsaddle trees. Hearing the grumbling and cussing of the animal, Guthrey went around the building. He could see the tall man's back and the knee-high hiking boots he had on.

"You leaving this country, Jim?"

"No. Just going prospecting. Oh, you're the Texas Ranger I've been hearing so much about. Noble, how are you doing? What can I do for you?"

"You know a ranch hand named Horace Woodward?"

"Oh, I don't think so. Why?"

"When we arrested him yesterday he had in his possession a watch he said he won off you at cards. Maybe you can recall that watch if I showed it to you."

"I don't know anything about losin' a watch."

"Noble, take his pistol. I think you know all about the watch I have in my pocket. I imagine you have been hurrying around fixin' to get forty miles south of here across the Mexican border this morning. Being that word was out we had all these tough guys in jail over in Soda Springs, you knew you'd made one mistake staying in a poker hand and betting a dead man's watch. I don't know how a man kills another man he called his friend in cold blood and then ignores the act."

"I have nothing to say."

"You will before they hang you. Put the cuffs on him behind his back, Noble."

"Jim? Jim, are you ready to leave?" The dark brunette in a divided riding skirt came into view.

"Jim has other plans, Steffany."

"Oh," she said. "It's you, ah, Guthrey. Jim, what's going on here? You said —"

Burroughs shook his head, looking crestfallen.

"Jim's going to jail for killing Harold Bridges. He'll probably be hung. You better take one of his horses, a bedroll, canteen, and some food and go the other way. We don't need you here anymore in Crook County."

"I swear to God, Guthrey, I never knew he killed Dan's father. I swear —"

"I'm telling you what you must do. Don't stop and tell a soul. Just ride east."

Tears began to stream down her full cheeks. "I will. I will. I just need my things from the house."

She ran off to the back door. He trusted she understood that she was a person not wanted in this county.

"Noble, can you deliver him to the Crook County jail and look up the law clerk Jory Wisdom? Have Wisdom file first-degree murder charges against him. I'll be back up there in the morning. Tonight is my wife's night."

"I savvy that fine, Sheriff. I'll handle the matter, and you tell Miss Cally I sure miss her good cooking."

"I will, Noble McCoy, chief deputy for

my outfit."

"Makes me feel young again, and I wouldn't mind except having to ride back over there with this worthless piece of shit is almost too much to ask."

"I'll sure think about giving you a raise for doing this for me." After the two loaded the prisoner in the saddle, Guthrey used a pair of leg irons under the horse's belly to lock Burroughs in the saddle. Noble rode off, leading his prisoner's horse.

There would be lots to tell Cally and Dan about the man who shot their father. He'd never mention to Dan that Steffany was set to leave with Burroughs. Another dove had left Steward's Crossing. Who could blame her? That kind of girl had no roots.

An hour later, he had ridden Lobo hard and they went under the crossbar of the 87T Ranch in a cloud of dust. He slid the gelding to a stiff-legged stop and swung down to run over, sweep his wonderful bride in the air, and swing her around until they were both dizzy. Then he set her on her feet.

"We have your father's killer. We have solid evidence. He's on his way to jail, and he will hang. I have, I believe, every criminal in Crook County in jail tonight. Except the pair who Gus and his posse went to find over there in the Chiricahua Mountains and he'll bring them in the next few days."

He smothered her to his chest. He couldn't get enough of her in his arms. She pulled down his face for the longest kiss of his life. Then he swept her up and carried her in his arms to the house. *By damn, we've done it.*